HOW TO STUDY
General Editors: John Peck and Martin Coyle

HOW TO STUDY A JANE AUSTEN NOVEL

Second Edition

How to Study
Series Editors: John Peck and Martin Coyle

IN THE SAME SERIES

HOW TO STUDY A
JANE AUSTEN NOVEL

Second Edition

Vivien Jones

MACMILLAN

First edition 1987
Reprinted 1993
Second edition 1997

Published by
MACMILLAN PRESS LTD
Houndmills, Basingstoke, Hampshire RG21 6XS
and London
Companies and representatives
throughout the world

ISBN 0-333-67074-4

A catalogue record for this book is available
from the British Library.

10   9   8   7   6   5   4   3   2   1
06   05   04   03   02   01   00   99   98   97

Printed in Hong Kong

For Anna and Luke

Contents

General editors' preface

EVERYBODY who studies literature, either for an examination or simply for pleasure, experiences the same problem: how to understand and respond to the text. As every student of literature knows, it is perfectly possible to read a book over and over again and yet still feel baffled and at a loss as to what to say about it. One answer to this problem, of course, is to accept someone else's view of the text, but how much more rewarding it would be if you could work out your own critical response to any book you choose or are required to study.

The aim of this series is to help you develop your critical skills by offering practical advice about how to read, understand and analyse literature. Each volume provides you with a clear method of study so that you can see how to set about tackling texts on your own. While the authors of each volume approach the problem in a different way, every book in the series attempts to provide you with some broad ideas about the kind of texts you are likely to be studying and some broad ideas about how to think about literature; each volume then shows you how to apply these ideas in a way which should help you construct your own analysis and interpretation. Unlike most critical books, therefore, the books in this series do not simply convey someone else's thinking about a text, but encourage you and show you how to think about a text for yourself.

Each book is written with an awareness that you are likely to be preparing for an examination, and therefore practical advice is given not only on how to understand and analyse literature, but also on how to organise a written response. Our hope is that although these books are intended to serve a practical purpose, they may also enrich your enjoyment of literature by making you a more confident reader, alert to the interest and pleasure to be derived from literary texts.

John Peck
Martin Coyle

Acknowledgements

I AM grateful to my colleagues John Whale and David Lindley for reading and improving earlier drafts of this book; to school teachers who attended day courses on *Mansfield Park* organised by the School of English at the University of Leeds, for valuable discussions of the problems of teaching Jane Austen; and to my general editors, particularly Martin Coyle, for their help.

Preface

JANE Austen's novels are as popular with readers as they are with examiners of papers in English Literature, but there are many students who find it very difficult to get on with a world which can seem remote and inconsequential. And, judging from the kinds of comments made by examiners, even those students who enjoy Jane Austen don't always find it very easy to translate that enjoyment into the kind of confident analysis required in essay and examination questions. To many, in fact, there appears to be a very definite gap between the enjoyment of reading the novels and the task of critical analysis.

There are all sorts of reasons for this, some of which are relevant to the study of any novel, some of which arise more specifically from Jane Austen's subject-matter and method. Because of the sheer length of a novel, selecting and arranging material can be a problem and here the gap between reading and analysis might seem particularly difficult to bridge. The pleasure of reading a novel over a period of time depends on such things as suspense, a desire to know what happens in the end, or a sense of close involvement with characters as we watch them develop. A critical analysis of the text, on the other hand, involves trying to see it complete and all at once, in terms of significant patterns rather than as a sequence. These two ways of seeing a novel are not, of course, mutually exclusive, but expressing whatever it was that made you eager to keep reading the novel in the first place in terms suitable for essay-writing can be difficult. Sometimes it seems easier to abandon your own first impressions altogether and to rely instead on the often rather different points made by teachers and critics.

This can be a particularly strong temptation when reading Jane Austen's novels. If you are reading Jane Austen for the first time the peculiarity and limited social scope of her world can be off-putting and her concern with the fairly uneventful progress of her heroine to a happy-ever-after marriage can seem rather unimportant. Yet you quickly find that critics and teachers claim that these novels offer subtle and incisive social and moral analysis. What can seem far from clear is just how that is achieved and what form it takes. What makes these novels different from other enjoyable romantic fiction? Or, for those who don't find this kind of fiction particularly appealing anyway, what makes them more than expressions of a narrow snobbery with no obvious relevance to a modern reader? Again, from a practical point of view, how do you begin to select significant episodes from a series of very ordinary events? Can you really analyse a Jane Austen text confidently unless you have a thorough knowledge of the historical context, or of Jane Austen's other novels, or both?

This book is an attempt to help you tackle some of these problems, not by offering an interpretation of Jane Austen's work which you have to learn and regurgitate, but by suggesting ways in which your first responses to a novel can be used to lead to further questions and further analysis. In other words, I shall be trying to help bridge the gap between reading and studying. Reading, even a very quick reading, is in fact a complicated process, and yet it is something we're all good at. Even if your experience of novels is fairly limited, your experience of stories, of narratives – from television, film, magazines, wherever – is probably extensive and helps you to make sense of all the other kinds of fiction you encounter. So, although your initial impressions of set texts might *feel* vague and unfocused, more often than not they are based on quite sophisticated responses to the ways in which the novel is organised – and this is true whether you actually *like* the book or not. Responding to a novel in this way is usually an unconscious process, but one of the main differences between reading and producing a critical analysis lies simply in the degree to which we are aware of how this process works.

One of the things I try to do in this book, then, is to suggest the kinds of questions and the critical vocabulary which will help you to be more conscious of what is actually going on when you read and make sense of a novel. Reading is a combination of two elements: the experiences, expectations, assumptions, prejudices that each individual reader brings to a text; and the characteristics of that particular text which subtly encourage certain kinds of response, organising, shaping, perhaps even changing readers' preconceptions. Though it would be impossible ever to give a complete account of all the factors in that process, it helps enormously if, as a student of literature, you have some sense of what's happening as you read. So one of the things this book attempts is to help you develop the habit of self-conscious reading. The aim is to make you more confident about your own ideas and responses to Jane Austen's novels, to help you use them as the starting-point for more complex analysis and as the basis for generalisations about the novel as a whole, instead of abandoning them in favour of those offered by a more experienced reader.

Obviously, this basic approach should be of value when you read any novel, but, since this is a book about how to study a Jane Austen novel, it is applied here in the context of the particular responses and problems raised in reading Jane Austen's work. In the introductory chapter I suggest ways in which the early chapters of a novel, in this case *Northanger Abbey*, set up expectations and establish a pattern of reading for the whole work. I do this by using three basic questions to analyse passages chosen to illustrate several different ways in which Jane Austen presents material – the introduction of characters, characters in conversation, a social gathering, a passage in which the author analyses the heroine's feelings – and to suggest the different kinds of things we learn from these different kinds of narration and the ways in which we begin to put them together into a general impression. This basic method of starting from an analysis of different kinds of passage is used throughout the book and will, I hope, provide a useful model for your own analyses of the novels. In the second part of the introductory chapter, I look at Jane Austen's basic plot structure, using *Sense and Sensibility* as my example, and suggest a way of getting to grips with the overall pattern of the novel which you can again apply to any of Jane Austen's novels.

It is important that you read the introductory chapter because as well as establishing the analytic method used in the whole book, it raises important basic questions which you can ask of any other Jane Austen novel and which will only be briefly summarised in other chapters. Don't worry if you are not studying or haven't read *Northanger Abbey* or *Sense and Sensibility*. Short plot summaries are provided to put you in the picture and the aim of the chapter is to provide a general framework rather than specific points about these particular novels. If you read the first chapter together with the relevant chapter on the novel you are studying, you should have a useful set of questions and vocabulary which will help you shape your own ideas into a critical analysis of that novel.

I deal with the four later novels, the ones most commonly set on exam syllabuses, in the order in which they were written, with the exception of *Mansfield Park* which I have chosen to deal with last. This is because it seems to me in some ways more complex than the other novels, so it provides a useful opportunity for suggesting how you might extend the basic analytic method. The chapters on individual novels can be read separately, but together they also provide an overall view of Jane Austen's work which will extend your ideas of your particular set text and suggest to you new questions and critical angles. So, ideally, you will read the whole book and, much more important, one or two of Jane Austen's other novels in addition to your set text. As I've already suggested, the way we read is the result of our previous experience of different kinds of texts: the more we read, the better we get at reading and the more enjoyment we get out of it. The aim of this book is not to tell you what to think about Jane Austen but to suggest a basic analytic method which will not simply help you to write better essays on her novels (though I hope it *will* do that) but, by showing you how to use and clarify your first impressions, will help to make you a more confident reader in general and, as a result, help you to get new kinds of enjoyment from studying a Jane Austen novel.

Chapter 6 is for those of you who want to move on to read critical material on Austen. It uses a very similar analytic method to that used throughout on the novels, but applied this time to passages from important representative critical readings of Austen from the past fifty years or so.

As so many editions of Austen's novels are available, references throughout are restricted to chapter references.

1

Introduction: *Northanger Abbey* and *Sense and Sensibility*

YOU are studying one of Jane Austen's novels as a set text. It's the first time you have come across anything by Jane Austen, you have read the novel through in an attempt to gain your own first impression and you are about to start studying it in more detail in preparation for writing an essay. You are confident about what happens in the story and you have formed opinions about the main characters, both what they are like and how you feel about them, and in spite of some difficulties with the novel's language and the unfamiliar society it deals with you might be prepared to say what you think it's 'about' in general terms. The problem now is where to start. How were those initial impressions gained and how do you select episodes from the whole novel which will illustrate your points?

One of the most important things to remember when you are studying a novel is that you should constantly be asking yourself not just 'What happens?' but '*Why* and *how* does it happen?'; not just 'What is such-and-such a character like?' but 'What makes us think they are like that?' and 'What role do they play in the novel as a whole?' Examiners commonly complain that many answers to questions on novels don't do much more than retell the story or give a series of character sketches, that they don't take into account how those things are presented, how the material of the novel is structured. So, though it's important to begin work on a novel by forming impressions of what happens and of the characters involved, rather in the way that we form judgements of people we meet, it's equally important to try to analyse why the story takes a particular course and what has made you react to it in the way that you have. Virginia Woolf, a novelist writing in the first half of this century, said that in novels 'Life conflicts with something that is not life' and a good critical analysis of a novel must deal with both elements, both with the 'life-like' features and with the particular way in which they are presented, with the novel's *form*.

Novelists use all sorts of techniques to present their material. In many novels an *authorial* or *narrative voice* tells us a lot of the things we know about characters and events; at other times we might just be presented with, say, a conversation between various characters and left to draw our own conclusions from what we hear or observe. Sometimes for parts of the novel the narrative voice merges with the thoughts of one of the characters so that we see things from their point of view; and sometimes the narrative voice is actually an 'I' and we are given the whole story through the first-person narration of someone involved. Jane Austen uses all these techniques, except first-person narration, and a very good way of getting into the habit of paying attention to her method is to begin by analysing passages in which different techniques of presentation, different *narrative methods*, are used. This is a useful basic approach which can be applied to the work of any novelist you are studying.

To illustrate what I mean, I'm going to look at a few passages from the early part of Jane Austen's first novel, *Northanger Abbey* (written 1797; published 1818). I have chosen passages in which the authorial voice gives us information about characters, conversations, descriptions of social events, and an analysis of the heroine's feelings. Jane Austen employs these four main kinds of narration in all her novels so I hope that my focusing on them right at the beginning will give you a starting-point for your own analysis of the text you are studying. It doesn't matter if you haven't read *Northanger Abbey*: the important element here is not *Northanger Abbey* itself but the analytic method I am applying which you can apply to your own set text.

Introductory analysis: Northanger Abbey

I have chosen my passages for analysis from the first fifty pages of the novel when, on a first reading at least, we are still forming opinions about the characters and have very little idea how things will turn out. I shall be examining the part these different passages play in forming those early judgements of the characters and impressions of what the novel is about. In other words, I'm going to suggest an analytic method which will help you to become conscious of the processes by which our responses are created, processes we're not usually aware of, but which are at work constantly as we read through a novel, establishing, adjusting and changing our views of characters and events. An awareness of these processes will help you to make the step from reading a novel to writing a critical analysis of it. However, my analysis will also depend to some extent on my knowledge of the whole novel because, though you should get into the habit of asking questions about your responses *as* you read, your own main analyses should be made on the basis of having *read through* the novel you are working on, so your own work will be influenced and helped by a knowledge of what happens in the end.

Northanger Abbey is about a young girl, Catherine Morland, who has been brought up in a large happy family in the country and is introduced to the ways of wider society when she is invited by some neighbours, Mr and Mrs Allen, to accompany them to Bath. There she meets and becomes friends with Isabella Thorpe and her brother John, and with Eleanor Tilney and her brother Henry, with whom Catherine falls in love. Catherine's views of the world have been largely formed by reading romantic novels and when she is invited to stay at the Tilneys' home, Northanger Abbey, she indulges in melodramatic speculations about their father's ill-treatment of his wife. She is brought down to earth by Henry's criticism of her unrealistic fantasies and by the news that her friend Isabella, who had been engaged to Catherine's brother James, has eloped with Captain Frederick Tilney, who is the brother of Eleanor and Henry. After some difficulties with Henry's father, who discovers that Catherine is not heiress to a fortune as he had at first thought and who as a result abruptly sends her home from Northanger, Henry and Catherine are married, 'to begin perfect happiness at the respective ages of twenty-six and eighteen'.

I'm going to begin with the first chapter. The opening of any novel is obviously very important in setting up our expectations about subject-matter and the *kind* of novel we are about to read, so it is always worth while paying particular attention to beginnings. The opening chapter of *Northanger Abbey* is devoted to an introduction of Catherine Morland. It begins: 'No one who had ever seen Catherine Morland in her infancy, would have supposed her born to be an heroine.' The rest of the first paragraph describes the circumstances which make her such an unlikely heroine: the ordinariness and respectability of her parents, her own looks – 'a thin awkward figure, a sallow skin without colour, dark lank hair, and strong features', her preference for boys' games over 'the more heroic enjoyments of infancy, nursing a dormouse, feeding a canary-bird, or watering a rose-bush', and her dislike of lessons.

> What a strange, unaccountable character! – for with all these symptoms of profligacy at ten years old, she had neither a bad heart nor a bad temper; was seldom stubborn, scarcely ever quarrelsome, and very kind to the little ones, with few interruptions of tyranny; she was moreover noisy and wild, hated confinement and cleanliness, and loved nothing so well in the world as rolling down the green slope at the back of the house.
>
> (ch. 1)

By the age of fifteen, however, 'appearances were mending': Catherine's looks improved, she began to take an interest in clothes and dancing and to read 'all such works as heroines must read to supply their memories with those quotations which are so serviceable and so soothing in the vicissitudes of their eventful lives'.

> So far her improvement was sufficient – and in many other points she came on exceedingly well; for though she could not write sonnets, she brought herself to read them; and though there seemed no chance of her throwing a whole party into raptures by a prelude on the pianoforte, of her own composition, she could listen to other people's performance with very little fatigue. Her greatest deficiency was in the pencil – she had no notion of drawing – not enough even to attempt a sketch of her lover's profile, that she might be detected in the design. There she fell miserably short of the true heroic height. At present she did not know her own poverty, for she had no lover to pourtray. She had reached the age of seventeen, without having seen one available youth who could call forth her sensibility; without having inspired one real passion, and without having excited even any admiration but what was very moderate and very transient. This was strange indeed! But strange things may be generally accounted for if their cause be fairly searched out. There was not one lord in the neighbourhood; no – not even a baronet. There was not one family among their acquaintance who had reared and supported a boy accidentally found at their door – not one young man whose origin was unknown. Her father had no ward, and the squire of the parish no children.
>
> But when a young lady is to be a heroine, the perverseness of forty surrounding families cannot prevent her. Something must and will happen to throw a hero in her way.
>
> (ch. 1)

I have quoted at some length from this opening chapter because, as is so often the case in Jane Austen's novels, it contains a lot of hints about things which are going to be important later on. As I've already suggested, it's always useful in your own analyses to spend time examining your responses to beginnings. I will look at the more general points in a minute, but since they arise out of the presentation of the chapter's central subject, Catherine herself, I will start with her. What impression of Catherine do we get from this description? She is kind and good-natured, something of a tomboy as a child, rather inexperienced, above all very ordinary and familiar in her early preference for physical fun over lessons and her shift of interest with adolescence to romantic reading and her appearance. It's easy enough to identify with this unspectacular heroine, even across a gap of almost two hundred years.

All the evidence for this brief character sketch is very obviously present in the text. We are clearly told by the authorial voice that Catherine was kind to her younger brothers and sisters, that she preferred 'boys games', that she 'had reached the age of seventeen, without having inspired one real passion'. The next step is to build on this initial impression by asking further questions about the *way* Catherine has been presented.

I'd like to suggest three questions which will help you to develop your analysis, questions which can be asked of any passage picked out for close attention:

1. *From what point of view is the passage presented and what is the effect of this?*
2. *Do there seem to be any particularly important words, key words, in the passage and if so why?*
3. *Are there any obvious contrasts or oppositions at work in the passage which might throw light on the work as a whole?*

What answers do I get when I ask these questions of Jane Austen's introduction of her ordinary heroine?

1. Point of view. The voice telling us about Catherine is clearly that of someone who knows all about her – and who shows confident knowledge not only of Catherine, but of the assumptions of the world in general: '*No one* who had ever seen Catherine Morland . . . would have supposed.' The speaker is obviously much more experienced than Catherine herself and is therefore prepared to judge her, describing her 'improvement' at the age of fifteen, for example, as 'sufficient' in some respects, though falling 'miserably short' in others. What effect does this judgemental authority have on readers' reactions to Catherine? Do we identify with Catherine or with the speaker? I suggested earlier that here is a character with whom we identify easily, but if we identify with her can we also judge her in the way that the authorial voice suggests everyone must? Do we, in fact, agree with the authorial voice's interpretations of the evidence? What about the description of her in the first paragraph I quoted as a 'strange, unaccountable character' showing 'symptoms of profligacy'? This seems rather strong language for what seems to a modern reader at least a small girl's understandable preference for active 'boys' games' over such docile pastimes as 'feeding a canary-bird, or watering a rose-bush'. And, from the second quoted paragraph, is it really 'strange indeed' that a girl should have reached seventeen 'without having inspired one real passion'? So, from the very beginning of the novel, though we rely on the narrative voice for information about characters and events, we feel free to disagree with the narrator's judgements. It's possible, in fact, that the narrator is being *ironic*, saying things which are the opposite to what she really means, or using language which is obviously excessive, in order to provoke readers into making judgements.

You have probably come across references to Jane Austen as an ironic novelist and in a later chapter I shall be looking at this aspect of her method in more detail, but because it's so central to her technique I think it's important to start thinking about its effects straight away. Essentially, as the exploration of point of view in the opening chapter makes clear, it is a narrative technique which encourages readers constantly to make *judgements*, it makes us immediately aware that this is a novel concerned with evaluation.

So, having decided that we are prepared to distance ourselves from the narrator, let's go back to my question about where we stand in relation to Catherine. We certainly feel that we understand her better than the narrator does, but it's also true that in judging the narrator's comments as inappropriate, we are implicitly relying on wider experience than Catherine's own. In other words, our sympathy for and identity with her still allow us to maintain a slight distance from her. This is important because it means that we are in a position to judge her sympathetically but independently as her story develops and to see her as part of the overall scheme of the novel. It's not enough, then, just to say what kind of person Catherine is, we must also see her as an element in the novel's method.

2. *Key words*. The word which seems to me to carry the most weight in

this chapter is 'heroine' and, associated with it, 'heroic'. 'Heroine' is used in the very first sentence as the starting-point for the introduction of Catherine and this gives it immediate importance as a kind of reference point. It describes both what Catherine is – the heroine of this novel; and what she is not – the usual type of heroine. This opposition governs the way she is presented in the rest of the chapter: she doesn't like the 'more heroic enjoyments of infancy'; in not having a lover to draw 'she fell miserably short of the true heroic height'. And even when the word is not actually used, the text creates an image of the usual, ideal heroine by implicitly defining her as the opposite to Catherine herself. Catherine is rather plain, so the ideal heroine must be beautiful; Catherine is a tomboy, so heroines must be feminine; Catherine's literary and musical skills are very mediocre, so heroines presumably shine at everything they do; and Catherine has no lovers, so heroines must usually be inundated by admirers.

What might be the purpose of this very specific focus in Jane Austen's presentation of her main character? At this stage we can only hazard a guess, but our initial sympathy with Catherine's ordinariness will help to give an answer. Heroines, as implicitly defined here, appear rather unreal, certainly much less normal than the girl who 'loved nothing so well in the world as rolling down the green slope at the back of the house'. They seem, in fact, much less attractive than the plain but lively Catherine. 'Heroine' is of course a technical term given to the main female character in a work of literature, which is why Catherine still is a heroine in spite of her shortcomings. Jane Austen seems to be making a point here not just about Catherine herself, but about the kinds of characters novels usually deal with, and by evoking our sympathy for her own ordinary heroine, she also enlists our sympathy for her kind of novel.

3. *Oppositions.* The answers to my three suggested questions will inevitably often overlap and examining Jane Austen's use of the key term 'heroine' in these opening passages also involved attention to the opposition between the usual type of heroine and this one. This was based on several contrasts: between beauty and plainness; social accomplishments and lack of ability; success and lack of success in love, and so on. What sorts of expectations do these various contrasts create in the reader who is trying to get his or her bearings in the novel? What sense do they give of what the novel is going to be 'about' in general terms? Three elements look particularly interesting. The first of these

has already arisen out of responses to Catherine: an opposition between the specialness (but unreality?) of conventional heroines with their 'eventful lives', and the attractive ordinariness of Catherine herself. This could be generalised in various terms as the opposition between *fiction* and *real life*; or between the *ideal* and the *real*; or between *fantasy* and *actuality* – and you can no doubt think of other ways of putting it.

The other two oppositions are more specific. As a child, Catherine resists girlish pastimes. She prefers 'boys' games'. Her 'improvement' as an adolescent is seen as dependent on her becoming better-looking – which will presumably make her more attractive to the opposite sex – and on her change of interest to more feminine pursuits. Being a successful heroine according to the usual model seems to depend on conforming to social expectations of how girls ought to behave. How will the novel develop this concern with the opposition between male and female social roles? So far, one of the most attractive things about Catherine, to a modern reader at least, has been her early resistance to any such conformity.

The third opposition is closely related to the others. This is the contrast between Catherine's innocence ('she did not know her own poverty, for she had no lover to pourtray') and the usual assumption not only that heroines will inspire undying passion but that their main interest will be in love affairs, that they will be mistresses of intrigue, however harmless: 'she had no notions of drawing – not even enough to attempt a sketch of her lover's profile, *that she might be detected in the design*'. This moral contrast between openness and deception, innocence and sophistication, might also receive further development as part of the examination of this particular, slightly unusual, heroine.

What is made clear at the end of the chapter, though, is that in one respect at least, Catherine *is* to be the expected heroine. In spite of the differences which have received so much attention between conventional heroines and this one, hers is still, apparently, to be a love story. 'Something must and will happen to throw a hero in her way', and the plot is set in motion. Questions immediately arise which make us want to read on. What kind of hero will be supplied for this ordinary heroine? We are clearly not to expect a prince in disguise on the fairy-tale model of the 'young man whose origin was unknown', since Jane Austen firmly states there are none of those around in this particular neighbourhood. Catherine is invited to Bath, where she will presumably meet her hero. How will she react to this new environment?

Before going on to look at passages which develop those questions further, I want briefly to sum up the aim of my analysis so far. I have deliberately spent quite a lot of time looking at this first extract so that you have a model for your own analyses which illustrates the kinds of answers you can get from a chosen passage by asking the three questions I have suggested. In examining the first chapter of *Northanger Abbey*, I have been able to make general observations about techniques and issues which characterise Jane Austen's work as a whole (authorial irony, for example, or the opposition of ideal and real). I have done so by asking further questions about the presentation of Catherine Morland, about readers' responses to the character of the heroine. Feelings about her, the 'life-like' part of the text, led on to technical questions, the 'something that is not life', and perhaps the most important thing to stress is that there need not be a gap between your initial reactions to a text and studying it in order to write on it, between reading and analysis.

We left Catherine about to go to Bath, to encounter a much wider social circle, and, presumably, to meet her hero. Having looked at Jane Austen's introduction of her heroine, I want now to look at passages in which other main characters are presented and to explore further what effect the method of presentation has on the reader's developing idea of the novel's main concerns. One of the first people Catherine meets in Bath is Isabella Thorpe, and the two become close friends. Here are two conversations between Catherine and Isabella. The first, reported by the narrator, takes place when they have just met:

> Their conversation turned upon those subjects, of which the free discussion has generally much to do in perfecting a sudden intimacy between two young ladies; such as dress, balls, flirtations, and quizzes. Miss Thorpe, however, being four years older than Miss Morland, and at least four years better informed, had a very decided advantage in discussing such points; she could compare the balls of Bath with those of Tunbridge; its fashions with the fashions of London; could rectify the opinions of a new friend in many articles of tasteful attire; could discover a flirtation between any gentleman and lady who only smiled on each other; and point out a quiz through the thickness of a crowd. These powers received due admiration from Catherine, to whom they were entirely new; and the respect which they naturally inspired might have been too great for familiarity, had not the easy gaiety of Miss Thorpe's manners, and her frequent expressions of delight on this acquaintance with her, softened down every feeling of awe, and left nothing but tender affection.
>
> (ch. 4)

The second, after a few days of intimacy:

> The following conversation, which took place between the two friends in the Pump-room one morning, after an acquaintance of eight or nine days, is given as a specimen of their very warm attachment, and of the delicacy, discretion, originality of thought, and literary taste which marked the reasonableness of that attachment.
>
> They met by appointment; and as Isabella had arrived nearly five minutes before her friend, her first address naturally was – 'My dearest creature, what can have made you so late? I have been waiting for you at least this age!'
>
> 'Have you indeed! – I am very sorry for it; but really I thought I was in very good time. It is but just one. I hope you have not been here long?'
>
> 'Oh! these ten ages at least. I am sure I have been here this half hour. But now, let us go and sit down at the other end of the room, and enjoy ourselves. I have an hundred things to say to you. In the first place, I was so afraid it would rain this morning, just as I wanted to set off; it looked very showery, and that would have thrown me into agonies! Do you know, I saw the prettiest hat you can imagine, in a shop window in Milsom-street just now – very like yours, only with coquelicot ribbons instead of green; I quite longed for it. But, my dearest Catherine, what have you been doing with yourself all this morning?'
>
> (ch. 6)

Like Catherine, we are interested in this new acquaintance, but also in assessing Catherine's response to her. What impression of Isabella is given in these two extracts? She is experienced, even worldly, compared with Catherine and perhaps rather frivolous in her interests, but we are told that her easy manner inspires 'tender affection' and at the beginning of the second extract their friendship is described as a 'very warm attachment'. Bearing in mind the three main questions which I suggested you ask of every passage, what more can be said about the relationship between these two friends?

Both passages are controlled by the authorial voice – though in the second this gives way to directly reported conversation – but here we have two examples which show how much that voice can vary in its tone and effects. In the first passage we might assume at first that the narrator is giving an objective view of Isabella's greater experience, that it is the narrator who sees Isabella as having a 'very decided advantage' over Catherine and thus the ability to 'rectify the opinions of her new friend' on details of fashion. But, on further consideration, isn't this a view of Isabella that Catherine herself might have expressed? The authorial voice, in other words, is here very close to the point of view of one of the characters and as readers trying to judge for ourselves we need to be aware that such a point of view might have its limitations. Here, for example, Catherine is, as the narrator clearly points out, encountering something 'entirely new'. In fact the central opposition in this passage is between Isabella's experience and Catherine's lack of it, a contrast between the two characters which picks up the opposition between innocence and sophistication which was present in the first chapter. As we read, our first concern is whether Catherine's new friendship will be good or bad for her. Given the difference between them, will Catherine be able to judge Isabella wisely? Is she mistaken in feeling such 'respect' for her? But because of the narrative voice's sympathetic closeness to Catherine's point of view, the reader's first impression of Isabella is influenced by the attraction Catherine feels to her 'easy gaiety'. We reserve judgement, and keep on reading to see how the friendship will turn out.

At the beginning of the second passage, on the other hand, the narrator is very much detached from the characters, in fact much closer to the reader to whom she is offering 'a specimen' of the girls' attachment. And in this second passage the irony is much more obvious. It soon becomes clear, from the contents and style of Isabella's conversation, that 'delicacy, discretion, originality of thought' are the very *opposite* of what characterises this friendship, at least on Isabella's side, and that in describing it in those terms the narrator is inviting readers to disagree. Isabella's conversation is clearly exaggerated and trivial rather than delicate ('at least this age'; 'these ten ages'; 'an hundred things to say to you'; 'agonies') and, far from showing 'originality of thought', is rather boringly predictable in its concern with the weather and new bonnets. 'Delicacy, discretion, originality' are positive terms and could even be described as key words in this second passage, so the contrast between this authorial judgement and what Isabella actually says is obviously an important influence on our view of her. The passage tends, in fact, to set up an opposition between these positive values and Isabella herself.

The different conversational styles of the two girls again draw attention to the way in which the characters themselves are being opposed. Isabella's extravagant language contrasts with Catherine's reasonable tone and polite concern: it's easy to believe that Catherine means what she says whereas Isabella's inflated clichés make it very difficult to tell what she really thinks. The way Jane Austen's characters speak is usually a good indication of how they are to be judged. Here,

Catherine and Isabella's very different styles of conversation are indicative of a *moral* difference between them: Catherine's straightforwardness is a sign of honesty whereas Isabella's exaggerations suggest unreliability. (And it's interesting to note in the light of this that in the first passage Isabella judges others not by innocent appearances but according to her own suspicious interpretations of things: she can 'discover a flirtation between any gentleman and lady who only smiled on each other'.) This opposition between sincerity and insincerity reinforces and extends the contrast of innocence with sophistication, inexperience with knowledge, which characterised Isabella's introduction in the first passage. Because of the narrator's ironic comments at the beginning of this second conversation, the reader now has a much clearer view of Isabella than does Catherine. It is becoming clear that the two characters stand in the novel not only for different kinds of experience, but for two very different attitudes to life. At the moment these differences seem innocent enough – their conversations are after all only the rather unimportant chat of two young girls – but one of the questions which keeps us reading might be how, or whether, Jane Austen is going to develop this contrast between her characters. And readers who know the whole novel will see the connection between Isabella's apparently mild dishonesty and deception here and the fact that she later jilts Catherine's brother James for a richer man.

As you have probably noticed, I haven't applied my three questions systematically in my analysis of these two passages as I did when I looked at the opening chapter, but I have kept them constantly in mind. In other words, I have a method which helps me to get the most out of my impressions without producing an analysis which looks too rigidly schematic. I am trying to get some sense of the novel as a whole, so I have looked whenever possible for further examples of the techniques and oppositions which seemed to be important in the opening chapter, and I have noticed that the contrast between the characters themselves seems to be another version of some of those major oppositions. This suggests a very important point about Jane Austen's technique: that her characters are not just interesting individually but are *part of the pattern of the novel*. The differences between them, as with the contrast between Catherine and Isabella here, give important clues to the book's general concerns.

Bearing this in mind, I'm going to look at short extracts from the scenes in which Catherine meets the two major male characters, Henry Tilney and John Thorpe, examining any points of contrast which might alert us to their roles in the novel's overall scheme. In both cases, as with Isabella, I have chosen examples of their conversation.

Catherine is introduced to Henry Tilney by the master of ceremonies at the Lower Rooms (these were public dancing rooms where young people went to meet each other). After their dance, they have tea together and Henry Tilney teases Catherine about how she will write of him in her journal:

> 'My dear madam, I am not so ignorant of young ladies' ways as you wish to believe me; it is this delightful habit of journalizing which largely contributes to form the easy style of writing for which ladies are so generally celebrated. Every body allows that the talent of writing agreeable letters is peculiarly female. Nature may have done something, but I am sure it must be essentially assisted by the practice of keeping a journal.'
>
> 'I have sometimes thought,' said Catherine, doubtingly, 'whether ladies do write so much better letters than gentlemen! That is – I should not think that the superiority was always on our side.'
>
> 'As far as I have had the opportunity of judging, it appears to me that the usual style of letter-writing among women is faultless, except in three particulars.'
>
> 'And what are they?'
>
> 'A general deficiency of subject, a total inattention to stops, and a very frequent ignorance of grammar.'
>
> 'Upon my word! I need not have been afraid of disclaiming the compliment. You do not think too highly of us in that way.'
>
> 'I should no more lay it down as a general rule that women write better letters than men, than that they sing better duets, or draw better landscapes. In every power, of which taste is the foundation, excellence is pretty fairly divided between the sexes.'
>
> (ch. 3)

John Thorpe's topics of conversation are rather different. Catherine and Isabella bump into him, together with Catherine's brother James, one morning when they are walking through Bath. John Thorpe engages Catherine in conversation, mainly about his gig and horse, offering to take her for a drive the following day:

> 'Rest! he has only come three-and-twenty miles to-day; all nonsense; nothing ruins horses so much as rest; nothing knocks them up so soon. No, no; I shall exercise mine at the average of four hours every day while I am here.'
>
> 'Shall you indeed!' said Catherine very seriously, 'that will be forty miles a day.'
>
> 'Forty! aye fifty, for what I care. Well, I will drive you up Lansdown tomorrow; mind, I am engaged.'

'How delightful that will be!' cried Isabella, turning round; 'my dearest Catherine, I quite envy you; but I am afraid, brother, you will not have room for a third.'

'A third indeed! no, no; I did not come to Bath to drive my sisters about; that would be a good joke, faith! Morland must take care of you.'

This brought on a dialogue of civilities between the other two; but Catherine heard neither the particulars nor the result. Her companion's discourse now sunk from its hitherto animated pitch, to nothing more than a short decisive sentence of praise or condemnation on the face of every woman they met; and Catherine, after listening and agreeing as long as she could, with all the civility and deference of the youthful female mind, fearful of hazarding an opinion of its own in opposition to that of a self-assured man, especially where the beauty of her own sex is concerned, ventured at length to vary the subject. . . .

(ch. 7)

The contrast between Catherine and Isabella which I have looked at already could be seen in terms of the true and the false heroine (taking up the stress on heroines in the opening chapter), and even a very quick reading of these extracts suggests that Henry Tilney and John Thorpe might complete the pattern by providing a similar contrast between the good and bad hero. I want now to look at aspects of that opposition in more detail. With the exception of the paragraph at the end of the second passage, the authorial voice is not present here, so we have to judge these characters entirely from the evidence of their conversation. What immediate points of contrast are there between the two? To start with, they talk about very different topics. John Thorpe can only converse about horses and carriages, otherwise he is silent, and Catherine, not surprisingly, is soon bored; Henry Tilney, on the other hand, flatters her and stimulates her interest both by concentrating on 'young ladies' ways', which she feels she knows something about, and by disguising his real views behind ironic generalisations which make them fascinatingly uncertain. The fact that he tailors his conversation to try to interest Catherine indicates some sensitivity to others, and when he does offer an opinion which seems to be genuine, about the fair division of excellence between men and women, it shows unprejudiced common sense and a willingness to judge each case on its individual merits. This is strikingly unlike John Thorpe's dogged indifference to anything, including the well-being of his horses, except his own pleasure and interests, and his readiness to pronounce judgement simply on the appearance of every woman who passes, as if they too were horses or gigs.

I have put these passages side by side to draw attention to the process of comparison and choice which goes on constantly as we read, though we are often barely aware of it. Judgements often start from attitudes brought from outside the novel (here, for example, your initial view of John Thorpe might well depend on how you feel about 'macho' males!). These attitudes are influenced and modified as we read by such things as the role of characters within the story and the influence of the narrative voice (as was the case with the increasingly negative view of Isabella). In setting John Thorpe against Henry Tilney here, the reader reflects Catherine's own process of choice, a choice which will be vital for her whole future since, as we know from the first chapter, 'something must and will happen to throw a hero in her way'. Bath is, of course, a marriage market and Catherine's choice will be for life.

The two men are themselves very much aware of this. In spite of differences between them, they are both clearly showing off, using their social advantage as men to impress an inexperienced girl. The wry authorial comment at the end of the second extract about the 'civility and deference of the youthful female mind' faced with a 'self-assured young man' makes clear the novel's awareness of the differences between male and female roles, something we noted as a potentially important opposition in the first chapter, and the authorial voice is surely ironic here in suggesting that Catherine's unwillingness to offer an opinion is understandable '*especially* where the beauty of her own sex is concerned'. Why should a man's opinion on the subject be so much more valuable? We are encouraged by Catherine's attraction to feel that Henry Tilney is *nicer* than John Thorpe, certainly he's more interesting and better-looking, but he's just as self-assured, just as willing to offer judgements about 'young ladies'. He is of course older and more experienced than Catherine but to what extent does that give him authority over her? (And you might want to compare his guidance with that of Isabella as another source of contrast and pattern in the novel.) Will he always give her the right advice? Though we almost certainly decide straight away that he *is* the hero, we reserve judgement about him and the detailed development of their relationship promises to be another source of interest as we read on.

In these analyses of passages from *Northanger Abbey* which introduce the heroine and other main characters, I have tried to demonstrate some of the ways in which our early impressions of a novel are established, how they accumulate and shift or strengthen as we are presented with different kinds of evidence (authorial comments, conversations, and so on) given to us through different narrative techniques (such as irony or patterns set up through comparison and contrast). The first forty pages or so of the novel, from which these extracts are taken, are largely introductory, concerned to set the story in motion and to give a fairly full picture of Catherine's position in relation to the other main characters. In the eighth chapter, we see all the characters together for the first time, at a ball in the Upper Rooms. Social gatherings are important events in all Jane Austen's novels. They show us characters in action, and so provide another source of evidence by which to judge and, because they bring characters together, they are often points of crisis in the story, events where some kind of revelation or change takes place. Because of this importance, I suggested earlier that a social gathering should always be one of the *kinds* of narrative that you look at in detail when you are analysing a Jane Austen novel.

I'm going to look now at extracts from the ball in Chapter 8 of *Northanger Abbey*. Catherine has promised in advance to be John Thorpe's partner. When the ball begins, however, he leaves her to talk to a friend in the card-room and Isabella, in spite of protestations that she won't leave Catherine, is persuaded to do so and goes off to dance with Catherine's brother James:

Catherine, though a little disappointed, had too much good-nature to make any opposition, and the others rising up, Isabella had only time to press her friend's hand and say, 'Good bye, my dear love,' before they hurried off. The younger Miss Thorpes being also dancing, Catherine was left to the mercy of Mrs Thorpe and Mrs Allen, between whom she now remained. She could not help being vexed at the non-appearance of Mr Thorpe, for she not only longed to be dancing, but was likewise aware that, as the real dignity of her situation could not be known, she was sharing with the scores of other young ladies still sitting down all the discredit of wanting a partner. To be disgraced in the eye of the world, to wear the appearance of infamy while her heart is all purity, her actions all innocence, and the misconduct of another the true source of her debasement, is one of those circumstances which peculiarly belong to the heroine's life, and her fortitude under it what particularly dignifies her character. Catherine had fortitude too; she suffered, but no murmur passed her lips.

From this state of humiliation, she was roused, at the end of ten minutes, to a pleasanter feeling, by seeing, not Mr Thorpe, but Mr Tilney, within three yards of the place where they sat; he seemed to be moving that way, but he did not see her, and therefore the smile and the blush, which his sudden reappearance raised in Catherine passed away without sullying her heroic importance. He looked as handsome and as lively as ever. . . .

The group Henry Tilney is with stop, close to where Catherine is sitting:

> Catherine, catching Mr Tilney's eye, instantly received from him the smiling tribute of recognition. She returned it with pleasure, and then advancing still nearer, he spoke both to her and Mrs Allen, by whom he was very civilly acknowledged. 'I am very happy to see you again, sir, indeed; I was afraid you had left Bath.' He thanked her for her fears, and said that he had quitted it for a week, on the very morning after his having had the pleasure of seeing her.

Henry and Mrs Allen continue their conversation, then:

> . . . after a few minutes consideration, he asked Catherine to dance with him. This compliment, delightful as it was, produced severe mortification to the lady; and in giving her denial, she expressed her sorrow on the occasion so very much as if she really felt it, that had Thorpe, who joined her just afterwards, been half a minute earlier, he might have thought her sufferings rather too acute. The very easy manner in which he then told her that he had kept her waiting, did not by any means reconcile her more to her lot; nor did the particulars which he entered into while they were standing up, of the horses and dogs of the friend whom he had just left, and of a proposed exchange of terriers between them, interest her so much as to prevent her looking very often towards that part of the room where she had left Mr Tilney. Of her dear Isabella, to whom she particularly longed to point out that gentleman, she could see nothing. They were in different sets. She was separated from all her party, and away from all her acquaintance; – one mortification succeeded another, and from the whole she deduced this useful lesson, that to go previously engaged to a ball, does not necessarily increase either the dignity of enjoyment or a young lady.

> (ch. 8)

    This ball at the Upper Rooms is a critical event in Catherine's experience: she is forced by what happens to her there to make judgements and decisions. In a similar way, seeing all the characters in action together helps the reader to clarify and confirm the impressions and judgements which have been building up in the preceding chapters, and so I'm going to use this passage to summarise some of the points made so far.

    The behaviour of the various characters at the ball does nothing to change our opinion of them. Isabella and John Thorpe leave

Catherine alone, Isabella being quickly persuaded to break her vow not to dance until her 'dear love' Catherine does so, and John Thorpe, in spite of his engagement to dance with Catherine, disappearing to discuss, as we later discover, horses and dogs. Their selfishness – even rudeness in the case of John Thorpe – is once again contrasted with Catherine's self-restraint ('no murmur passed her lips') and with Henry Tilney's faultless good manners in acknowledging Catherine's acquaintance, politely talking to Mrs Allen and asking Catherine to dance. The difference between what Isabella says and what she actually thinks or does again draws attention to a kind of dishonesty, a readiness to mouth phrases (like 'my dear love') which actually have very little substance, which is very different from Catherine's sincere attachment to her friend and from the unaffected openness of her regret at being unable to dance with Henry Tilney – no thought of playing hard to get by pretending she doesn't mind! Henry himself is still something of an unknown quantity – is he genuinely interested in Catherine or is he just being polite? – but, compared with the Thorpes' behaviour, his politeness is a very positive quality.

What techniques are involved in confirming these impressions of the characters? The extract is controlled throughout by the authorial voice telling the reader what is happening, but it's important to note that events are recounted very much from Catherine's point of view. This is not to say that there is no distance between Catherine and the narrator – when we look at the passage closely, in fact, it becomes clear that the distance between them varies considerably. Catherine would be unlikely to say of herself that she had 'too much good-nature' to object to Isabella leaving her – that is surely the narrator giving us a very clear reminder of how much nicer Catherine is than her friend. On the other hand, the description of Henry Tilney, 'as handsome and as lively as ever', probably comes pretty close to Catherine's own thoughts, and it's surely Catherine rather than the narrator who refers to Isabella as 'her dear Isabella'. Once again, the narrative position allows us to sympathise with Catherine but at the same time to see her as part of an overall pattern.

Our sympathy with Catherine, which is encouraged by the fact that we see these events predominantly from her point of view, plays an important part in directing our judgement. Catherine suffers because of the Thorpes' behaviour and the reader shares her indignance at the way she has been treated and her frustration in being unable to dance with Henry. The moral oppositions between sincerity and dishonesty, thoughtfulness and selfishness, which seemed earlier to characterise the contrasts between the various characters, are here confirmed as they are seen in action, in their effects on the character with whom we are closely involved, and this sympathetic involvement directs us into making the right choice between them.

At the same time, we can see Catherine as part of a larger scheme; the narrator refers to her in a rather distanced way as 'the heroine', for example, and her irritation at being left alone and thought to be without a partner is dramatically described as 'infamy' and 'debasement'. These could be Catherine's own terms of course, taken from her reading of romantic novels to describe her own situation, but however sympathetic we are to Catherine's sufferings, our judgement as readers is alerted by this obviously inflated way of describing a young girl's disappointments at her first major ball. The term 'heroine' and this disproportion between tragic language and the actual experience to which it refers, recall the opening chapter where the contrast was set up between the characteristics and experiences of the usual heroines of novels and those of Catherine herself. Conventional novels, in which the heroines really *are* 'disgraced in the eyes of the world' so that their 'fortitude' is put to the test, are here implicitly opposed to this novel in which the 'disgrace' is simply appearing to have no dancing partner. Fiction, in which important and dramatic events take place, is contrasted with very ordinary and apparently unimportant reality. But what is the effect of the comparison? Is it to ridicule Catherine's view of the importance of her experience? This would be one obvious answer. Or is it to ridicule conventional novels for depicting events most girls never do experience? Perhaps a bit of both. It certainly makes us ask questions about what *is* important, about why such weighty terms might even be thought to be appropriate to describe such an ordinary experience, about, indeed, why a novel takes as its subject a young girl's unspectacular progress through the familiar excitements and setbacks of courtship.

Again, these are important questions not just for *Northanger Abbey* but for any of Jane Austen's novels. You might have found yourself wondering what this concern with good manners and trivial conversation is all about – the more so perhaps if you are a male reader: men often get on with Jane Austen's novels much less readily than women. If you do find these novels inconsequential it's important not simply to dismiss them, but to try to use this impression to ask further questions. *Why* do they seem so? Is it something to do with the kinds of events we are trained to consider important and, in consequence, the kinds of subject-matter we expect in novels? And do those things differ for men and women? Jane Austen writes about the private lives of young women, whose experience is limited in their society to a small group of acquaintance and a restricted round of social events. This passage about the ball makes clear Catherine's comparative powerlessness to put her own desires into action. Social convention means that she can neither ask Henry Tilney to dance nor explain to him the reality of her feelings and situation. Yet, as I've already suggested, what happens in Bath could affect her happiness for the rest of her life and the ability to see through surface manners, through what people actually say, to their deeper moral implications is crucial. Jane Austen might not write about the large public events which are generally considered to be 'important', but the private world she does depict is of at least as much consequence for the women involved. And though we read her novels from a distance of two hundred years, it's worth asking whether this distinction between the private and the public worlds, with its associated assumptions about what really matters, doesn't still operate. Why is it still women rather than men who read romantic fiction? Does this have anything to do with the fact that they tend to get on better with Jane Austen? And aren't all these questions part of Jane Austen's point in thus drawing attention to the difference between her own novels and the unreal melodrama of more conventional stories?

Catherine herself learns a lesson about what is and is not important at the end of this extract. She had assumed that above all else it was vital to have a partner rather than be thought unable to attract anyone, but after what happens she learns that 'to go previously engaged to a ball, does not necessarily increase either the dignity or the enjoyment of a young lady'. She learns, in fact, that who the partner is and the freedom to choose matter much more than the mere appearance of having someone to dance with. She is beginning to discover the difference between attractive appearance and real value, an important lesson given what we have seen of Isabella, and it is in this sense that the ball is a turning-point, a kind of crisis, for Catherine. Until now, Catherine has treated everything that has happened to her and the people she has met with the same good-natured acceptance; it has been the reader, directed by the narrative voice in the ways I have examined, who has judged between them. Now Catherine too begins to discriminate good from bad, the important from the trivial, and in doing so she begins to lose some of her naïvety and to become morally *active* rather than passive.

To make this point more clearly I have chosen one last, short, extract from *Northanger Abbey*. It comes from the chapter following the ball. Catherine has to fulfil her earlier promise to John Thorpe to go for a drive with him, an experience which only confirms her impression of the previous evening:

> Little as Catherine was in the habit of judging for herself, and unfixed as were her general notions of what men ought to be, she could not entirely repress a doubt, while she bore with the effusions of his endless conceit, of his being altogether completely agreeable. It was a bold surmise, for he was Isabella's brother; and she had been assured by James, that his manners would recommend him to all her sex; but in spite of this, the extreme weariness of his company, which crept over her before they had been out an hour, and which continued unceasingly to increase till they stopped in Pulteney-street again, induced her, in some small degree, to resist such high authority, and to distrust his powers of giving universal pleasure.
>
> (ch. 9)

And to add insult to injury, when she gets home she finds that she has missed meeting Henry Tilney and his sister!

The passage makes clear how unused and unwilling Catherine is to judging for herself or contradicting others' authority. It also makes clear how right she is to do so in this case: the authorial voice endorses Catherine's feelings about John Thorpe in its damning descriptions of 'the effusions of his endless conceit'. The reader is delighted by Catherine's show of independence, however small. She is prepared to contradict the male authority of her adored brother and even to doubt Isabella's perfection – progress indeed towards a moral maturity which will, we hope, protect her against mistakes and unhappiness.

I am going to leave *Northanger Abbey* there and I want now to summarise what I have tried to do in my analysis of these extracts from the early part of the novel. My main aim has been to offer you an analytic model, a method which will help you choose and examine passages from any of Jane Austen's novels so that in your essays you can show how your arguments and ideas grow out of a close reading of the text. This method has five main elements:

1. Read the whole novel through first.

2. Choose examples of different narrative methods for analysis: a description of character, a conversation, a passage in the authorial voice, a social event. Sometimes, of course, these categories will overlap (a social event might be mainly in the authorial voice but contain several conversations), but the important thing is that you are aware as you read of the way different narrative techniques are involved in forming your impressions.

3. Start from your own impressions, however simple or vague you might feel they are, and begin your analysis by asking questions about how you arrived at those impressions. This will help you to start thinking about the relationship between your own assumptions (the 'life' bit, in Virginia Woolf's phrase) and the effect of the way the novel is organised (the 'something that is not life').

4. As a way into your examination of each of your chosen passages, use the three questions I gave you earlier. Look at the point of view from which the passage is presented. Read the passage carefully to see whether it contains any words which seem to be given particular importance and try to decide why. Look for oppositions and contrasts in the passage which might point towards the novel's general preoccupations: these might be contrasts between characters or they might be more abstract. In my analysis of passages from *Northanger Abbey* I focused on several of these, all of which recur in Jane Austen's fiction. I looked, for example, at oppositions between fiction and ordinary life, fantasy and reality; between surface appearance and the reality underneath; between moral qualities like deviousness and sincerity, selfishness and thoughtfulness; and between male and female roles and different ideas of what is and is not important. This is by no means a full list – you will be able to add many others from your own analyses – but it might help as an initial guide.

5. Look for ways in which your observations on the individual passages help to build up a sense of the novel's overall themes and patterns. Thematic oppositions obviously contribute to this, as do patterns of contrast and comparison between characters, and the way the story or plot develops is also important.

I want to focus on plot in my discussion of Jane Austen's second novel, *Sense and Sensibility* (written 1797; published 1811). The first point to make clear is that this is not quite the same thing as the story. An account simply of the events in the order in which they happen (the story) doesn't really give an accurate idea of what a novel is 'about' in any important sense. For that, we need an account of how those events relate to each other and how they are organised in order to make us see their significance. If our interest in a novel depended just on finding out what happens in the end, we would be unlikely ever to reread it and studying novels would be a very tedious business. Though the events in a novel are obviously important, they are organised by the plot into patterns which alert the reader to the thematic concerns which are going to keep us interested in the novel long after we know how things turn out, and a good critical analysis of a novel should always be concerned with *how* the events and characters are used in the overall thematic or moral pattern. In *Northanger Abbey*, for example, what happens in the first few chapters can be summed up very simply – Catherine goes to Bath, meets various people and goes to her first major ball – but that gives no idea at all of the significance of those events. A satisfactory account would have to describe the differences between her new acquaintances, the ways in which those differences can be seen to set up a significant moral pattern which reaches a kind of provisional climax at the ball, and the effect of that event on Catherine's development. The pattern of the *plot*, in other words, is dependent on the juxtaposition and interpretation of the events of the story. *Northanger Abbey* is really as much 'about' Catherine Morland's growth to maturity, her moral education, as it is about her going to Bath and finding a husband.

There is a basic plot pattern which recurs in Jane Austen's novels and works both within sections of the novels and over whole works. This is the pattern of progression which I have just described from the opening chapters of *Northanger Abbey*: the setting up of characters and issues, the movements to a climax or crisis, and the changed judgements which result from that. I'm going to look now at this pattern as it works in *Sense and Sensibility*. In order to highlight the novel's overall pattern, I shall be analysing *Sense and Sensibility* in a much less detailed way than I did *Northanger Abbey*. Again, my analysis of this particular novel is intended to provide you with a model which you can then apply to whichever novel you are studying.

Looking at plot: *Sense and Sensibility*

Sense and Sensibility is about two sisters, Elinor and Marianne Dashwood. The unexpected death of Mr Dashwood forces the sisters and their mother to live on a much reduced income because the family estate is left to the male line, to a son by their father's first marriage. They are persuaded to move from Norland, their home in Sussex, to a cottage on the estate of a cousin, Sir John Middleton, of Barton Park in Devonshire. Before they leave Norland, an attachment has formed between Elinor and Edward Ferrars, the brother of her sister-in-law and heir to a large estate. At Barton, Marianne meets and falls deeply in love with Willoughby, the cousin of a neighbour.

Both relationships encounter problems. Elinor discovers that Edward has been engaged for some years to Lucy Steele, an ambitious and unpleasant young woman. He feels bound to honour their engagement, though he no longer loves her. Willoughby abruptly disappears from Barton with no explanation and, when the sisters spend some time in London, fails to get in touch with Marianne in spite of her notes to him and in spite of the fact that many people, including Marianne herself, had taken their engagement for granted. They then hear that he has married a rich heiress, and also that in the past he was responsible for seducing and then abandoning the close relation of Colonel Brandon, a neighbour at Barton Park who is in love with Marianne. The shock of Willoughby's behaviour makes Marianne dangerously ill. However, things work out for the two sisters in the end. Lucy Steele elopes with Edward's younger brother, now the heir since Edward's mother disinherited him when she found out about his engagement to Lucy. This leaves Edward free to marry Elinor. And when Marianne recovers from her illness, she has realised her fault in being so infatuated with Willoughby and eventually marries her much older but loyal and respectable admirer, Colonel Brandon.

The account I have just given describes the basic story-line of *Sense and Sensibility*, the bare outline of two love stories. But to get any sense of the significance of the plot, of what the novel is really 'about', I need to look more closely at *how* the details of the story are organised, to look for a pattern other than that of the mere events themselves. At the end of my analysis of *Northanger Abbey* I described a plot pattern which I suggested was common to most of Jane Austen's novels: introductory material establishing thematic oppositions; a crisis leading to a change of judgement; and the effects of that change. I'm going to look at *Sense and Sensibility* now, bearing that pattern of development in mind, and I'm going to begin, as I did with *Northanger Abbey*, with Jane Austen's introduction of her main characters, looking for clues about their positions in the plot pattern.

Elinor and Marianne are introduced at the end of the first chapter; they are in mourning for their father and angered by the way their step-brother and his wife have moved into Norland straight after the funeral. Elinor dissuades her mother from leaving immediately:

> Elinor, this eldest daughter whose advice was so effectual, possessed a strength of understanding, and coolness of judgment, which qualified her, though only nineteen, to be the counsellor of her mother, and enabled her frequently to counteract, to the advantage of them all, that eagerness of mind in Mrs Dashwood which must generally have led to imprudence. She had an excellent heart; – her disposition was affectionate, and her feelings were strong; but she knew how to govern them: it was a knowledge which her mother had yet to learn, and which one of her sisters had resolved never to be taught.
>
> Marianne's abilities were, in many respects, quite equal to Elinor's. She was sensible and clever; but eager in every thing; her sorrows, her joys, could have no moderation. She was generous, amiable, interesting: she was every thing but prudent. The resemblance between her and her mother was strikingly great.
>
> Elinor saw, with concern, the excess of her sister's sensibility; but by Mrs Dashwood it was valued and cherished. They encouraged each other now in the violence of their affliction. The agony of grief which overpowered them at first, was voluntarily renewed, was sought for, was created again and again. They gave themselves up wholly to their sorrow, seeking increase of wretchedness in every reflection that could afford it, and resolved against ever admitting consolation in future. Elinor, too, was deeply afflicted; but she could still struggle, she could exert herself. She could consult with her brother, could receive her sister-in-law on her arrival, and treat her with proper attention; and could strive to rouse her mother to similar exertion, and encourage her to similar forbearance.
>
> (ch. 1)

The narrative voice controls the passage, giving us an objective comparative assessment of Elinor and Marianne. The narrator's account seems at this stage to be free of irony and though she sees good qualities in both sisters, our own views of the two are inevitably affected by the fact that judgement is clearly weighted in favour of Elinor. What is this judgement based on? The description of the sisters focuses on their capacity for and control over their feelings and various words take on particular importance. In Elinor's case it is her *understanding* and *judgement* which are stressed and which make her able to *govern* both her own strong feelings and her mother's '*eagerness* of mind which must generally have led to *imprudence*'. Marianne, like her mother, is *eager* and 'everything but *prudent*', her feelings lack *moderation*. At the beginning of the third paragraph, we meet one of the terms from the book's title: 'Elinor saw, with concern, the excess of her sister's *sensibility*'. It looks as though the opposition suggested by the title is to be represented by the two major characters. They are contrasted in this extract in terms of their ability to *govern* their feelings, the degree to which, perhaps, they show *sense*. But the importance of paying close attention to exactly how words are used is clearly demonstrated here. Marianne's fault is not just a matter of her sensibility (which might be an unfamiliar term to a modern reader but which seems here to have to do with strong feelings), but the *excess* of that sensibility. It might seem that Elinor is, according to modern terminology, the 'sensible' one, but Marianne too is described as '*sensible* and clever' (and in the paragraph which follows this extract the third sister is described as having 'already imbibed a good deal of Marianne's romance, without having much of her *sense*') – and the narrator is also concerned to point out that Elinor has strong feelings.

The words 'sense', 'sensible', 'sensibility' have shifted slightly in meaning since Jane Austen wrote, though they were beginning to be used as we use them today. You needn't worry too much at this stage about the details of those shifts in meaning, though it *is* important that you are aware that Jane Austen sometimes uses words in a slightly different way from us. (If you are studying *Sense and Sensibility* you might be interested to look these terms up in a historical dictionary like the *Oxford English Dictionary* which shows the ways in which definitions of words have changed.) What I want to point out here is the way in which attention to key terms can alert us to central issues in a novel and the quite complex way in which Jane Austen uses her terms. Though there is an important opposition present, a careful reading makes it clear that it isn't simply a matter of sense being a good thing and sensibility bad, or vice versa. Both sisters have something of both. What *does* seem to be significant is the degree to which individuals control and use the feelings they have.

The effects of this control or lack of it are made clear in the third paragraph. Marianne and her mother indulge their feelings and leave Elinor to cope with her brother and sister-in-law, to give them '*proper* attention'. Another opposition is implicitly set up, between selfishness and social duty or, to put it in even bolder terms, between the different demands of *self* and *society*. And the novel clearly approves of Elinor's ability to hide her own grief in the interests of good manners.

The way in which the two main characters are introduced, then, makes it clear that the plot of *Sense and Sensibility* is to deal not just with the Dashwood sisters' love affairs but with the ways in which two rather different personalities react to their experiences of love and of society in general. In other words, this is to be a drama of *values* rather than of events. Their taste in men, for example, illustrates the moral contrast between them. Marianne is disappointed by Elinor's fondness for Edward. She finds, ' "a something wanting – his figure is not striking; it has none of that grace which I should expect in the man who could seriously attach my sister" ' (ch. 3). Willoughby, of course, is very good-looking and, unlike Edward, shows his feelings in an obvious way. What Marianne reveals here is a tendency to confuse *outer* signs with *inner* qualities and her hasty judgements according to surface evidence make her vulnerable to Willoughby's cruelty. Elinor on the other hand, as she says at one point, prefers to give herself ' "time to deliberate and judge" ' (ch. 17). She sees through Edward's quiet manner to his real worth.

With Elinor and Marianne established as joint heroines, each with an attendant hero, the main events of the novel get underway and our interest lies in finding out how their different attitudes will affect their relationships. The thematic contrast between the sisters is made very clear by the way in which their experiences run in parallel. Willoughby's abrupt departure from Devonshire is closely followed by that of Edward and both girls are left without any explanation of their lovers' motives or assurance of their feelings. Though the girls' experiences are similar, however, their reactions to them are rather different and the reader is very clearly invited to make comparisons. On the day Willoughby leaves, no one sees Marianne until dinner-time when she reappears with eyes 'red and swollen', avoiding everyone's looks and unable to eat or speak:

> This violent oppression of spirits continued the whole evening. She was without any power, because she was without any desire of command over herself. The slightest mention of any thing relative to Willoughby overpowered her in an instant; and though her family were most anxiously attentive to her comfort, it was impossible for them, if they spoke at all, to keep clear of every subject which her feelings connected with him.
>
> (ch. 15)

Marianne's behaviour here is explicitly recalled by the narrator when Edward takes leave of Elinor: 'she did not employ the method so judiciously employed by Marianne, on a similar occasion, to augment and fix her sorrow, by seeking silence, solitude and idleness'. Instead:

Elinor sat down to her drawing-table as soon as he was out of the house, busily employed herself the whole day, neither sought nor avoided the mention of his name, appeared to interest herself almost as much as ever in the general concerns of the family, and if, by this conduct, she did not lessen her own grief, it was at least prevented from unnecessary increase, and her mother and sisters were spared much solicitude on her account.

Such behaviour as this, so exactly the reverse of her own, appeared no more meritorious to Marianne, than her own had seemed faulty to her. The business of self-command she settled very easily; – with strong affections it was impossible, with calm ones it could have no merit. That her sister's affections *were* calm, she dared not deny, though she blushed to acknowledge it; and of the strength of her own, she gave very striking proof, by still loving and respecting that sister, in spite of this mortifying conviction.

(ch. 19)

In these explicit comparisons between the sisters' reactions to similar events the narrator's sympathies are very obviously with Elinor, who is gradually being established as a model of self-control in contrast with Marianne's self-indulgence. The two characters are clearly part of the novel's *didactic* purpose, its aim to teach a moral lesson, and we might expect the plot's overall development to be organised to the same end. As always, it's important to consider *how* our responses are being manipulated to fit this didactic purpose. In these passages, for example, the oppositions between selfishness and concern for others which we have already noted are again emphasised in the stress on the ways in which the two girls do or do not involve the whole family in their distress.

The position of the narrator is also crucial. The account of Marianne's grief remains fairly detached: it is described through her external symptoms and effect on her family, and we are allowed to see her state of mind only through the negative observation that she was unable to control herself because she had no desire to do so. When Elinor's suffering is first contrasted with Marianne's she is described as not adopting 'the method so *judiciously* employed by Marianne' and the immediate impression is that the narrator is treating Marianne positively. In fact, of course, 'judiciously' is used ironically: the actual suggestion is that Marianne's grief was the result of her melodramatic behaviour rather than the other way round, that her feelings were in large part a matter of surface. Elinor's suffering is quite the opposite: she hides her feelings from her family so successfully that Marianne, judging as usual by appearances, thinks she doesn't really care. The reader, however, should not make the same mistake. The narrator, though still mainly describing Elinor from the outside, makes her feelings very clear. She only *'appeared* to interest herself' in her family's concerns, and by doing so she *'did not lessen* her own grief'. Although she is silent, her suffering is none the less acute.

Many readers find Elinor much less attractive than Marianne, in spite of her positive role within the didactic plot. She is much less lively than her sister, she can even seem priggish, and her willingness to compromise, to tell white lies in difficult social situations, can look like dishonesty. It is important that you don't assume that a response which goes against what seems to be the narrative's didactic purpose is therefore *wrong*. It is easy to overlook the fact that Elinor suffers a great deal silently and so deserves sympathy, but if you do find that your own sympathies are primarily with Marianne then, as always, it is better to use your responses to raise further questions than to assume they have to give way to someone else's reading. In *Sense and Sensibility* Elinor seems to stand for the view that to behave in a socially acceptable way is at least as important as being true to your own feelings; in the opposition between self and society she is on the side of society. Any doubts we might have about her can lead on to legitimate questions about the relative claims of self and others, about what degree of compromise actually is acceptable. They can also alert us to the fact that a modern view might differ from Jane Austen here, reminding us of the historical differences which inevitably affect our judgements. And they can be very important as the plot develops in encouraging us to question the ways in which Marianne seems to be punished for her earlier mistakes.

So far my analysis of the plot of *Sense and Sensibility* has concentrated on the moral contrasts demonstrated by the sisters' reactions to events, moral contrasts whose importance is made clear by the plot's organisation of those events, thus establishing the novel's didactic pattern. I have looked at passages from what I have described earlier as the first section of the plot, where characters and issues are being established and events set in motion. I'm going to leap now to much nearer the end of the novel to look at the way this pattern is worked out through the crises in the plot. Willoughby is now married to his heiress and the full story of how he seduced and ruined Eliza, the daughter of Colonel Brandon's adopted sister, is known. Marianne is ill from emotional and nervous exhaustion. When Willoughby arrives at the house where she is staying to explain his conduct, Elinor unwillingly listens to what he has to say. Marianne's illness and Willoughby's account of his conduct stand as the final crises in the novel: they precipitate judgement both in Marianne and in Elinor and it's this I want to look at now. To give you an idea of Willoughby's conversation with Elinor I'm going to quote first from his account of his affair with Eliza:

> 'I do not mean to justify myself, but at the same time cannot leave you to suppose that I have nothing to urge – that because she was injured she was irreproachable, and because *I* was a libertine, *she* must be a saint. If the violence of her passions, the weakness of her understanding – I do not mean, however, to defend myself. Her affection for me deserved better treatment, and I often, with great self-reproach, recall the tenderness which, for a very short time, had the power of creating any return. I wish – I heartily wish it had never been. But I have injured more than herself; and I have injured one, whose affection for me – (may I say it?) was scarcely less warm than her's; and whose mind – Oh! how infinitely superior!' –
>
> [Elinor:] 'Your indifference, however, towards that unfortunate girl – I must say it, unpleasant to me as the discussion of such a subject may well be – your indifference is no apology for your cruel neglect of her. Do not think yourself excused by any weakness, any natural defect of understanding on her side, in the wanton cruelty so evident on yours. You must have known, that while you were enjoying yourself in Devonshire pursuing fresh schemes, always gay, always happy, she was reduced to the extremest indigence.'

(ch. 44)

Willoughby's broken sentences and exclamations indicate his agitation. This state of extreme feeling and apparent suffering at what he has done to Marianne are very likely to evoke sympathy, particularly when combined with our memories of his old attractiveness. His attempt to lay much of the blame on Eliza, however, is rather less attractive and Elinor's sharp criticism that his not loving Eliza was no excuse for ruining her is an important reminder of the effects of his behaviour. Marianne, after all, has escaped comparatively lightly; Eliza's life has been ruined. However much Willoughby protests that he loves Marianne, his treatment of Eliza raises the possibility that he might have treated Marianne in the same way. He describes himself as a libertine and it's important that as modern readers we recognise the full implications of that term for Jane Austen's contemporaries. Eliza is a victim of the double sexual standard: men's sexual adventures were largely taken for granted and overlooked, even if they were not approved of; for women on the other hand any sexual misdemeanour meant disgrace unless followed by marriage to the man concerned, and even then it might take society a long time to forgive and forget. Willoughby, on the other hand, is respectably married to his heiress. Jane Austen's novels almost all include elopements or seductions, whose role in the plot is to stand as warnings of the dire consequences of wrong judgement. The revelations about Willoughby's past suggest one possible outcome of Marianne's (and many readers') response to Willoughby's external attractiveness. Her belief that her own feelings arc trucr than social forms, her assumption that she and Willoughby were engaged though he had never publicly acknowledged the fact, is made to look positively dangerous.

To this extent, then, the plot is used to endorse Elinor's concern for social form, her judgement according to sense rather than sensibility. Her prudence (to use a key word from the very first extract I quoted) at least provides a degree of protection from men like Willoughby. But a full analysis of plot must deal not only with the climax of events but with the judgements which follow. So my final extracts from the novel are chosen to illustrate the *effects* on both girls of their experiences.

Her conversation with Willoughby leaves Elinor with mixed feelings:

> Willoughby, he, whom only half an hour ago she had abhorred as the most worthless of men, Willoughby, in spite of all his faults, excited a degree of commiseration for the sufferings produced by them, which made her think of him as now separated for ever from her family with a tenderness, a regret, rather in proportion, as she soon acknowledged within herself – to his wishes than to his merits. She felt that his influence over her mind was heightened by circumstances which ought not in reason to have weight; by that person of uncommon attraction, that open, affectionate, and lively manner which it was no merit to possess; and by that still ardent love for Marianne, which it was not even innocent to indulge. But she felt that it was so, long, long, before she could feel his influence less.
>
> (ch. 45)

The narrative voice is here wholly within Elinor's point of view as she analyses her response and we see first-hand the power of Willoughby's person and manner, the very features which attracted Marianne, even over Elinor. Key words in the passage seem to me to be *felt*, used three times to describe her process of response, and *in reason*, used to describe the way she knows she ought to be responding. These terms, feeling and reason, often appear as opposites and are versions of the opposition between sensibility and sense which broadly characterises the two sisters throughout the novel. The crisis with Willoughby is a real test of Elinor's 'sense', and evidence of the strength of her 'sensibility'. In the end, her judgement of Willoughby remains firm, but through the narrative closeness to her point of view here we share her struggle to maintain that judgement in spite of her sympathetic feelings towards him. (A short time later, in the happier circumstances of discovering that Lucy Steele has married Robert and not Edward Ferrars, Elinor is allowed the relief of giving in wholly to her feelings: 'She almost ran out of the room, and as soon as the door was closed, burst into tears of joy, which at first she thought would never cease' (ch. 48).)

Marianne's struggle takes the form of her illness which, as she admits to Elinor when she recovers, gives her the opportunity to think:

> 'It has given me leisure and calmness for serious recollection. Long before I was enough recovered to talk, I was perfectly able to reflect. I considered the past; I saw in my own behaviour since the beginning of our acquaintance with him last autumn, nothing but a series of imprudence towards myself, and want of kindness to others. I saw that my own feelings had prepared my sufferings, and that my want of fortitude under them had almost led me to the grave. My illness, I well knew, had been entirely brought on by myself, by such negligence of my own health, as I had felt even at the time to be wrong. Had I died, – it would have been self-destruction.'
>
> (ch. 46)

Because this is conversation, we are given Marianne's experience in her own words without authorial intervention. It's worth asking, though, whether this is more or less vivid than the previous account of Elinor's reactions to Willoughby, which was in the authorial voice but presented from Elinor's point of view. In this speech Marianne seems to be speaking for the author, so well has she learned her lesson, and the terms she uses are familiar pointers to the novel's moral pattern. She accuses herself, for example, of *imprudence*, and of selfishness in her 'want of kindness to others', and she recognises that her 'want of fortitude' in coping with her feelings led to her sufferings. This self-accusation is the result of having had time to *reflect*, in contrast with her earlier impetuosity. It's possible of course that Marianne's capacity for self-dramatisation has something to do with this apparently complete change of heart – and, not surprisingly, she finds it difficult to live up to her own ideal of 'finding her only pleasures in retirement and study' (ch. 50). But the important point for an analysis of the plot is that she is able to learn from her mistakes, and in the terms which govern the novel's moral pattern: ' "my *feelings* shall be *governed*" ' she promises (ch. 46); in the extract from the first chapter which I quoted earlier it was said of Elinor that 'her *feelings* were strong; but she knew how to *govern* them'.

So both Elinor and Marianne can be seen as part of the novel's didactic scheme. Both suffer as a result of their capacity for feeling and both, though with different degrees of difficulty, exert sense over sensibility. And they are rewarded at the end with marriage – Elinor to Edward Ferrars and Marianne to Colonel Brandon, the man 'whom, two years before, she had considered too old to be married' (ch. 50) but who has throughout been devoted to her. Like all romantic love stories, Jane Austen's novels invariably end with marriage so it's an aspect of the novels I shall be looking at again. What I hope this analysis of *Sense and Sensibility* makes clear is that marriage plays an important role in the plot's moral scheme. It is not just a matter of providing a happy ending to the story, but of symbolically rewarding the heroines for reaching the right judgement.

I hope this analysis of *Sense and Sensibility* has demonstrated that a full account of the plot of a novel must deal with far more than simply what happens. In your own analyses, you should be constantly asking questions about the significance of the way events are organised, about the didactic patterns set up by the plot. Jane Austen's novels, I have suggested, all work on a very similar basic plot pattern, so my account of that in *Sense and Sensibility* is intended to provide a model for whichever novel you are studying. This basic pattern has three main stages: the introduction of characters and, through them, the setting up of the issues they represent; the movement, through their interactions, to a crisis or climax of some sort which often changes either their judgement or ours, or both; and an exploration of the effects of that crisis. This basic pattern might be repeated a few times in one novel. To illustrate this in *Sense and Sensibility* I have chosen passages from each of the three stages, trying as far as possible to use examples of different kinds of narrative, and analysing them using the method I gave you in the first half of this chapter. This combines an overview, a sense of the overall pattern of a novel, with close analysis of individual passages.

This combination of a sense of overall pattern illustrated by a detailed analysis of particular passages, beginning with your own responses, is the basis of the method I have been trying to establish in this chapter. It's a method which you can apply to any Jane Austen novel and throughout the rest of the book I shall be using it as the basis for my analysis of the four major novels. In the following chapters I shall be looking in more detail at many of the issues and narrative techniques which I have introduced here, and I shall be asking other questions and raising different, sometimes more complex, problems. (How satisfied are we, for example, by Marianne being married off rather suddenly at the end of *Sense and Sensibility* to a much older man, and what questions does this raise about Jane Austen's didactic endings?) By basing this further analysis firmly in the method introduced in this chapter I hope to give you the confidence to go on yourselves to ask more searching questions of Jane Austen's novels.

2

Money and marriage:
Pride and Prejudice

AT the end of both *Northanger Abbey* and *Sense and Sensibility* the heroines marry the men they love. In each case these happen to be men whose incomes are large enough to ensure that they will be able to live comfortably for the rest of their lives. What it means to 'live comfortably' varies according to the heroine concerned – Marianne needs rather more than Elinor to make her content – but they all end up considerably better off than they began. Money is extremely important in all Jane Austen's work and it's an aspect of her fiction which some readers find difficult to cope with. They feel that in some cases both she and her heroines are more interested in money than in more important considerations when it comes to choosing husbands, or that the novels' concern with characters who are comparatively well-off suggests a kind of snobbery. In this chapter on Jane Austen's third novel, *Pride and Prejudice* (published 1813; begun 1796–7), I'm going to continue my focus on plot, suggesting how this kind of response can be used to raise important questions about the relationships between marriage and money, the two essential elements in the plots of all the novels.

Pride and Prejudice is about the Bennets, a family with five daughters whose rather irresponsible mother's only concern is to see them all well married. By the end of the novel she has succeeded with three of them, Jane, Elizabeth and Lydia, though in Lydia's case disgrace is only narrowly avoided when the family manage to secure her marriage to the worthless Wickham, with whom she has eloped. Jane marries Mr Bingley, a charming and rich young man whom she meets when he rents nearby Netherfield Park, and Elizabeth, the heroine of the novel, marries his proud and even richer friend Darcy, but not before Darcy has tried to remove Bingley from Jane's influence because he thinks the marriage would be beneath him. Elizabeth is already prejudiced against Darcy because he snubs her at a ball and because she believes he has behaved badly to Wickham, whose true character has not yet been revealed. When she discovers the way in which he has influenced Bingley she spiritedly refuses his first offer of marriage. It gradually becomes clear, however, that though proud, Darcy is not guilty of mistreating Wickham and when Wickham and Lydia elope he pays Wickham's debts in order to secure their marriage. This, together with the experience of visiting Darcy's home, Pemberley, convinces Elizabeth that she loves him after all. He and Bingley return to Netherfield, propose to the Bennet sisters and are accepted.

In my introductory chapter I suggested to you a pattern of development which underlies all Jane Austen's plots. A good way of beginning your analysis of an Austen novel is to decide what you think is the main focus of the plot and to choose passages for analysis which seem to you to illustrate its main stages of development: from introductory material to some kind of crisis to the effects of that crisis, using where possible examples of different narrative methods. In *Pride and Prejudice* the plot's main concern is the development of the relationship between Elizabeth and Darcy, so in this chapter I'm going to use passages which trace that development, starting with Darcy's first appearance in the Bennets' neighbourhood. But my choice of passages is also influenced by my interest in marriage and money, much as your own examples will be chosen with specific essay questions in mind. As I suggested in the first chapter, it's often worth paying particular attention to the beginnings of novels, so before turning to the introduction of Darcy I'm going to look at the novel's famous opening lines. The immediate focus here is on the link between money and marriage:

> It is a truth universally acknowledged, that a single man in possession of a good fortune, must be in want of a wife.
> However little known the feelings or views of such a man may be on his first entering a neighbourhood, this truth is so well fixed in the minds of the surrounding families, that he is considered as the rightful property of some one or other of their daughters.
>
> (ch. 1)

Our immediate assumption is that the point of view in the opening sentence is that of the narrator, because of the authority with which this 'truth' seems to be presented, but closer analysis suggests this is perhaps not the case. The opening lines claim that it is a truth '*universally* acknowledged' that a young man should be in want of a wife. But who is actually included in that? Apparently not even the young man himself since, according to the second paragraph, his feelings on the matter are in fact unknown. This contradiction between the claim to 'universal' truth in the first paragraph and the explanation in the second that this is simply the opinion of 'the surrounding families' suggests that the two statements are presented from different points of view: that of the families themselves, followed by the assessment of a more objective observer. Jane Austen's irony is immediately at work, drawing the reader's attention to the motivation of these surrounding families whose 'universal truth' depends on their hopes for their own daughters. They see marriage as the natural consequence of having a 'good fortune', whereas the reader might want to argue that affection ought to be the important factor. Jane Austen's irony here depends partly on our bringing that assumption from outside the novel, but it is reinforced by the reference to the *feelings* or views' of the man concerned. In this way an opposition is established from the very beginning between money and love.

In the context of this immediate opposition, the word *property* takes on interesting importance and can be seen as a key word in the passage. It suggests that for these families marriage is about possession, not only of a fortune but of a person – indeed the two seem to be completely identified. Again, the reader (and particularly a modern reader) might want to argue that marriage should be about partnership, a *moral* contract between individuals, rather than a financial takeover of ownership, and these two opposing ideas of marriage reinforce the basic oppositions between money and love.

At this point I want to introduce one extra factor which slightly complicates this straightforward opposition between moral and economic criteria. When Jane Austen was writing (and until 1870) married women legally owned nothing: all their property belonged to their husbands. Yet the only way to financial security for many women of the time was through marriage to a richer man (so that a contemporary reader might be less quick than a modern reader to see affection as the only important reason for marriage). So there is an added irony in these families seeing the eligible young man as the 'rightful property' of one of their daughters. If anyone was to be in possession in financial terms, it would be the young man himself and the daughter's parents (whose point of view this expresses) would effectively sell their daughter, like a piece of property, in exchange for financial relief. Lying behind these two opening sentences, therefore, there is also the opposition between male and female roles familiar from the last chapter, and questions are raised about the different kinds of power open to men and women.

Bearing these introductory oppositions in mind, I'm going now to turn to the main plot, which begins when Bingley and Darcy, two eminently eligible young men, arrive in the Bennets' neighbourhood. The surrounding families meet the young men properly for the first time at a ball in the local assembly rooms:

> Mr Bingley was good looking and gentlemanlike; he had a pleasant countenance, and easy, unaffected manners. His sisters were fine women, with an air of decided fashion. His brother-in-law, Mr Hurst, merely looked the gentleman; but his friend Mr Darcy soon drew the attention of the room by his fine, tall person, handsome features, noble mien; and the report which was in general circulation within five minutes after his entrance, of his having ten thousand a year. The gentlemen pronounced him to be a fine figure of a man, the ladies declared he was much handsomer than Mr Bingley, and he was looked at with great admiration for about half the evening, till his manners gave a disgust which turned the tide of his popularity, for he was discovered to be proud, to be above his company, and above being pleased; and not all his large estate in Derbyshire could then save him from having a most forbidding, disagreeable countenance, and being unworthy to be compared with his friend.
>
> (ch. 3)

By the end of the paragraph, Darcy has been dismissed by the onlookers for being too proud. Are we, as readers, so ready to write him off? Probably not, I suspect, and for at least two reasons, one based on our experience outside the novel, one internal. First, he is tall and handsome (and no doubt dark!) and, for most female readers at least, the experience of reading other romantic fiction suggests that he therefore qualifies as a hero. And his apparently unattractive pride simply makes him more interesting, particularly since, given the title of the novel, his pride takes on immediate thematic importance. To most readers, then, his presentation suggests the type of apparently unattractive character who wins our sympathy and admiration in the end. We are therefore prepared to reserve judgement. Secondly, we have already learned to distrust neighbourhood opinion, and the confusion between feelings and material possessions from the opening of the novel is clearly operating here. The passage is presented very much from the neighbours' point of view, so that we follow their shifting opinions closely but have to supply their motivation. Darcy is at first singled out for attention and his looks admired because he is rumoured to have ten thousand a year. This makes him 'much handsomer' than Bingley (who is rather less rich). By the end of the paragraph, however, he has a 'forbidding, disagreeable countenance' and is unworthy of comparison with his friend because of his bad manners. *Manners* is an important word in the passage. Bingley's manners are 'easy' and 'unaffected' whereas Darcy's manners excite 'disgust'. Manners can be seen in opposition to money, to the economic criteria by which he is initially judged, so that the immediate assumption might be that the neighbours have judged admirably, allowing moral criteria – their objections to his pride – to overcome the attraction even of a 'large estate in Derbyshire', and they are no doubt congratulating themselves on their selfless discrimination. But is it so selfless?

A close examination of the judgements in the passage suggests other possible explanations. The interest the young men arouse is entirely dependent on their eligibility. Mr Hurst, already married, 'merely looked the gentleman' and excites no more attention. Might it not be that Darcy's obvious indifference to the gathered neighbours – 'above his company, and above being pleased' – arouses in them not so much an objective assessment of his bad manners but a resentful recognition that their match-making schemes are likely to be lost on such a man? And what would the scene look like from Darcy's point of view? Perhaps he *is* guilty of bad manners in making his feelings so obvious, but might he not be registering the same distaste for materialistic scheming that we have already felt? Might not his pride in fact have some justification?

An examination of the reader's inclination to reserve judgement on Darcy at this stage thus raises important questions and illustrates the way in which the text invites us to make fine discriminations between various apparently similar positions. In this passage the neighbours operate a *warped* version of the opening opposition between moral and economic criteria. The effect on us as readers is to make us side, if anything, with the proud Darcy. In fact several different kinds of pride are operating in this passage: Darcy's, which seems to be a mixture of snobbery and a more justified moral distaste; Darcy's as seen by the onlookers; theirs, angry at being rejected; and, perhaps, our own in being able to see through and reject the neighbours' motives. Another opposition which is thus implicitly established is between justified and unjustified forms of pride.

My next two extracts focus on Elizabeth as she responds both to Darcy and to other events in the story, and I have chosen passages which illustrate her role in the plot's exploration of the issues of money, marriage and pride. My first extract is from another social occasion, a ball held by Mr Bingley at Netherfield. Elizabeth has by now decided she dislikes Darcy but is nevertheless made thoroughly uncomfortable during the evening by imagining how the behaviour of various members of her family must look to him. At dinner, for example, she is deeply embarrassed by her mother, who is gloating loudly over Bingley's attraction to Jane and assuming that their marriage is imminent:

> In vain did Elizabeth endeavour to check the rapidity of her mother's words, or persuade her to describe her felicity in a less audible whisper; for to her inexpressible vexation, she could perceive that the chief of it was overheard by Mr Darcy, who sat opposite to them. Her mother only scolded her for being nonsensical.
>
> 'What is Mr Darcy to me, pray, that I should be afraid of him? I am sure we owe him no such particular civility as to be obliged to say nothing *he* may not like to hear.'
>
> 'For heaven's sake, madam, speak lower. – What advantage can it be to you to offend Mr Darcy? – You will never recommend yourself to his friend by so doing.'
>
> Nothing that she could say, however, had any influence. Her mother would talk of her views in the same intelligible tone. Elizabeth blushed and blushed again with shame and vexation.
>
> (ch. 18)

Elizabeth's fears about Darcy's reactions are later proved right: he acknowledges that her family's behaviour at the Netherfield ball was instrumental in persuading him to try to separate Bingley and Jane, and Elizabeth agrees with his judgement if not with his action. On various occasions during the novel she is embarrassed by her relations – most obviously when her sister Lydia elopes with Wickham.

How does a modern reader react to Elizabeth's 'shame and vexation'? Some readers find the novel's apparent endorsement of what looks like a rather snobbish set of values impossible to cope with. Indeed I think most readers have experienced something of this reaction, though to different degrees, and if this *is* your response the important thing, as usual, is to *use* it to raise further questions rather than assuming it's 'wrong'. The first thing to ask is exactly what it is about her mother's behaviour that Elizabeth is ashamed of? Is this simply social snobbery or something closer to the moral distaste I suggested even we might feel for self-seeking materialist values? Mrs Bennet is certainly used to exemplify such values in the novel and she is dismissed at the end of the first chapter as 'a woman of mean under-standing, little information, and uncertain temper'. In this passage she is selfishly, and prematurely, gloating over her friend Lady Lucas whose daughter Charlotte is unlikely to make any such match and the novel's opposition between morality and self-interested economics tends to justify Elizabeth's view.

Mrs Bennet has a point though in asking Elizabeth why Darcy's opinion should matter. Elizabeth gives the obvious practical answer: that Darcy's opinion might influence Bingley. Another possibility could be that Elizabeth cares more about Darcy and his opinion of herself than her overt determination to hate him might suggest. So we are perhaps justified in feeling slightly critical of Elizabeth's 'shame': her pride is hurt at having been snubbed by Darcy and she is unwilling to give him any more ammunition against her.

Asking further questions about Elizabeth's reactions has thus helped to establish her position within that essential opposition between economic and moral values; and it has introduced more variations on the theme of pride. But has it done anything to change our unease with the heroine's pride, with the fact that her 'shame and vexation' are occasioned by her own mother? Though Elizabeth might be mildly criticised for failing to understand her own motives, the novel does, as I have pointed out, eventually suggest she was right. Jane Austen's novels are very much about making choices, as I suggested when I looked at *Northanger Abbey*. They are about accepting some values (and the people who represent them) and rejecting others, about arranging things in evaluative order. Accusing Jane Austen of 'snobbery' is an understandable reaction to this aspect of her work – and a valuable one, because analysing its implications at least helps you to explore important features of the novels, even if you never feel entirely happy about the apparent harshness of some of the judgements which result from it.

My second extract focusing on Elizabeth analyses her response to the news that her friend Charlotte Lucas, 'at the age of twenty-seven, without ever having been handsome' (ch. 22), has agreed to marry Elizabeth's cousin, Mr Collins. Mr Collins is the heir to Mr Bennet's estate (again, as in *Sense and Sensibility*, property is left to the male line). He is a stupid clergyman, the worst kind of snob in his uncritical admiration for his arrogant patroness, Lady Catherine de Bourgh, Darcy's aunt. He has also just proposed to Elizabeth and been refused. Charlotte explains her decision to her friend:

'. . . when you have had time to think it all over, I hope you will be satisfied with what I have done. I am not romantic, you know. I never was. I ask only a comfortable home; and considering Mr Collins's character, connections, and situation in life, I am convinced that my chance of happiness with him is as fair, as most people can boast on entering the marriage state.'

. . . It was a long time before [Elizabeth] became at all reconciled to the idea of so unsuitable a match. . . . She had always felt that Charlotte's opinion of matrimony was not exactly like her own, but she could not have supposed it possible that when called into action, she would have sacrificed every better feeling to worldly advantage. Charlotte the wife of Mr Collins, was a most humiliating picture! – And to the pang of a friend disgracing herself and sunk in her esteem, was added the distressing conviction that it was impossible for that friend to be tolerably happy in the lot she had chosen.

(ch. 22)

The views of marriage represented by Charlotte and Elizabeth are obviously versions of those established at the very beginning of the novel and various key words in the passage reinforce that link. Charlotte's interest in a 'comfortable home' is seen by Elizabeth as '*worldly advantage*' and opposed by her to 'every *better feeling*'. Her own idea of happiness in marriage, we gather, has to do with individual compatibility and affection, what Charlotte presumably means by *romantic*. Another set of key words describes Elizabeth's reactions again in terms of pride: Charlotte as Mr Collins's wife is a '*humiliating* picture'; she will be '*disgracing* herself', *sunk* in Elizabeth's *esteem*. And again this seems to be a pride in moral standards. Elizabeth feels ashamed that a friend of hers can fall so far below her own ideals of conduct.

The oppositions in the passage, then, are those already familiar from the earlier extracts: between material and ideal, economic and moral criteria. I want to return, though, to the implications of Charlotte's term 'romantic', the opposite of which is usually 'realistic', because the choice between these two alternatives is rather less clearcut. Though 'romantic' refers here to Elizabeth's view of marriage, it is a term which can have negative associations, suggesting something impractical and hopelessly idealistic, and 'realistic' can be very positive. This opposition puts Charlotte's decision in a slightly different light and complicates our judgements. Charlotte is fully conscious of her motives when she accepts Mr Collins, for she is aware that she is unlikely to get a better, or indeed any other, offer of marriage. Perhaps this *is* a compromise of principle as Elizabeth thinks; perhaps it is a realistic choice in a world where marriage is the only career for a woman in Charlotte's social position. Elizabeth, after all, can afford to be romantic; she is younger and more attractive than Charlotte. So the novel again suggests subtle differences within its main oppositions: Charlotte might be materialistic, but her self-awareness differentiates her markedly from, say, Mrs Bennet with her blind desperation for marriage at all costs. As so often in Jane Austen, judgements are far from cut and dried.

I have used these extracts from the introductory sections of the plot to explore both Darcy and Elizabeth and ways in which the reactions and attitudes of these main characters contribute to our sense of the novel's important thematic concerns. There are interesting similarities between the two characters – they are both clearly capable of justified and unjustified forms of pride, for example – and we are fascinated to know how they will develop as their attitudes are challenged in encountering each other. In order to explore this I have chosen next a passage from one of the main crises in the plot, Darcy's first proposal, a scene in which we see Darcy and Elizabeth together and can therefore begin to analyse their *effects* on each other.

Darcy's offer of marriage seems to burst from him involuntarily:

'In vain have I struggled. It will not do. My feelings will not be repressed. You must allow me to tell you how ardently I admire and love you.'

Elizabeth's astonishment was beyond expression. She stared, coloured, doubted, and was silent. This he considered sufficient encouragement, and the avowal of all that he felt and had long felt for her, immediately followed. He spoke well, but there were feelings besides those of the heart to be detailed, and he was not more eloquent on the subject of tenderness than of pride. His sense of her inferiority – of its being a degradation – of the family obstacles which judgment had always opposed to inclination, were dwelt on with a warmth which seemed due to the consequence he was wounding, but was very unlikely to recommend his suit.

In spite of her deeply-rooted dislike, she could not be insensible to the compliment of such a man's affection, and though her intention did not vary for an instant, she was at first sorry for the pain he was to receive; till, roused to resentment by his subsequent language, she lost all compassion in anger. She tried, however, to compose herself to answer him with patience, when he should have done. He concluded with representing to her the strength of that attachment which, in spite of all his endeavours, he had found it impossible to conquer; and with expressing his hope that it would now be rewarded by her acceptance of his hand. As he said this, she could easily see that he had no doubt of a favourable answer. He *spoke* of apprehension and anxiety, but his countenance expressed real security. Such a circumstance could only exasperate further . . .

Elizabeth challenges Darcy with his behaviour towards her sister, and makes clear she is refusing him on grounds of principle. Darcy continues to assume she is refusing simply out of hurt pride, because of his honesty in admitting he struggled against making so low a connection. Elizabeth replies:

> 'You are mistaken, Mr Darcy, if you suppose that the mode of your declaration affected me in any other way, than as it spared me the concern which I might have felt in refusing you, had you behaved in a more gentleman-like manner.'
> She saw him start at this, but he said nothing, and she continued,
> 'You could not have made me the offer of your hand in any possible way that would have tempted me to accept it.'
> Again his astonishment was obvious; and he looked at her with an expression of mingled incredulity and mortification.
>
> (ch. 34)

The power play between these two haughty characters who find their feelings for each other very difficult to cope with is both exciting and funny. The reader knows that they will marry in the end – even on a first reading it is clear that Darcy is the hero – so our interest lies not in *what* will happen, but in *how* it will come about. What changes have to take place before their marriage becomes a possibility and how do they relate to the debate about motives for marriage already established in the novel?

What light does an analysis of this passage thrown on these questions? The scene is presented from Elizabeth's point of view with the result that we share her indignation at Darcy's grudging acknowledgement of the power of his love. At this point it is Elizabeth who seems to be in the right and therefore Darcy who must change. In the first long paragraph the nature of Darcy's struggle is made clear through pairs of important terms: he is 'not more eloquent on the subject of *tenderness* than of *pride*' and is much concerned with Elizabeth's inferior social status which '*judgment* had always opposed to *inclination*'. Feeling, which clearly includes a strong sexual attraction, is opposed to judgement or reason, personal response to social acceptability, and personal feeling has won. We might expect Elizabeth to respond positively to this, given her views on marriage as a personal rather than a social contract, and indeed 'she could not be insensible to the compliment of such a man's affection', but the way Darcy presents his case makes clear that the power of his feelings has really done nothing to change his sense of superiority: his values remain essentially the same. This would not, in fact, be the kind of marriage Elizabeth seeks, but one in which she was made to feel constantly grateful for Darcy's regard: 'she could easily see that he had no doubt of a favourable answer'. Darcy has not considered her feelings at all.

Because of her 'deeply-rooted dislike', her prejudice against him, Elizabeth is in the supremely powerful position of being able to refuse Darcy in the most effective way possible. She makes it abundantly clear that nothing, even 'a more *gentleman-like* manner' of behaviour, would have induced her to accept him. That term 'gentleman-like', and the realisation that Elizabeth's decision is based not on *social* gratitude but on *moral* principle, clearly hit Darcy hard. (And we learn later, of course, that her description of his failure as a gentleman 'tortured' him (ch. 58).) 'Gentleman' is an important term in Jane Austen's fiction and, as its use here suggests, it implies far more than simply social status. Darcy's birth makes him a gentleman socially, but Elizabeth is using the term to describe a kind of behaviour, a moral quality. Again, an opposition is implicit between social and moral criteria. Unlike Darcy, Elizabeth is here indifferent to social status, or at least she expects someone who is a gentleman in social terms to live up to that label morally.

To deserve Elizabeth, therefore, Darcy has to go much further in his rejection of personal and social pride. He has yet to recognise her as an equal in the *moral* terms which really matter. But what about Elizabeth herself? To achieve an ideal marriage both characters must learn to compromise, so my next extract is chosen to illustrate another crisis in the plot, this time one which is important for Elizabeth's process of adjustment and moral education.

Elizabeth prides herself on her judgement, but the day after Darcy's proposal she receives a letter from him which explains his treatment of the unscrupulous Wickham and convinces her that she is capable of making mistakes. As a result of this, and partly perhaps because she knows Darcy loves her, her feelings towards him begin gradually to soften. Some time later, Elizabeth goes on a tour with her aunt and uncle, the Gardiners, in the course of which they visit Darcy's home, Pemberley (on the assurance that Darcy is away). The visit is a further important influence on Elizabeth's feelings towards Darcy, so I want now to look at the way her impressions of Pemberley are presented. Her first view is of the house itself:

> It was a large, handsome, stone building, standing well on rising ground, and backed by a ridge of high woody hills; – and in front, a stream of some natural importance was swelled into greater, but without any artificial appearance. Its banks were neither formal, nor falsely adorned. Elizabeth was delighted. She had never seen a place for which nature had done more, or where natural beauty had been so little counteracted by an awkward taste.

Inside, the house is equally pleasing:

> The rooms were lofty and handsome, and their furniture suitable to the fortune of their proprietor; but Elizabeth saw, with admiration of his taste, that it was neither gaudy nor uselessly fine; with less of splendour, and more real elegance, than the furniture of Rosings.
>
> 'And of this place,' thought she, 'I might have been mistress! With these rooms I might now have been familiarly acquainted! . . .

The housekeeper's account of Darcy himself reinforces her positive impression:

> 'He is the best landlord, and the best master,' said she, 'that ever lived. Not like the wild young men now-a-days, who think of nothing but themselves. There is not one of his tenants or servants but what will give him a good name. Some people call him proud; but I am sure I never saw any thing of it. To my fancy, it is only because he does not rattle away like other young men.'
>
> (ch. 43)

Though we here see Pemberley very much through Elizabeth's eyes, her view is given the narrator's implicit approval since the opening sentences have the weight of an objective, accurate description: 'It was . . .'. What impression do we get of the reasons for judging Pemberley so positively? We might well suspect Elizabeth of responding simply to the richness and grandeur of the place, giving in to the economic criteria she scorned previously. Is Elizabeth then developing some of Charlotte Lucas's realism and beginning to compromise her principles?

How does an analysis of the key words and oppositions in these extracts help us define Elizabeth's response? One word which occurs in the descriptions both of the grounds and the interior of the house is *taste*. Elizabeth admires Darcy's taste in decoration and furniture, described as 'neither gaudy nor uselessly fine', and, we gather, the same standard of taste has been responsible for landscaping the grounds. The description of the stream in the first paragraph is based on a clear opposition between the *natural* and the *artificial*, good taste apparently consisting of fitting in with rather than 'counteracting' the natural surroundings. Darcy's good taste is thus established in opposition to the 'awkward' taste which has to do with artificiality, false adornment, gaudiness and *uselessness* ('uselessly fine'); it seems to be a matter of *balance*, of discreetly and *responsibly* enhancing and using nature, rather than imposing useless and obviously man-made features upon it. So what appears at first to be simply an *aesthetic* judgement, a judgement about the beauty of appearances, or indeed an even cruder response to evident wealth, in fact involves important *moral* criteria. Darcy's house thus becomes an expression of his personality, and the sense of responsibility suggested by his physical surroundings is then confirmed in the more obviously moral sphere by the housekeeper's praise for his care of his servants and tenants.

Elizabeth is undeniably responding to the power of wealth, to the aesthetic pleasure that would have been involved in being mistress of Pemberley, but the comparison with Rosings (Lady Catherine de Bourgh's house) makes clear that 'real elegance' depends on more than just income. The *responsibility* and *taste* with which that income is used are at least as important. Once again we are faced with economic and moral criteria, but here they are in combination rather than being presented simply as opposites. Wealth brings with it responsibilities (such as acting like a gentleman as well as simply being one in social terms), but it also makes it easier to carry out moral ideals, to live up to the 'real elegance' which seems to be a moral as well as an aesthetic category. Elizabeth's response to Pemberley is rather different from Charlotte Lucas accepting Mr Collins, because the two men are so different, but it involves the same acknowledgement that material comfort as well as personal feelings, realism as well as romance, matter in the choice of a partner.

Jane Austen's novels contain comparatively few descriptions of place and this is the first one that I have analysed, but *because* such descriptions occur infrequently, it's worth paying particular attention to those that are present. What I hope my analysis of the description of Pemberley has made clear is that it is not just 'background', scene-setting which we can afford to skip over as we read, but that it has an important contribution to make to the novel's exploration of particular themes. Just as the characters are arranged to represent particular attitudes within the overall pattern of the novels, so place has a thematic and not just a decorative role in the novels' didactic scheme, and your analysis of descriptions of place should always ask '*how does this fit into the novel's argument?*' The novel which illustrates this most clearly is *Mansfield Park*, and I shall be coming back to this aspect of Jane Austen's method in my chapter on *Mansfield Park*.

The housekeeper's account of Darcy suggests that the impression he gives of pride is mistaken, that it is only reserve, in contrast with the 'wild young men now-a-days' who 'rattle away'. She is judging not by appearances, but by long experience of Darcy's character in action. Darcy's letter explaining his relationship with Wickham has already forced Elizabeth to acknowledge that she had jumped to rather superficial conclusions about Darcy's behaviour, a blow to her pride in her powers of judgement. The housekeeper here confirms that lesson, and the incident emphasises the importance of going beyond *appearances* to the *reality* beneath, an opposition we are already familiar with from *Sense and Sensibility* and which recurs throughout Jane Austen's work.

Elizabeth's original view of Darcy is finally overturned when her sister Lydia elopes with Wickham. In spite of Wickham's abominable treatment of him in the past, and in spite of his dislike of Elizabeth's family, Darcy searches for the couple, pays Wickham's debts and so ensures that he will marry Lydia and save her from social disgrace. My last two passages from *Pride and Prejudice* illustrate the *effect* of these crises in the plot which so radically change Elizabeth's judgement, making her recognise that she loves Darcy. The first describes her coming to this realisation when she thinks their marriage has become an impossibility:

> She began now to comprehend that he was exactly the man, who, in disposition and talents, would most suit her. His understanding and temper, though unlike her own, would have answered all her wishes. It was an union that must have been to the advantage of both; by her ease and liveliness, his mind might have been softened, his manners improved, and from his judgment, information, and knowledge of the world, she must have received benefit of greater importance.
>
> But no such happy marriage could now teach the admiring multitude what connubial felicity really was. An union of a different tendency, and precluding the possibility of the other, was soon to be formed in their family.
>
> How Wickham and Lydia were to be supported in tolerable independence, she could not imagine. But how little of permanent happiness

could belong to a couple who were only brought together because their passions were stronger than their virtue, she could easily conjecture.

(ch. 50)

The second describes her feelings after their engagement, when Elizabeth 'did all she could' to shield Darcy from her mother:

and was ever anxious to keep him to herself, and to those of her family with whom he might converse without mortification; and though the uncomfortable feelings arising from all this took from the season of courtship much of its pleasure, it added to the hope of the future; and she looked forward with delight to the time when they should be removed from society so little pleasing to either, to all the comfort and elegance of their family party at Pemberley.

(ch. 60)

I want to use my analysis of these passages which are again like so much of the novel, presented primarily from Elizabeth's point of view, to draw together the ideas of marriage and money on which I have been focusing in this chapter. As always the key words and oppositions in the passages direct attention to the important concerns, and as we might expect at the end of the novel many of these are by now familiar.

The first passage defines Elizabeth's view of a '*happy marriage*', the marriage which of course takes place at the end of the story, rewarding Elizabeth and Darcy for their ability to change and learn. It also sets this ideal against the 'union of a different tendency' between Lydia and Wickham, who are described as 'brought together because their passions were stronger than their virtue'. The attention to different kinds of marriages in the passage recalls the other views of marriage which have so far been examined in the novel, notably that of Charlotte Lucas when she accepts Mr Collins, and that of the neighbours in the opening chapter who see marriage as a purely economic contract. Three factors are now present: Elizabeth's ideal; the mercenary view we are already familiar with; and the 'passions', the sheer sexual attraction of Wickham and Lydia. What then is involved in this ideal of 'connubial felicity'? Elizabeth imagines their union as being 'to the advantage of both': Darcy will be 'softened' by her influence; she will benefit from his wider experience. It is an image of *balanced* harmony, an idea we have met already in the description of Pemberley, where nature is complemented by taste. It is important to recognise that this balanced union is not a simple rejection of the other two versions of marriage. We have already seen the power of Darcy's sexual attraction to Elizabeth, and her recognition at Pemberley of the attractions of wealth, so their marriage will *include* both the 'passion' of Lydia and Wickham and a realistic view of the importance of financial comfort (something which, as this passage incidentally makes clear, Lydia and Wickham lack). Unlike Lydia and Wickham, it will control *passions* with *virtue*, and unlike someone like Mrs Bennet or Lady Catherine de Bourgh, it will see *wealth* as a form of *moral* responsibility. No wonder Elizabeth can still afford to be proud, in her vision of teaching 'the admiring multitude what connubial felicity really was'!

As this analysis of the elements combined in Elizabeth and Darcy's marriage suggests, it has an important *symbolic* role in the novel. As I pointed out at the end of my discussion of *Sense and Sensibility*, this is true of the marriages at the end of all Jane Austen's novels. They provide a satisfactory romantic ending to the events in the *story*, but also a significant culmination of the moral concerns of the *plot*. Jane Austen's novels are *romantic comedies*. That is, they are love stories with happy endings. 'Comedy' here is used not so much to suggest something which makes us laugh, though Jane Austen's novels often do that as well, but as the opposite of 'tragedy'. In other words, it describes a positive, celebratory view of life, one which presents happiness and ideals as possibilities. Jane Austen's novels are often compared with Shakespeare's comedies, and if you are familiar with any of these you will know that the plays end in a very similar way, with marriages which symbolise reconciliation and harmony.

Modern readers particularly are often sceptical of comedy of this kind, and you might feel that happy endings are a kind of escapist, unrealistic fantasy. This is a valid point of view which, again, can be used as the basis for further questions about the effects of Jane Austen's method. To what extent do her happy endings mean she has to gloss over some of the problems raised in the earlier parts of the novels? I want to end my discussion of *Pride and Prejudice* by using the second passage quoted above to begin to explore this question, and it's something I shall be coming back to in later chapters.

The passage describes Elizabeth's desperation to get away from her family and you might find yourself objecting to the fact that the novel seems uncritical of her attitude. She longs for the '*comfort* and *elegance* of their family party at Pemberley', the qualities she enjoyed during her visit there. When I looked at the description of that visit I suggested that these can be moral as well as simply material or aesthetic terms, and here they are applied to the *family* rather than to the surroundings, which tends to confirm that interpretation. Elizabeth is exchanging the family of her birth, the family she finds so unsatisfactory, for her family by marriage where, it is implied, she has found her true place. She can only find real happiness in an environment which represents her values as opposed to the superficial materialism of her mother. Elizabeth can't change Mrs Bennet; she can only move away from her influence. To that extent, the end of the novel is not offering a simplistic view of happiness but one which recognises that, though the heroine might find contentment, things on the whole go on much as before.

But that recognition still involves Elizabeth rejecting her background for a much richer life-style. The novel has been concerned throughout to make us judge between material and moral criteria, yet at the end the heroine is rewarded with both. Wealth is not criticised in itself, only if it is used in the wrong way. Similarly, the plight of Charlotte Lucas makes it clear that women's choices in Jane Austen's society were severely limited, yet at the end her heroine achieves perfect happiness within society's limits. Elizabeth and Darcy have been presented throughout the novel as equal moral adversaries, but when Elizabeth imagines their marriage she expects to receive 'benefit of greater importance', suggesting that her 'softening' feminine influence is less valuable than his masculine experience. The novel is critical of the superficialities and injustices in Jane Austen's society, but not of the way that society is fundamentally organised.

In other words, Jane Austen is in many ways a *conservative* novelist, in spite of her powerful criticism of many aspects of her society. If you do feel uncomfortable with her 'snobbery' it is in reaction to this conservative element in her novels, an aspect which should be examined and defined rather than dismissed, and in the next chapter I shall be using the basic analytic method to look at *Emma*, a novel which again raises these questions.

3

Judgement and irony: *Emma*

THE main focus of *Emma* (1815), as the title suggests, is the heroine
herself. Like Elizabeth in *Pride and Prejudice*, and like so many of Jane
Austen's heroines, she undergoes a process of *moral education* in the
course of the novel, learning by the end both to acknowledge her
faults and to understand herself better. Because Emma is the dominant
character, the reader's position is very close to hers, and so the reader
shares Emma's process of self-discovery. But, at the same time, readers
usually feel that they see things more clearly than Emma does and so
are able to judge her better than she can judge herself.

As I said at the beginning, and as I hope my discussion of the
novels I have looked at so far has made clear, in reading Jane Austen's
novels we are constantly engaged in making judgements. This kind of
double view of the main character − sympathy *and* judgement − was
evident in my analysis of the reader's relationship with Catherine in
Northanger Abbey in the introductory chapter, and with Elizabeth in *Pride
and Prejudice*. How is this achieved? So far I have shown how, by applying the analytic method I have suggested and asking the three basic
questions about point of view, key words and major oppositions of
each passage you choose for analysis, you can begin to explain the reasons for your responses and judgements of characters and events in
these novels. At the same time, this method helps you to get a clearer
idea of the thematic patterns at work in the novels and in the last
chapter, I took the theme of money and marriage, which is particularly
important in Jane Austen's novels, as my focus. Because of the way in
which *Emma* focuses so closely on its heroine and her judgements and
misjudgements, I want to look in more detail at the question of judgement, and to use my analysis of passages from the novel to illustrate
some of the main methods used in all the novels to encourage the
reader to make particular moral choices. In other words, I am going

to examine Jane Austen's *didactic* method, the ways in which her novels teach particular moral lessons.

On various occasions I have described Jane Austen's method as *ironic*, by which I mean the way in which the reader is often forced into making judgements because the authorial voice, sometimes speaking from the point of view of one of the characters, offers a very obviously limited or mistaken view of a particular person or situation, which the reader feels obliged to correct. In other words, irony is dependent on readers feeling that they *know more*, or *understand more*, either than the narrator or than one or more of the characters. Irony of this kind is often used in *Emma* in establishing the reader's 'double vision' of the heroine, so I shall be looking at passages which illustrate this technique. In addition to these ironic effects, however, *Emma* is a particularly good example of a larger form of irony which is again a feature of all Jane Austen's novels. This is the irony which becomes apparent on reading the novel for the second time. On a first reading, we are mainly interested in what will happen, in the events of the *story*; like the characters themselves we are in the dark about many things. In reading the novel again, we know what happens so our interest necessarily shifts to other elements, to the *plot's* organisation of events into particular patterns; we are now in the position of knowing more than the characters and with this hindsight we can, for example, understand their motives better than they can themselves. Again, the ironic effect is dependent on the reader being in a position of greater knowledge or understanding. (In *Emma*, for example, when we know that she is really in love with Mr Knightley all the time, we can appreciate the irony of Emma's careful examination of her feelings for Frank Churchill: she is proud of her self-knowledge, but we know she is still ignorant of her real feelings.) This irony of plot again plays an important part in directing judgement, and I shall be drawing attention to the way it works in some of the passages chosen for analysis.

Emma is the story of Emma Woodhouse, the rich, beautiful daughter of a rather feeble old father who has been willing to let her have her own way since the death of her mother when she was a child. The only person prepared to criticise her is her brother-in-law, Mr Knightley. The Woodhouses are at the top of the social tree in their very restricted neighbourhood, Highbury, so that although Emma has a high opinion of herself, her experience is actually extremely limited. When the story begins Emma is feeling particularly isolated because her governess has just married a local gentleman, Mr Weston. To fill her time she takes an interest in Harriet Smith, a young woman from the local boarding school, persuading her to refuse an offer of marriage from a respectable farmer, Robert Martin. Instead, Emma decides to engineer a match between Harriet and the local clergyman, Mr Elton. Her scheme collapses, much to Harriet's disappointment, when Mr Elton turns out to be in love not with Harriet, but with Emma herself. When Emma refuses his proposal, he goes to stay in Bath, and returns with a brash, dominant woman as his wife.

Two new figures arrive in Highbury: Jane Fairfax, the poor niece of Miss Bates, a single, well-meaning, but rather irritatingly talkative elderly woman, and Frank Churchill, the son of Mr Weston. Emma for a while believes herself to be in love with Frank Churchill, and tells him about her speculation that Jane Fairfax has come to Highbury to escape from an emotional commitment to a married man. In various ways Emma is made aware of her misjudgements: she is rude to Miss Bates and reprimanded for it by Mr Knightley; Harriet confesses that she is in love with Mr Knightley, making Emma realise that she loves him herself; and it is revealed that Frank Churchill and Jane Fairfax have been secretly engaged for some time. In the end both Harriet and Emma marry the appropriate man: Robert Martin proposes again to Harriet, and Emma and Mr Knightley acknowledge their love for each other and look forward to a married life of 'perfect happiness'.

As this summary suggests, *Emma* offers a particularly clear example of the plot pattern which is by now familiar: introductory material, crisis, and the effects of that crisis on characters' judgements. It is a pattern which repeats itself several times as Emma's growth to self-knowledge progresses and in this chapter I have chosen two groups of passages for analysis which illustrate two movements of this kind. The first group, from near the beginning of the novel, concerns Emma's relationship with Harriet; the second, from later in the book, illustrates her growing recognition of her feelings for Mr Knightley. As I have said, I am interested in exploring techniques – especially irony – which persuade us into making particular judgements, but as always I shall be doing so by means of my three basic analytic questions.

I am going to start by looking at two views of the friendship, between Emma and Harriet, beginning with that of Emma herself when she first meets Harriet:

She was not struck by anything remarkably clever in Miss Smith's conversation, but she found her altogether very engaging – not inconveni-
ently shy, not unwilling to talk – and yet so far from pushing, shewing so
proper and becoming a deference, seeming so pleasantly grateful for
being admitted to Hartfield, and so artlessly impressed by the appearance
of every thing in so superior a style to what she had been used to, that
she must have good sense and deserve encouragement. Encouragement
should be given. Those soft blue eyes and all those natural graces should
not be wasted on the inferior society of Highbury and its connections.
The acquaintance she had already formed were unworthy of her. The
friends from whom she had just parted, though very good sort of people,
must be doing her harm. They were a family by the name of Martin,
whom Emma well knew by character, as renting a large farm of Mr
Knightley, and residing in the parish of Donwell – very creditably she
believed – she knew Mr Knightley thought highly of them – but they
must be coarse and unpolished, and very unfit to be the intimates of a
girl who wanted only a little more knowledge and elegance to be quite
perfect. She would notice her; she would improve her; she would detach
her from her bad acquaintance, and introduce her into good society; she
would inform her opinions and her manners. It would be an interesting,
and certainly a very kind undertaking; highly becoming her own situation
in life, her leisure, and powers.

(ch. 3)

Mr Knightley, however, thinks that the friendship can only damage
Harriet, as he tells Mrs Weston:

'She will grow just refined enough to be uncomfortable with those among
whom birth and circumstances have placed her home. I am much mistaken if Emma's doctrines give any strength of mind, or tend at all to
make a girl adapt herself rationally to the varieties of her situation in life.
– They only give a little polish.'
    'I either depend more upon Emma's good sense than you do or am
more anxious for her present comfort; for I cannot lament the acquaintance. How well she looked last night!'
    'Oh! you would rather talk of her person than her mind, would you?
Very well; I shall not attempt to deny Emma's being pretty.'
    'Pretty! say beautiful rather. Can you imagine any thing nearer perfect
beauty than Emma altogether – face and figure?'
    'I do not know what I could imagine, but I confess that I have seldom
seen a face or figure more pleasing to me than her's. But I am a partial
old friend.'

(ch. 5)

I have put these passages side by side to illustrate the way in which we
make judgements by a process of constant comparison between different points of view. They occur within fifteen pages of each other near

the beginning of the novel, when we are still getting our bearings and forming impressions, and Mr Knightley's opinion gives us an importantly different perspective on Emma and her schemes. How do we choose between Emma's view of the relationship with Harriet and Mr Knightley's?

The first passage is presented very much from Emma's point of view, following the progress of her thoughts very closely. At various points, for example, we see her drawing conclusions: 'she *must have* good sense'; 'they *must* be coarse and unpolished'. We know nothing about Harriet, but by this stage in the novel we have formed some opinion of Emma, so as we read this passage we are both using this new evidence to confirm or change our views on Emma herself, and using our initial impressions to assess Emma's view of Harriet. We know, for example, that Emma is bored and so predisposed to find Harriet interesting, and we have been told by the narrator on the first page that 'the real evils' of her situation were 'the power of having rather too much of her own way, and a disposition to think a little too well of herself' (ch. 1). This 'disposition' is certainly in evidence here. Emma is pleased with Harriet for showing '*proper*' and '*becoming*' deference, for being '*grateful*' that Emma has noticed her, and towards the end of the passage, the repetition of '*she*' ('*she* would notice her; she would improve her') draws attention to Emma's concern with herself. Emma thinks she is encouraging Harriet for Harriet's good; we begin to suspect that in fact Emma is using Harriet for her own ends. She thinks first, for example, that taking Harriet up will be 'interesting' but only second 'a very kind undertaking'; and she sees the relationship as a kind of ornament: 'highly *becoming* her own situation'. We begin to suspect, then, that Emma's thoughts are being presented *ironically*; we are aware of a gap between what we see as her real motives, and her own view of what she is doing.

How does this confusion of motives affect Emma's assessment of Harriet? She is determined to see her positively, indeed as someone who needs 'only a little more knowledge and elegance to be quite perfect' (and that 'only' has its own ironic force – to need both knowledge and elegance is no small demand), and she tends to assume that Harriet actually possesses the qualities she wants her to have. Harriet's deference, for example, is taken to mean that she '*must have*' good sense. In the same way, later in the passage, her own desire to raise Harriet socially leads to the assumption that the Martins '*must be* coarse and unpolished', regardless of Mr Knightley's good opinion of them, and by the end of the passage this social judgement has become a moral one: the Martins are Harriet's '*bad* acquaintance'. Emma also slips too easily between attractive physical appearance and qualities of character in her eagerness to praise Harriet: from her assumed 'good sense', for example, to her 'soft blue eyes'.

The passage thus implicitly sets up various sets of oppositions which we are drawing on, probably largely unconsciously, as we judge Emma. She confuses *self-interest* with a *disinterested* concern for others; *social* status with *moral* status; and *internal* features and *external* appearance – or, in other words, *moral* and *physical* qualities; and she jumps to conclusions based on *speculation* or *imagination* rather than *knowledge* or *reason*. If we do suspect that Jane Austen is presenting Emma ironically here, it's interesting to note that her ironic effect partly depends on the reader bringing certain presuppositions from *outside* the novel. It relies, for example, on the assumption that concern for others is preferable to self-interest, that there is an important difference between people's internal and external qualities, that social status is not at all the same as moral value, and that reason is more reliable than imagination. (In the same way, at the beginning of *Pride and Prejudice*, the reader is expected to see that economic reasons for marriage are mistaken.) But these novels don't only rely on the reader agreeing already with what they have to teach. They try to prove their case through the organisation of the plot and the juxtaposition of characters.

Here, for example, the second passage offers a different point of view on Emma and Harriet. We can see the same oppositions at work in this second passage, suggesting, perhaps, that they will take on thematic importance in the novel as a whole. Rather than confusion, however, Mr Knightley's judgement of Emma and Harriet is based on careful choice between the various criteria and this contrast between his method of judgement and that of Emma herself clearly affects our view of the heroine. Like Emma, Mr Knightley is very much aware of Harriet's social inferiority but his worries about her being introduced to the habits of a different class show a *disinterested* concern for Harriet's well-being – he fears that she will be made unhappy by feeling socially displaced – which is rather different from Emma's more *selfish* assumption that what she herself wants will also be good for Harriet. He is also very much aware of the difference between *external* and *internal* qualities: Emma might give Harriet 'a little *polish*' but he doubts that she will gain 'strength of *mind*' or learn to deal '*rationally*' with her changed situation; and when Mrs Weston praises Emma's appearance, he makes a firm distinction between her *person* and her *mind*. And, again unlike Emma whose speculations quickly become certainties in her mind, Mr Knightley apparently makes a point of judging only from the evidence before him. When Mrs Weston presses him on Emma's beauty, he refuses to compare it with anything he could *imagine*, preferring to judge by the evidence of the faces he has actually seen, but he is self-aware enough to see that his judgement might be affected by the fact that he is a 'partial old friend'.

So the doubts we might have had about Emma's attitude to Harriet are echoed by Mr Knightley, whose views seem to be based on a firm grasp of distinctions Emma herself doesn't see, and whose criticism carries even more weight since he is, by his own admission, fond of Emma. If we have already read the novel at least once, we know of course that Mr Knightley is proved right, that Harriet *does* suffer because Emma gives her expectations above her social position, so that Emma's dismissal of his high opinion of the Martins here carries even greater ironic weight, since it is an opinion she later has to accept. Our sense that Emma is presented ironically is thus confirmed by comparing one point of view with another *within* the novel, and Mr Knightley's moral case is given authority by the plot.

The next extract I have chosen for analysis is from the scene in which Emma draws Harriet's portrait in an effort to secure Mr Elton's interest in her. Emma is pleased with the portrait after the first sitting:

> . . . and as she meant to throw in a little improvement to the figure, to give a little more height, and considerably more elegance, she had great confidence in its being in every way a pretty drawing at last, and of its filling its destined place with credit to them both. . . .

Emma's friends comment on the portrait in various ways, again offering the reader the chance to compare different views.

> 'Miss Woodhouse has given her friend the only beauty she wanted,' – observed Mrs Weston to him – not in the least suspecting that she was addressing a lover. – 'The expression of the eye is most correct, but Miss Smith has not those eye-brows and eye-lashes. It is the fault of her face that she has them not.'
> 'Do you think so?' replied [Mr Elton]. 'I cannot agree with you. It appears to me a most perfect resemblance in every feature. I never saw such a likeness in my life. We must allow for the effect of shade, you know.'
> 'You have made her too tall, Emma,' said Mr Knightley.

Emma knew that she had, but would not own it, and Mr Elton warmly added,

'Oh, no! certainly not too tall, not in the least too tall. Consider, she is sitting down – which naturally presents a different – which in short gives exactly the idea – and the proportion must be preserved, you know. Proportions, fore-shortening. – Oh, no! it gives one exactly the idea of such a height as Miss Smith's. Exactly so indeed!'

'It is very pretty,' said Mr Woodhouse. 'So prettily done! Just as your drawings always are, my dear. I do not know any body who draws as well as you do. The only thing I do not thoroughly like is, that she seems to be sitting out of doors, with only a little shawl over her shoulders – and it makes one think she must catch cold.'

(ch. 6)

The introductory paragraph is presented primarily from Emma's point of view, but the scene as a whole again allows the reader to stand back slightly and judge her. It is made quite clear that Emma's portrait is not in fact an accurate likeness of Harriet, that she has intentionally given 'a little improvement to the figure' in the interests of furthering her match with Mr Elton. Emma sees this as perfectly justified, though the reader might want to disagree. *Improvement* is an important word in this first paragraph because it repeats the terms in which Emma saw Harriet – 'she would *improve* her' – in the first passage I looked at, and so recalls the doubts about Emma's motives that we felt then. The repetition also invites us to identify Emma's attitude to the portrait with her attitude to Harriet herself, so that we see the portrait incident as *representative* or *symbolic* of their relationship.

When Emma's point of view gives way to the conversation between the other characters, the reader's position is detached even further from that of the heroine, and we are again involved in judging between different opinions – here, of Emma's portrait and therefore, implicitly, of her treatment of Harriet. This kind of scene, in which we see different characters' reactions side by side, is quite common in Jane Austen's fiction. It is sometimes called a *touchstone* situation, because by showing characters responding to the same thing it offers a kind of comparative test of their reactions. In other words, it tells us as much about the characters themselves as about the object of their attention. Here, for example, Mr Knightley is most critical: offering simply the curt comment, ' "You have made her too tall" '; he is right but seems perhaps over-severe. Mrs Weston recognises that the portrait has 'improved' Harriet's eyes but blames Harriet's face rather than Emma for the change – ' "It is the fault of her face that she has them not" '

- turning her accurate vision of the portrait, a measure of her good sense, into much more indulgent and short-sighted praise of Emma. Emma's father, ineffectual and obsessed with health as always, sees neither the portrait nor Emma with any accuracy, and Mr Elton's reaction is very similar. These two are the comic figures in the passage, almost caricatures in fact, with Mr Woodhouse as the hypochondriac, and Mr Elton as the besotted lover whose broken sentences and repetitions suggest his lack of control.

We are thus given a range of reactions, from the severity of Mr Knightley to the indulgence of Mr Woodhouse, from Mr Knightley's *clarity* of judgement to Mr Woodhouse's *blindness*. As readers we are concerned both to decide whether to accept any of these positions and to supply motives for what the various characters say. This makes the comedy of Mr Elton's reaction more complicated. On a second reading irony again comes into play since we know that it is Emma and not Harriet whom he is trying to flatter through his uncritical admiration of the portrait. Some of our amusement is therefore at Emma's expense, whereas on a first reading we might well have shared her mistaken interpretation of Mr Elton's motives and assume he was attracted to Harriet. So, on a first reading at least, we too are implicated in that opposition between clarity and blindness of judgement; we too perhaps are guilty of the kinds of mistakes which Emma finds so painful, and the process of reading the novel becomes a process of learning for the reader as well as for Emma herself.

Mr Elton's real feelings are revealed, and Emma's treatment of Harriet reaches its first crisis, when he proposes to Emma herself and she is forced to recognise that her plans for Harriet have been misguided. My final extract in this first group is from the chapters which examine the effects of that crisis. Emma reflects on what she has done:

> The first error and the worst lay at her door. It was foolish, it was wrong, to take so active a part in bringing any two people together. It was adventuring too far, assuming too much, making light of what ought to be serious, a trick of what ought to be simple. She was quite concerned and ashamed, and resolved to do such things no more.
>
> (ch. 16)

How are we to judge Emma's self-criticism here? Her ability to see that she has been wrong is clearly in her favour, but how serious is she? How long will her resolution 'to do things no more' actually last? If we have read the novel before, judgement is easier: we know that

Emma still has a long way to go before she understands the full implications of her self-centredness so we are quicker to respond here to
any clues that her remorse is as yet limited. But even on a first reading
we might feel inclined to doubt the quality of Emma's remorse. What
then are the clues which invite such doubts? The language Emma uses
to judge herself is comparatively gentle and shows no signs of deep
emotional disturbance. The first word she uses to describe her 'error'
is *'foolish'*, a fairly mild term of moral disapproval; she sees what she
has done as a *'trick'*; and at the end of the paragraph, she is described
as being *'quite* concerned and ashamed'. It is unclear here whether this
is the narrator's judgement, or Emma's own description of her state of
mind but it hardly matters: 'quite' suggests a very lukewarm kind of
concern. These terms of mild criticism tend to suggest that when
Emma does use a stronger word, describing what she has done as
'wrong', she is not fully aware of what that term really implies. The
rest of Chapter 16, which I haven't room to look at here but which
you can go back to for yourself, confirms this impression of superficial
repentance. Though she dreads having to tell Harriet the truth, she is
quickly able to find consolation for her initial uneasiness, notably in
the fact that 'there could be no necessity for any body's knowing what
had passed'.

    Emma's view of her fault is very specific; she focuses on her role
as match-maker rather than seeing this as part of her general influence
over Harriet, and the oppositions which she uses to describe her mistake – *'making light* of what ought to be *serious*, a *trick* of what ought to
be *simple'* – do not really coincide with the more serious kinds of moral
confusion illustrated by Mr Knightley's judgements which I looked at
earlier. As always, comparison from incident to incident and character
to character is part of our process of judgement here, and Mr Knightley's views are bound to be an important point of comparison, particularly since he has so far been proved right. Emma still lacks his *clarity*
of judgement, remaining *blind* to many of her faults.

    Emma's first moral crisis shows that she is capable of remorse and
self-criticism but suggests too that she has much further to go in her
process of self-knowledge. The passages which I want to look at in the
rest of this chapter come from much later in the novel and lead up to
the final crisis and Emma's most painful process of realisation. They
focus on her relationship with Mr Knightley and the first comes from
a conversation about Mr Knightley between Emma and Mrs Elton:

'And who do you think came in while we were there?'

Emma was quite at a loss. The tone implied some old acquaintance – and how could she possibly guess?

'Knightley!' continued Mrs Elton; – 'Knightley himself! – Was it not lucky? – for, not being within when he called the other day, I had never seen him before; and of course, as so particular a friend of Mr E.'s, I had a great curiosity. "My friend Knightley" had been so often mentioned, that I was really impatient to see him; and I must do my caro sposo the justice to say that he need not be ashamed of his friend. Knightley is quite a gentleman. I like him very much. Decidedly, I think, a very gentleman-like man.'

Happily it was time to be gone. They were off; and Emma could breathe.

(ch. 32)

What impression does this example of Mrs Elton's speech give of her and of what she has to say? It is taken from the end of a much longer conversation, all in much the same style, and it might be that, like Emma, you feel suffocated by her over-bearing manner. Or, like many readers, you might enjoy Mrs Elton for the comedy she provides. What seems clear is that, whether we find her irritating or amusing, Mrs Elton is not to be taken seriously, even though she is so aware of Mr Knightley's virtues. What are the reasons for this negative judgement? The most obvious clue to how we should judge her is her language, the style of her speech. We have already had one example of the comic effects of a character's speech in Mr Elton's disjointed responses to Emma's portrait of Harriet, and in the introductory chapter, when I looked at Isabella Thorpe's extravagant language, I suggested that you pay particular attention to the way characters speak in Jane Austen's novels since this is such an important indicator of how they are to be judged. The abbreviations and the Italian phrase which characterise Mrs Elton's speech here violate the strict code of behaviour of the time: 'Mr E.', 'caro sposo', 'Knightley', suggest an intimacy which was not acknowledged publicly even where it existed; and in dropping 'Mr', Mrs Elton refers to Mr Knightley not as an equal but as though he were of lower social status. She is thus effectively insulting the people she refers to in this way – and all the more so given that she hardly knows Mr Knightley. The comedy arises from the absurd pretentiousness of her style of speech, and also from what the style ironically reveals about Mrs Elton.

Mrs Elton describes Mr Knightley as 'quite the *gentleman*'. When I looked at Elizabeth's refusal of Darcy's proposal in *Pride and Prejudice*, I pointed out the importance of this term in Jane Austen's fiction: that it is not just a description of *social* position, but a term of *moral* approval suggesting that the person so described has the good manners and consideration for others appropriate to that position. Mrs Elton's language reveals her own lack of good manners and makes us doubt whether she fully understands the meaning of the term she uses. The full *moral* meaning of 'gentleman', as exemplified by what we have seen of Mr Knightley in the novel so far, is thus contrasted with Mrs Elton's misuse of the term in the interests of her own *social* status, which seems to be the motive behind her attempt to prove that Mr Knightley is ' "so particular a friend of Mr E.'s" '. The reader's response to Mrs Elton's language makes us aware of the irony that, far from demonstrating her own good sense and social respectability, Mrs Elton's description of Mr Knightley proves the impossibility of his ever being a close friend.

It is Mrs Elton's pretence about Mr Knightley, and the condescending way in which she talks of him (' "he need not be ashamed of his friend" ') which particularly annoys Emma. On a first reading, we might put this down purely to Emma's pride – both her legitimate pride in her own real friendship and respect for Mr Knightley, and her perhaps more dubious fondness for her own status as the lady of Highbury, which Mrs Elton is challenging. On subsequent readings, we are aware of a further irony: still unknown to herself, Emma is in love with Mr Knightley and so particularly sensitive to this attempt to appropriate him by a woman she dislikes.

I'm going to look next at a passage which suggests Emma's feelings for Mr Knightley even more clearly. It occurs during the ball. Emma dances with Frank Churchill for most of the evening, though she is by now sure she is not in love with him, but she is worried by the fact that Mr Knightley is not dancing:

> There he was, among the standers-by, where he ought not to be; he ought to be dancing, – not classing himself with the husbands, and fathers, and whist-players, who were pretending to feel an interest in the dance till their rubbers were made up, – so young as he looked! – He could not have appeared to greater advantage perhaps any where, than where he had placed himself. His tall, firm, upright figure, among the bulky forms and stooping shoulders of the elderly men, was such as Emma felt must draw every body's eyes; and, excepting her own partner, there was not one among the whole row of young men who could be compared with him. – He moved a few steps nearer, and those few steps were enough to prove in how gentlemanlike a manner, with what natural

grace, he must have danced, would he but take the trouble. – Whenever she caught his eye, she forced him to smile; but in general he was looking grave. She wished he could love a ballroom better, and could like Frank Churchill better. – He seemed often observing her. She must not flatter herself that he thought of her dancing, but if he were criticising her behaviour, she did not feel afraid.

(ch. 38)

In this passage, and particularly on a first reading, we are concerned, like Emma, to work out characters' feelings and motives from limited evidence. Along with Emma, we are trying to account for the feelings responsible for Mr Knightley's 'grave' looks; but we are interested primarily in the feelings of Emma herself.

What impression do we gain from her observation of Mr Knightley here? The stress throughout most of the passage is on Mr Knightley's powerful *physical* presence, on his 'tall, firm, upright figure', his 'natural grace'; and as used here, 'gentlemanlike' seems to refer primarily to physical characteristics. Like Colonel Brandon and Marianne in *Sense and Sensibility*, Mr Knightley is considerably older than Emma and you might find it difficult to come to terms with their marriage at the end of the novel because of this. Unlike Colonel Brandon and Marianne, however, Emma's view of Mr Knightley here, her inability to take her eyes off him, provides ample evidence of her strong sexual attraction. She is struck by how *young* he looks, comparing him favourably with the much younger Frank Churchill and putting him in a different category from the 'husbands, and fathers' who surround him, and though she dismisses the possibility, she wants him to be similarly physically aware of her: 'She must not flatter herself that he thought of her dancing'. It is a mistake to think that Jane Austen's novels are unaware of sexuality just because they don't deal with it in an obvious way. Like the interchange between Darcy and Elizabeth in *Pride and Prejudice*, this passage is highly charged with strong sexual feelings, both on Emma's part as this analysis suggests and on Mr Knightley's – as the end of the novel makes clear, his 'grave' looks here can be attributed to his jealousy of Frank Churchill.

The irony of the passage lies in Emma's unawareness of the real state of her feelings, feelings we strongly suspect on a first reading and which are confirmed at the end of the novel. She shows no sign of understanding *why* it is that she is so worried by Mr Knightley's not dancing. There is thus an ironic opposition between her *ignorance* of her own emotional state and the *self-awareness* on which she prides herself, particularly when she examines her feelings for Frank Churchill (ch. 31); between her *blindness* here and the *self-knowledge* which she has to reach by the end of the novel, a thematic opposition we have come across before, both in other characters and in Emma herself.

Though I have chosen to stress the *physical* aspect of Emma's response to Mr Knightley here, it's important to note that this is just a part of their relationship. Her use of '*gentlemanlike*' to describe his appearance, particularly after her criticism of Mrs Elton for misusing the term, is an indication that she is attracted by *moral* qualities as well. And at the end of the extract, though she wishes he were watching her dancing, she implicitly recognises him as a moral authority in her suspicion that he is actually 'criticising her behaviour'. It is this moral authority which is stressed later in the novel when, on the outing to Box Hill which is an important crisis in the novel, Emma is rude to Miss Bates and Mr Knightley points out to her how wrong that was:

> While they talked, they were advancing towards the carriage; it was ready; and, before she could speak again, he had handed her in. He had misinterpreted the feelings which had kept her face averted, and her tongue motionless. They were combined only of anger against herself, mortification, and deep concern. She had not been able to speak; and, on entering the carriage, sunk back for a moment overcome – then reproaching herself for having taken no leave, making no acknowledgement, parting in apparent sullenness, she looked out with voice and hand eager to show a difference; but it was just too late. He had turned away, and the horses were in motion. She continued to look back, but in vain; and soon, with what appeared unusual speed, they were half way down the hill, and every thing left far behind. She was vexed beyond what could have been expressed – almost beyond what she could conceal. Never had she felt so agitated, mortified, grieved, at any circumstance in her life. She felt it at her heart. How could she have been so brutal, so cruel to Miss Bates! – How could she have exposed herself to such ill opinion in any one she valued! And how suffer him to leave her without saying one word of gratitude, of concurrence, of common kindness!
>
> (ch. 43)

This passage, presented entirely from Emma's point of view, has the same function as the one I looked at earlier in which Emma reflected on her mistaken attempt to create a match between Harriet and Mr Elton: in the same way, a crisis has forced Emma to judge her behaviour. That earlier passage therefore provides a useful point of reference as we assess the quality of Emma's remorse here, illustrating the way in which our judgement is again partly dependent on a process of comparison – here, between incidents from different parts of the novel. So, bearing that earlier passage in mind, what impression does this one give of Emma's feelings?

In immediate contrast to her earlier self-criticism, the terms used here to describe Emma's state of mind suggest powerful feelings: '*anger*'; '*mortification*'; '*deep concern*'; and later, '*agitated, mortified, grieved*' and 'most *forcibly* struck'. In the earlier passage Emma's moral language was strikingly mild, such that when she did describe herself as 'wrong' it was doubtful that she fully understood the implications of the word. Here, she immediately recognises her behaviour as 'brutal' and 'cruel', terms which show her awareness of her own *selfishness*, her cruel *blindness*, to others' feelings, and so suggest that she is now much closer to understanding Mr Knightley's moral criteria. Again unlike the earlier incident, where Emma was soon able to console herself, here she is really suffering as a result of her error. But although Emma is now much closer to an understanding of her faults, we still, I think, feel that her self-knowledge is limited and that we understand her more fully than she understands herself. So *irony* is still operating in this presentation of Emma's remorse.

What then is ironic about Emma's state of mind here? An important word in this description of her feelings is *mortification*. It is used near the beginning of the passage, then again later she is described as '*mortified*'. Mortification, shame, is therefore an important element in Emma's response and as always in this novel we are concerned as readers to work out the motives behind a particular reaction. The obvious reason for her shame is a moral one: she has behaved selfishly towards Miss Bates. But is this the only reason? Having defined her treatment of Miss Bates as brutal and cruel, Emma goes on to wonder 'how she could have exposed herself to such ill opinion in any one she valued'. This suggests shame at having created a bad impression – and on whom? The person she values here is at first sight Miss Bates, but the final sentence in the extract makes it clear (and the use of the dash also suggests) that the person whose opinion she really cares about is actually Mr Knightley. If we reread the passage with this in mind, it becomes clear that her agitation is due at least as much to her failure to acknowledge him properly as the carriage moves away as it is to the Box Hill incident itself. Emma's real remorse is at having exposed her selfishness not to Miss Bates, but to Mr Knightley. It is her feelings for him ('She felt it at her *heart*') rather than a purely rational or moral realisation which has awakened her to her wrong behaviour, feelings of which she herself is still only partly aware, but which even the first-time reader now very strongly suspects.

My final extract describes the point at which, a few chapters later, Emma does finally realise what she feels for Mr Knightley. Harriet has told Emma that she is herself in love with him and that she has hopes that he loves her:

> Emma's eyes were instantly withdrawn; and she sat silently meditating, in a fixed attitude, for a few minutes. A few minutes were sufficient for making her acquainted with her own heart. A mind like her's, once opening to suspicion, made rapid progress. She touched – she admitted – she acknowledged the whole truth. Why was it so much worse that Harriet should be in love with Mr Knightley, than with Frank Churchill? Why was the evil so dreadfully increased by Harriet's having some hope of a return? It darted through her, with the speed of an arrow, that Mr Knightley must marry no one but herself!
>
> Her own conduct, as well as her own heart, was before her in the same few minutes. She saw it all with a clearness which had never blessed her before. How improperly had she been acting by Harriet! How inconsiderate, how indelicate, how irrational, how unfeeling had been her conduct! What blindness, what madness, had led her on! It struck her with dreadful force, and she was ready to give it every bad name in the world.
>
> (ch. 47)

Emma's first moral crisis was the result of discovering that the man she had planned Harriet should marry was in fact in love with her; now the man she loves appears to be in love with Harriet. The plot neatly reverses the situation and Emma has a taste of her own medicine. The strength of her own feelings shows her how wrong she has been to play with the feelings of others: Mr Knightley is proved right in the most painful way possible.

The terms in which Emma expresses her faults to herself are again important: she has been '*inconsiderate*', '*irrational*'; led on by '*blindness*' and '*madness*'. As so often in Jane Austen's fiction, attention to details of vocabulary, to the key words in a passage, is a means of defining the novel's major preoccupations, and here these terms take us back to the thematic oppositions set up in the first extracts I looked at. There, Mr Knightley's views on Emma's relationship with Harriet helped to establish moral oppositions between *self-interest* and *disinterestedness* and between judgements based on *reason* and those based on *speculation* or *imagination*, and Mr Knightley's *clarity* of judgement was contrasted with the *blindness* of various other characters. In this passage, Emma at last echoes Mr Knightley's terms and sees everything 'with a *clearness* which had never blessed her before'. 'Inconsiderate', 'indelicate', 'unfeeling' acknowledge her selfishness; 'irrational', 'blindness', 'madness' suggest the lack of reason and understanding in her behaviour, the way in which her schemes have been based on sheer fictions about people's feelings (including her own), the products of imagination rather than certain knowledge. In the end, Emma runs out of definite terms to describe her fault: 'she was ready to give it every bad name under the sun', and this provides an interesting contrast with the earlier crisis when she was happy to label her conduct as 'wrong' without really understanding what that meant. Now she fully understands her position and no term of moral disapproval is too strong to describe it.

But the very strongest of those terms – *evil* – is reserved for the idea that Mr Knightley loves Harriet. *Morally* speaking, there would be nothing wrong with such a situation (though from a *social* point of view it could be seen as wrong within the strict hierarchy of Highbury) and Emma's use of such a strong moral tone is a measure of the strength of her feelings rather than an accurate judgement. Her misuse of the word alerts us to what is perhaps the final irony in her situation. Emma is now aware of her fault *and* her feelings, but she is only aware of her fault *because* of her feelings: her moral and emotional self-awareness are inseparable, as the beginning of the second paragraph makes clear: 'Her own *conduct*, as well as her own *heart*, was before her in the same few minutes'. The question thus arises as to whether Emma would have seen her own selfishness if she hadn't been in love with Mr Knightley. In other words, is a kind of selfishness still one of her prime motives? How much has she really changed at the end of the novel?

Like all Jane Austen's heroines, Emma is rewarded by marriage to the man she loves and, in this case, the man who has represented moral authority, right judgement, throughout the novel. As with Elizabeth and Darcy in *Pride and Prejudice*, the marriage of Emma and Mr Knightley is presented as a *balance* of various elements: the powerful *feelings* which are evident in this last extract and in the sexual attraction illustrated at the ball; the *rational* self-knowledge which Mr Knightley has demonstrated throughout and which Emma seems to have achieved in the end; and the *social* equality which would not have been the case had Mr Knightley married Harriet. And as in *Pride and Prejudice*, the happy ending can be seen as offering a kind of ideal, suggesting that, given the right moral attitudes which Emma has to learn, reconciliation of these various elements, which could come into conflict, is possible. Emma has come through the various crises, two of which are illustrated in the groups of extracts I have chosen, has learned to recognise her mistakes and achieved self-knowledge and is rewarded appropriately.

But again as in *Pride and Prejudice* and as my question about how much Emma has really changed suggests, the ending could be seen as reconciling some of the novel's oppositions a bit too easily. Certainly it again supports a *conservative* social position. Emma has to learn to *deserve* her social status by treating other people with respect, to become a 'lady' as Mr Knightley is a 'gentleman', but her social position is not itself questioned: there is never a real possibility that Harriet will cross social boundaries by marrying Mr Knightley or even Mr Elton. Emma is a snob at the beginning of the novel and her social attitudes haven't really changed at the end. Another problem is raised by the difficulty some readers have in accepting Emma's marriage to Mr Knightley. Is the cost of her learning to deserve her social position too great? To what extent has she given up her independence of mind, however mistaken it sometimes proved to be? In spite of the sexual attraction I have pointed out, does Emma's marriage to a much older man, a man who has been a teacher rather than a lover – and whom she says she will only ever call 'Mr Knightley' (ch. 53) – involve too great a sacrifice of herself?

In the introductory chapter, one of the oppositions I suggested was at work in *Sense and Sensibility* was that of *self* and *society*, an opposition I suggested was present in most of Jane Austen's novels. In a similar way to Emma's marriage here, the change in Marianne and her marriage to Colonel Brandon raised questions about how far individuals should give up their own interests to those of society. Though we as readers might feel uncomfortable with the novels' conclusions, both *Sense and Sensibility* and *Emma* seem to argue that society has the more important claim. In *Persuasion*, however, Jane Austen's last completed novel, the argument seems to be rather different and in my next chapter I am going to use my analysis of *Persuasion* to explore this theme more fully.

4

Self and society: *Persuasion*

THE society of Highbury in *Emma* is extremely restricted and the novel never moves outside that society, making us acutely aware of its claustrophobic limitations. In the end, however, Emma settles down to 'perfect happiness' with Mr Knightley, apparently finding fulfilment without needing to move outside her immediate social circle. At the end of the last chapter I suggested that the ending expressed a *conservative* position, a defence of the establishment social order and of society's claims over those of the individual. *Persuasion* (1818), Jane Austen's last completed novel, is rather different. It begins with the heroine, Anne Elliot, and her father and sister leaving the family home; the action of the novel moves from the Somersetshire countryside to Lyme Regis and finally to Bath; and it ends with Anne Elliot's marriage to a naval officer, breaking entirely with family tradition and social expectations. It is thus very different not only from *Emma*, but also from *Pride and Prejudice* where Elizabeth similarly moves away from her family on her marriage but makes a brilliant match which again tends to support established social patterns.

Persuasion also has a heroine who is much older than those in Jane Austen's other novels, a heroine who at the beginning of the novel seems to have little hope of a successful marriage and so is much more like Charlotte Lucas than like Elizabeth or Emma. Eight years before the novel begins, Anne Elliot was engaged to Frederick Wentworth, a young naval officer with uncertain prospects, and was persuaded to break off the engagement by Lady Russell, who saw the match as socially and financially risky and whose opinion Anne respected because she had been a close friend of her mother's before her death. Lady Russell was proved wrong: Captain Wentworth was highly successful and Anne never got over her feelings for him.

As the novel begins, Anne's extravagant and vain father, Sir Walter Elliot, is forced by financial problems to let their home, Kel-

70

lynch Hall, to Admiral Croft, whose wife happens to be Captain Wentworth's sister. Sir Walter and his elder daughter Elizabeth move to Bath, together with Elizabeth's companion, Mrs Clay, who is suspected of wanting to marry Sir Walter. Anne goes to stay with her younger sister and her husband, Mary and Charles Musgrove, who live close by at Uppercross, near Charles's parents and lively younger sisters, Henrietta and Louisa. The change of company and the sense that she is of some use to the family do Anne good, and while there, she meets Captain Wentworth again. He is still unmarried but now wants to find a wife and seems to be attracted to Louisa Musgrove. On a trip to Lyme Regis, Louisa is badly injured jumping off the sea wall, the Cobb, into Captain Wentworth's arms and he is impressed by Anne's prompt, level-headed response to this crisis. Anne returns to Uppercross to look after the Musgrove children and Louisa stays with the Harvilles, naval friends of Captain Wentworth, until she recovers. There she becomes engaged to Captain Benwick, who when he first appears is still mourning the death of his first fiancée. Captain Wentworth is thus still free.

Anne and Lady Russell join Sir Walter in Bath where the Elliots are approached by their estranged cousin, William Walter Elliot, the heir to Kellynch, who had been expected some years before to marry Elizabeth. He now shows interest in Anne but she mistrusts him and her suspicions are confirmed when she hears from Mrs Smith, an old school friend and now a poor widow, of how he ruined herself and her husband. Mr Elliot's attentions to Anne reawaken further Captain Wentworth's love for her, and he is convinced of her continuing affection when he overhears a conversation between Anne and Captain Harville in which she defends women's constancy in love. Anne and Captain Wentworth are finally united and William Elliot, his plans thwarted, goes off to London with Mrs Clay.

How do we respond to Anne's earlier rejection of Captain Wentworth simply from this summary of the events of the *story*? Anne's life comes very close to being tragically wasted. But for the coincidences of Kellynch being let to the Crofts, and of Captain Wentworth being Mrs Croft's brother, Anne might never have been reunited with him, remaining the sad, unfulfilled figure we meet at the beginning of the novel: 'she was only Anne' (ch. 1). From the bare outline of the story, then, we get a strong impression that this is a novel which argues in favour of personal feeling and romantic love, that it suggests that Anne should have followed her own instincts and taken the risk of marrying

Captain Wentworth eight years before, regardless of all the apparently sensible reasons against doing so offered by other people.

In what ways is this initial impression confirmed or extended when we analyse it more fully by examining the organisation of these events in the *plot* of *Persuasion*? In this chapter I shall as usual be suggesting ways in which you might answer this question by applying the basic analytic method I suggested in the introductory chapter to passages from different parts of the novel. As the title I have chosen for this chapter suggests, the question of the novel's attitude to Anne's earlier decision is part of the general thematic opposition of *self* to *society*, an opposition present in all Jane Austen's novels, and I shall be focusing on this in the course of the chapter. The three groups with whom Anne is associated – her immediate family, the Musgroves, and the naval characters – are representative of different values and of different attitudes to this question, rather as Pemberley represents to Elizabeth a different set of values from those of home in *Pride and Prejudice*. Some of the passages I have chosen are as usual from crucial stages of the plot, and others illustrate the way in which the parts played by these different groups of characters within the plot influence the way we judge Anne's earlier rejection of Captain Wentworth's love.

I am going to begin by looking at extracts from the early chapter in which we were told about what happened eight years before. Anne and Captain Wentworth's 'exquisite felicity' was cut short by the objections of her father, and of Lady Russell:

> Anne Elliot, with all her claims of birth, beauty, and mind, to throw herself away at nineteen; involve herself at nineteen in an engagement with a young man, who had nothing but himself to recommend him, and no hopes of attaining affluence, but in the chances of a most uncertain profession, and no connexions to secure even his farther rise in that profession; would be, indeed, a throwing away, which she grieved to think of! Anne Elliot, so young; known to so few, to be snatched off by a stranger without alliance or fortune; or rather sunk by him into a state of most wearing, anxious, youth-killing dependance! It must not be. . . .
>
> Captain Wentworth had no fortune. He had been lucky in his profession, but spending freely, what had come freely, had realized nothing. But, he was confident that he should soon be rich; – full of life and ardour, he knew that he should soon have a ship, and soon be on a station what would lead to every thing he wanted. He had always been lucky; he knew he should be so still. – Such confidence, powerful in its own warmth, and bewitching in the wit which often expressed it, must

have been enough for Anne; but Lady Russell saw it very differently. – His sanguine temper, and fearlessness of mind, operated very differently on her. She saw in it but an aggravation of the evil. It only added a dangerous character to himself. He was brilliant, he was headstrong.

Anne's attitude as a result of her experience is made very clear:

> How eloquent could Anne Elliot have been, – how eloquent, at least, were her wishes on the side of early warm attachment, and a cheerful confidence in futurity, against that over-anxious caution which seems to insult exertion and distrust Providence! – She had been forced into prudence in her youth, she learned romance as she grew older – the natural sequel of an unnatural beginning.
>
> (ch. 4)

The point of view in these extracts is quite complicated, shifting between an external, objective narrative voice and a position much closer to the three characters who are involved. At the beginning we are given Lady Russell's view of the affair in such phrases as 'throw herself away' and 'it must not be'; the narrative voice then gives us information about Captain Wentworth, moving closer to his point of view with 'he knew that he should soon have a ship' and away again when his effect on Anne is described. 'He was brilliant, he was headstrong' is again Lady Russell; then in the final paragraph we are given Anne's present view of things in phrases which could come either from her or from the narrator – which, for example, describes her attitude as 'the natural sequence of an unnatural beginning'?

I have gone through these different points of view in detail because it is important to analyse the way in which our judgements as readers are affected by the extent to which the authorial voice seems to support a particular character's position. Here, for example, we probably feel inclined to agree with the judgement in the last paragraph that Lady Russell's persuasion of Anne was 'unnatural', that her caution was 'over-anxious', and this is partly because these judgements seem to come as much from the authorial voice as from Anne herself. In contrast, in the first paragraph we treat the opinions with scepticism because they are so clearly Lady Russell's. (And the intervening events are loaded in favour of Anne's position: in parts of the chapter which I haven't quoted here, we learn that Captain Wentworth's financial hopes were more than fulfilled and that for Anne her experience 'clouded every enjoyment of youth; and an early loss of bloom and spirits had been their lasting effect', making Lady Russell's fear that she would have been reduced to 'youth-killing dependance' through marriage to Wentworth sadly ironic.) What then were Lady Russell's criteria in dissuading Anne from marriage? What are the sets of values on which she based her opinion, which we are implicitly invited to reject? The vocabulary of that first paragraph suggests an overriding concern with *material* values: Anne's advantages, which she is thought to be 'throwing away' (as opposed to selling for a high price?) are, first and second, her '*birth*' and '*beauty*' and only lastly her 'mind'; and Lady Russell is worried because Captain Wentworth is a '*stranger* without *alliance* or *fortune*', he has little hope of '*affluence*' and no '*connexions*'. Lady Russell's primary concerns are with *material* comfort and *social* position – hence her worry that Wentworth is a 'stranger' and her mistrust of his 'uncertain profession'.

In the second paragraph these criteria are implicitly contrasted with a very different set of values associated with Captain Wentworth himself. The dominant vocabulary here expresses vitality and energy: '*confident*'; 'full of *life* and *ardour*'; '*powerful* in its own *warmth*'; '*sanguine* temper'; '*fearlessness* of mind'. These values are picked up in the last paragraph in Anne's continuing belief in 'early *warm* attachment', 'cheerful *confidence*' and '*exertion*'.

A very clear – and by now familiar – opposition is thus set up in this important early chapter between, to use the terms of the last paragraph, a *prudent* and a *romantic* attitude to marriage, between a belief in *material* values and a commitment to personal *feeling*, with romance and feeling being made very much more attractive because of the language of life and warmth used to express them. 'Warmth', used twice in the extracts I have chosen, is an important word in securing our sympathy for Anne's view, particularly when we know that her life at Kellynch with her father and sister is cold and loveless ('she was only Anne'). The concern of Lady Russell and Anne's family with social status is contrasted with Captain Wentworth's energetic individuality: he had '*nothing but himself* to recommend him', yet that self is enough to make Anne love him – and, as it turns out, to secure great success. Because Captain Wentworth is so successful and becomes very rich, it could be argued that, as so often, the novel is presenting a balance of these two sets of values as the ideal solution. Though this might be the case, there is an interesting difference between, for example, Elizabeth's marriage to Darcy in *Pride and Prejudice* and the marriage Anne would have entered eight years before: Elizabeth gets both love and material comfort, but takes no financial risks and breaks no social codes; *Persua-*

sion seems to be suggesting that the financial risk would have been worth taking and that Captain Wentworth's uncertain social status shouldn't have mattered when personal happiness was at stake.

I want now to explore further the thematic oppositions which are set up at the beginning of the novel by looking at two short passages from the plot's first crisis, from the chapter in which Anne and Captain Wentworth meet again for the first time. The first records Anne's responses:

> Mary talked, but she could not attend. She had seen him. They had met. They had been once more in the same room!
>
> Soon, however, she began to reason with herself, and try to be feeling less. Eight years, almost eight years had passed, since all had been given up. How absurd to be resuming the agitation which such an interval had banished into distance and indistinctness! What might not eight years do? Events of every description, changes, alienations, removals, – all, all must be comprised in it; and oblivion of the past – how natural, how certain too! It included nearly a third part of her own life.
>
> Alas! with all her reasonings, she found, that to retentive feelings eight years may be little more than nothing.
>
> Now, how were his sentiments to be read?

Anne's question is partly answered when Mary reports that Captain Wentworth found her 'so altered he should not have known her again':

> Frederick Wentworth had used such words, or something like them, but without an idea that they would be carried round to her. He had thought her wretchedly altered, and, in the first moment of appeal, had spoken as he felt. He had not forgiven Anne Elliot. She had used him ill; deserted and disappointed him; and worse, she had shewn a feebleness of character in doing so, which his own decided, confident temper could not endure. She had given him up to oblige others. It had been the effect of over-persuasion. It had been weakness and timidity.
>
> (ch. 7)

How does this first meeting contribute to our view of the main characters and extend our impressions of the novel's main thematic preoccupations? The passages are presented from the characters' points of view and it is very clear from the first that Anne is still in love with Captain Wentworth and deeply moved by seeing him again. The short sentences and exclamation at the beginning express the 'agitation' she acknowledges slightly later on, and the whole passage is thus an example of the 'retentive feelings' which are said at the end to be so powerful. At first sight, Captain Wentworth might be assumed to have got over their relationship rather more successfully – and indeed the chapter continues with a conversation in which he tells his sister that he is now ready to marry 'any pleasing young woman who came in his way, excepting Anne Elliot'. But the fact that he had 'not forgiven Anne Elliot', and the way in which we see his mind going over what he sees as her weakness, again in short sentences which suggest agitation, tend to contradict his own convictions and to imply that his feelings, too, have been permanently affected.

Captain Wentworth's main complaint against Anne is that she showed '*feebleness* of character' in giving in to others, and he compares what he sees as her '*weakness* and *timidity*' with his own '*decided, confident* temper'. 'Confident' picks up the dominant term used of Captain Wentworth in the first passages I looked at: he is again identified – and identifies himself – with confident self-reliance, with a strength of character which he thinks Anne lacked in giving him up 'to oblige others'. He is convinced Anne gave in to *social* pressure rather than following *personal feelings*, and the contrast which he angrily assumes exists between his confidence and her timidity can be seen as another version of the opposition between *self* and *society* established in the earlier passages. But how far is his view of Anne justified? Though Anne gave in to 'over-persuasion' at the time, this passage makes it clear that her feelings for Wentworth have not changed. We see her, in fact, trying to '*reason* with herself', to persuade herself that they must have done, that the 'changes, alienations, removals' of eight years must have made a difference, only to discover that 'to retentive feelings eight years may be little more than nothing'. So again here the power of *feeling* is demonstrated, and proved stronger than *reason*, another departure from the argument commonly offered in Jane Austen's novels – present in both *Pride and Prejudice* and *Emma*, for example – that feelings must be at least controlled by reason. Like Anne Elliot, *Persuasion* seems to be on the side of romance.

Captain Wentworth is still apparently a man of warm and immediate reactions: his comment here on Anne's changed appearance is said to have been 'spoken as he *felt*', suggesting how much they still have in common. Ironically, the physical alteration he sees in Anne is actually due to the strength and constancy of feelings he accuses her of lacking. Change and constancy are important ideas in these passages. Anne tries to persuade herself that things have changed and is only the more convinced of the steadfastness of her affection; Captain Wentworth wishes she had demonstrated firmness but accuses her of weakly shifting her position. This opposition between *change* and *constancy* has obvious associations with the novel's title, as Wentworth's accusation that Anne submitted to 'over-persuasion' makes clear, so it is a preoccupation worth looking out for as we read on in the novel. At the end of this chapter, for example, Wentworth tells Mrs Croft that the woman he is looking for will have ' "A strong mind" ' and, slightly later, Anne overhears a conversation between Captain Wentworth and Louisa Musgrove which makes it clear that he admires her for her boasted firmness of mind (ch. 10).

The incident of the overheard conversation is one that you can look up and analyse for yourself. Bearing in mind the various thematic oppositions established so far, I am going to move now to one of the major crises in the novel and to look at a short passage in which Anne reflects on Louisa's fall from the Cobb at Lyme. Louisa fell having insisted on jumping against Captain Wentworth's advice, and on her way back to Uppercross:

> Anne wondered whether it ever occurred to him now, to question the justness of his own previous opinion as to the universal felicity and advantage of firmness of character; and whether it might not strike him, that, like all other qualities of mind, it should have its proportions and limits. She thought it could scarcely escape him to feel, that a persuadable temper might sometimes be as much in favour of happiness, as a very resolute character.
>
> (ch. 12)

Anne here compares Louisa's 'very *resolute* character' unfavourably with her own '*persuadable* temper', hoping that the incident might have altered Captain Wentworth's perhaps rather rigid opinions in her favour. What effect does the incident at the Cobb and the terms of Anne's reflections here have on our view of the novel's interest in change and constancy? Anne's thoughts arise, of course, out of her own strong affection for Captain Wentworth – indeed, from her jealousy of his interest in Louisa – so that the passage demonstrates the constancy of her feelings even while she is defending a kind of flexibility of mind. This differentiation between *feelings* and qualities of *mind* extends the initial opposition between change and constancy and makes the novel's discussion of these qualities more interesting. Anne, Captain Wentworth and Louisa represent three different kinds of constancy – and further variations can be seen in other characters – and once again, the implicit comparison which the plot sets up between these invites the reader to form judgements.

Louisa's determination to have her own way shows a firmness of mind bordering on stubbornness, whereas her later shift of interest from Captain Wentworth to Captain Benwick suggests that her feelings are rather less fixed; Captain Wentworth, too, shows a stubbornness of mind against Anne but, as the outcome of the novel shows, events and the constancy of his feelings for her, which we already suspect but which he is as yet unaware of, make him willing to change; the firmness of Anne's feelings is in no doubt and she now thinks she was wrong to give in to the opinions of others eight years before, but her flexibility of mind can be an advantage in her dealings with other people: it makes her willing to adapt to the move from Kellynch, and useful and happy at Uppercross. The suggestion seems to be that constancy of feeling is not necessarily incompatible with a 'persuadable mind', and that though there are occasions on which feelings must come first, a concern for others is an important factor in personal happiness. In other words, that careful choices must be made between the sometimes rival claims of *self* and *society*.

At the beginning of this chapter I suggested that the different groups of characters in *Persuasion* could be seen as representing different attitudes to the novel's various preoccupations, just as Anne, Captain Wentworth and Louisa offer variations on the ideas of constancy and flexibility. So before examining the outcome of the plot at the end of the novel, I want now to look at a few passages which allow me to explore these differences in more detail, focusing particularly on Anne's family and the naval characters. In my discussion of *Pride and Prejudice* I pointed out that I was choosing passages partly because of their position in the development of the plot and partly because they focused on money and marriage, which were the topics I was particularly interested in exploring in that chapter. As I said then, you will find yourself choosing passages for their *thematic* interest in this way when you come to answer essay questions on particular topics. In this chapter, as in the chapter on *Pride and Prejudice*, the passages I have dealt with so far have been chosen with both plot and themes in mind; the next few passages, however, are included primarily for their thematic interest.

On the visit to Lyme, Captain Wentworth introduces the Musgrove party to his friend and fellow-officer Captain Harville and his wife:

Captain Harville, though not equalling Captain Wentworth in manners, was a perfect gentleman, unaffected, warm and obliging. Mrs Harville, a degree less polished than her husband, seemed however to have the same good feelings; and nothing could be more pleasant than their desire of considering the whole party as friends of their own, because the friends of Captain Wentworth, or more kindly hospitable than their entreaties for their all promising to dine with them. . . .

There was so much attachment to Captain Wentworth in all this, and such a bewitching charm in a degree of hospitality so uncommon, so unlike the usual style of give-and-take invitations, and dinners of formality and display, that Anne felt her spirits not likely to be benefited by an increasing acquaintance among his brother-officers. 'These would have been all my friends,' was her thought; and she had to struggle against a great tendency to lowness.

(ch. 11)

I'm going to put this description of the Harvilles beside one of Anne's cousin, William Walter Elliot, so that I can conveniently compare the two social groups they represent. My analytic method thus reflects the way the plot asks us to make constant comparisons as we read.

Mr Elliot was rational, discreet, polished, – but he was not open. There was never any burst of feeling, any warmth of indignation or delight, at the evil or good of others. This, to Anne, was a decided imperfection. Her early impressions were incurable. She prized the frank, the open-hearted, the eager character beyond all others. Warmth and enthusiasm did captivate her still. She felt that she could so much more depend upon the sincerity of those who sometimes looked or said a careless or a hasty thing, than of those whose presence of mind never varied, whose tongue never slipped.

Mr Elliot was too generally agreeable. Various as were the tempers in her father's house, he pleased them all. He endured too well, – stood too well with everybody.

(ch. 17)

In what ways do these descriptions direct our judgement of the characters concerned? In both passages, as in the first extract I looked at, the authorial voice merges with Anne's point of view, giving authority to her impressions and so encouraging the reader to see them as accurate. In the first passage, for example, Anne's response to the Harvilles in the second paragraph is in complete agreement with the very positive description of them already given by the narrator, so that we are in no doubt about how we as readers should judge these characters. In the second passage the opening sentences seem to come from the narrator so that we take them as a reliable description of Mr Elliot's mode of behaviour and thus are well prepared to agree with the negative reaction from Anne which follows.

Our judgement in both cases is influenced by the use of key words which are by now familiar to describe these characters, words which have already acquired positive or negative associations in the novel so far. Captain Harville, for example, is '*warm*' and his wife shows '*good feelings*'; Mr Elliot is quite the opposite: 'never any burst of feeling, or warmth of indignation or delight'. He is '*polished*' but not '*open*' whereas the Harvilles are less polished ('not equalling Captain Wentworth in manners'; 'a degree less polished than her husband') but show exactly that openness and sincerity which Anne feels Mr Elliot lacks. So it is clear where these characters fit into the oppositions between the individual and society, between feeling and reason, which I have been looking at so far. The naval characters are identified with warm *personal* affection, the Harvilles treating Captain Wentworth's friends like their own because of their attachment to him, and this is seen as far more important than the kind of *social* refinement Anne has been used to at home with the 'formality and display' of insincere 'give-and-take invitations'. Though they are seen by Anne's family as social outsiders, the naval characters can be described as 'perfect gentlemen'. Mr Elliot, like Anne's father, has the *external* manners of a gentleman, but not the *internal* qualities which are needed for him really to deserve the description. He is '*rational*' but shows no 'burst of *feeling*'.

The interest in change, constancy and flexibility which I discussed earlier is also present in these passages, extending our understanding of how the novel asks us to judge these qualities. It is made very clear, for example, that Mr Elliot is *too* flexible, 'too generally agreeable', that his ability to please everyone suggests a basic lack of sincerity, of firm principles. The Harvilles' accommodating willingness to offer dinner at short notice (something Anne's father, for example, would be incapable of doing) is, on the other hand, evidence of the constancy of their affection for Captain Wentworth. And Anne, in reacting so positively to the Harvilles in spite of their lower social status, shows a flexibility of judgement which puts personal qualities before rank and again differentiates her from her family.

The final quotation which I have chosen to illustrate the different qualities of the various social groups in the novel confirms that contrast between Anne and the rest of the Elliot family. Anne and her sister are attending a concert in Bath and Anne now has reason to believe that Captain Wentworth still loves her:

Very, very happy were both Elizabeth and Anne Elliot as they walked in.

Elizabeth, arm in arm with Miss Carteret, and looking on the broad back of the dowager Viscountess Dalrymple before her, had nothing to wish for which did not seem within her reach; and Anne – but it would be an insult to the nature of Anne's felicity, to draw any comparison between it and her sister's; the origin of one all selfish vanity, of the other all generous attachment.

Anne saw nothing, thought nothing of the brilliancy of the room. Her happiness was from within.

(ch. 20)

The authorial voice controls our view of Anne and her sister in this passage and very obviously directs our judgement in comparing their different sources of happiness. Elizabeth's is entirely dependent on *external* appearance, on the *social* status conferred by appearing publicly with the Countess Dalrymple; Anne's is 'from *within*', the result of *personal feeling*, of the warmth and affection associated throughout with Captain Wentworth in particular and the naval characters in general. The passage thus illustrates the novel's major opposition between self and society in very clear – almost schematic – terms and leaves us in no doubt as to how we should judge between them. It also makes it clear that, within that opposition, a belief in the importance of personal feelings is not the same as selfishness: it is Elizabeth and not Anne who is guilty of 'selfish vanity'. Anne's is a '*generous* attachment'.

Having looked at the way two of the major groups of characters fit into the novel's main thematic preoccupations, we can now sum up the values they seem to represent. The Elliots, clearly, are associated with an uncompromising and selfish concern with social status which almost destroys Anne's happiness. The naval characters are the complete opposite: in spite of their uncertain social position, Anne finds in them the kind of warm affection and faith in individual achievement on which, the novel seems to suggest, real happiness depends. They show a constancy of principle but a willingness to adapt and change their habits which Anne herself shares. Unlike *Emma*, then, where Emma finds happiness entirely within established society, *Persuasion* seems to argue that society must adapt to accommodate new social groups, indeed that its future happiness and vigour depend on such outsiders.

I have concentrated on the Elliots and on the naval characters in my analysis of the novel's representative use of the various social groups. You can go on to explore for yourself in a similar way the role of other characters – of Sir Walter Elliot at the beginning of the novel for example, or of the Musgroves or Lady Russell, in order to decide how they fit into the novel's thematic pattern of contrast and comparison. What I want to do in the rest of this chapter is to return to the development of the plot and to look at extracts from the final crisis: Anne's conversation with Captain Harville which finally convinces Captain Wentworth of her love.

They have been discussing Captain Benwick's transfer of affection from his dead fiancée to Louisa Musgrove. Captain Harville will not accept Anne's suggestion that men are more likely than women to forget their past loves:

> 'No, no, it is not man's nature. I will not allow it to be more man's nature than woman's to be inconstant and forget those they do love, or have loved. I believe the reverse. I believe in a true analogy between our bodily frames and our mental; and that as our bodies are the strongest, so are our feelings; capable of bearing most rough usage, and riding out the heaviest weather.'
>
> 'Your feelings may be the strongest,' replied Anne, 'but the same spirit of analogy will authorize me to assert that ours are the most tender. Man is more robust than woman, but he is not longer-lived; which exactly explains my view of the nature of their attachments. Nay, it would be too hard upon you, if it were otherwise. You have difficulties, and privations, and dangers enough to struggle with. You are always labouring and toiling, exposed to every risk and hardship. Your home, country, friends, all quitted. Neither time, nor health, nor life, to be called your own. It would be too hard indeed' (with a faltering voice) 'if woman's feelings were to be added to all this.'. . .

But Captain Harville is not to be persuaded:

> 'But let me observe that all histories are against you, all stories, prose and verse. If I had such a memory as Benwick, I could bring you fifty quotations in a moment on my side the argument, and I do not think I ever opened a book in my life which had not something to say upon woman's inconstancy. Songs and proverbs, all talk of woman's fickleness. But perhaps you will say, these were all written by men.'
>
> 'Perhaps I shall. – Yes, yes, if you please, no reference to examples in books. Men have had every advantage of us in telling their own story. Education has been theirs in so much higher a degree; the pen has been in their hands. I will not allow books to prove any thing.'
>
> (ch. 23)

In what ways is this important scene a climax in the novel's exploration of the various thematic oppositions I have examined so far? Anne is of course using this conversation to convince Captain Wentworth, who overhears their argument, of the constancy not only of women's love but of her own feelings, a fitting conclusion to the exploration of *change* and *constancy* which has been going on throughout the novel. It is the first occasion on which Anne really speaks up for herself, asserting her own beliefs and, implicitly, her own desires against those of others, in the way she failed to do eight years before. It can therefore be seen, too, as a climax in the novel's discussion of the rival claims of *self* and *society*. By her act of self-assertion, Anne wins happiness. In doing so she is true to her feelings but shows that flexibility, that willingness to change her characteristic behaviour, which we have noticed elsewhere as a feature of the characters whom the novel seems to approve. After being *passive* for much of the novel, she becomes *active* (a change which began with the earlier crisis of Louisa's fall). In the past, she has been the character who stays in the background, overhearing conversations between others (such as that between Captain Wentworth and Louisa Musgrove on the walk to Winthrop (ch. 10)); now the roles are reversed: Anne speaks and Captain Wentworth overhears.

This shift from passivity to a more active role is something we noticed in Catherine in *Northanger Abbey* in the introductory chapter, and it is also a feature of Fanny Price's development in *Mansfield Park*, which I shall be looking at next. And here, as in those other two novels, the heroine's growth in self-confidence is firmly linked with a discussion of the roles of men and women in society, a theme of constant importance in Jane Austen's fiction. In the introductory chapter, I suggested that male and female readers might react very differently to Jane Austen's novels and that this could be due to different reading experiences (such as the fact that women tend to read more romances) and to different expectations about what areas of experience are important (the *public* world, dominated by men, tends to be seen as more important than the *private*, domestic, world of women). In this conversation between Anne and Captain Harville, we see Anne's own acute awareness of the effects of these different kinds of experience. She sees a strong capacity for feeling as belonging essentially to women, as compared with men's more active role in the world. This idea of a balance of qualities, of men and women as *complementary* is something we have met already – in the marriage of Elizabeth and Darcy at the end of *Pride and Prejudice*, for example – and, again as I have already suggested, makes the marriages at the end of Jane Austen's novels such important images of harmony.

But Anne's defence of her sex is more radical than this suggests.

In the introductory chapter I also examined Jane Austen's idea of a 'heroine' and explored the way her irony in *Northanger Abbey* was directed against kinds of writing which bore no relation to her readers' usual experience so that the novel seemed to be arguing for the importance of young women's very ordinary experiences, so often undervalued. A very similar idea is present here. Anne defends women's capacity for feeling, their constancy, against what she sees as a male-dominated written tradition. Men, she argues, have had control of writing because they are given a better education, so ' "I will not allow books to prove any thing" '. In other words, Anne is suggesting that had society been organised differently, so that women had access to better education, and had women had the opportunity to write history and fiction, 'songs and proverbs', ideas about the abilities of the two sexes and about what is and is not important might have been very different. Bearing this in mind, you might be interested in going back to consider the figure of Mrs Croft in *Persuasion*. She is presented as an intelligent woman who has benefited from her experience of living alongside her husband on board ship. She has not conformed to society's expectations of how women ought to behave (unlike, for example, Mary Musgrove) – and it is surely significant that the Crofts' marriage is presented as one of the happiest in the novel.

As I pointed out at the beginning of this chapter, there are interesting differences between *Persuasion* and some of Jane Austen's other novels. One of these, I suggested, was a much less conservative attitude to society and, as we have seen, the novel's approval of the naval characters and harsh criticism of the Elliots suggest an openness to social change very different from the attitude we find in, for example, *Emma*. And this more radical social argument is combined with a similarly reformist defence of women's potential. At the end of *Persuasion*, however, Anne tells Captain Wentworth that she thinks she was right to give in to Lady Russell all those years ago, arguing that ' "a strong sense of duty is no bad part of a woman's portion" ' (ch. 23). Now that her story has a happy ending Anne can afford to be generous. Now that her own desires are fulfilled, she can afford to assert the importance of duty to society. But the reader is very unlikely to agree with her judgement since the whole novel seems to have been concerned to point out what a waste her life would have been if Captain Wentworth had not happened to return to Kellynch. Once again, the ending of the novel raises problems. There is an apparent desire for compromise between elements which have been opposed in the course of the novel – here the demands of the individual and those of society – elements which, we suspect, can't be quite so easily reconciled. Anne's story could so easily have been tragic and had that been the case, she might have been less willing to defend women's 'duty'.

Several of the questions raised in this chapter on *Persuasion*, will be raised again in the context of *Mansfield Park* which I shall be discussing in the next and final chapter on the novels. Like *Persuasion*, *Mansfield Park* is a novel about social change and deals with a comparatively wide range of characters and places. Like Anne Elliot, Fanny Price, its heroine, has to learn to assert and defend her own beliefs and desires, and like the naval characters in *Persuasion*, she is an outsider to established society. So I shall be using my discussion of *Mansfield Park* to focus on the relationship between character and place, and on Jane Austen's use of place to represent particular values, in order once again to try to define the novel's social and moral argument.

5

The importance of place: *Mansfield Park*

Mansfield Park (1814) was written more than ten years after *Pride and Prejudice* but before *Emma* and *Persuasion*. I have chosen to deal with it last because it is Jane Austen's most complex and also, I think, her most interesting novel. It is also, however, the novel many readers like least, or find most difficult to get on with when they first read it. I have already suggested that it's a good idea to read more of Jane Austen's novels than the one you are actually studying and, because of its comparative difficulty, this is particularly true if you are studying *Mansfield Park*. If you read it alongside something like *Pride and Prejudice* you should be in a position to approach *Mansfield Park* more confidently since the two novels, though so different in tone, have many themes and methods in common. Like Jane Austen's other novels, *Mansfield Park* is a love story in which the heroine's rejection of one man and love for another involve important moral decisions; it deals with the by now familiar opposition and confusion of material and moral values; and its plot structure – introduction, development to a crisis, and the effects of that crisis – is also the one you are already familiar with. So though you might find some aspects of the novel unfamiliar or off-putting, you can feel confident with many of its basic themes and techniques.

Because *Mansfield Park* is a more complex novel, I shall be using a slightly different version of the basic analytic method. In my discussions of Jane Austen's other novels, I chose particular passages for analysis mainly to illustrate the different stages in the development of the plot. Sometimes, however, I included passages for their *thematic* interest as well: in the case of *Pride and Prejudice*, for example, I chose passages which focused on money and marriage, and in the last chapter, some of the passages from *Persuasion* were chosen solely because they illustrated the way in which particular characters represented particular sets of values. I hope by now you are familiar enough with Jane Austen's basic plot structure to be able to work out its main stages in *Mansfield Park* for yourself and I shan't be paying much attention to that aspect of the novel. Instead, I shall be moving on to demonstrate the next stage of analysis, a development from the kind of simple thematic analysis I have used so far. In the introductory chapter, I defined the difference between the *story* and the *plot* of a novel, the plot being the way the story is organised, and I suggested that attention to plot is an important help in identifying the novel's main concerns, what it is 'about'. The progression of the plot from beginning to end is one kind of pattern which helps us to see a novel as a whole; but by using the plot to help us focus on the main thematic concerns we are made aware of another source of pattern, the *patterns created by the ideas* themselves. In my analysis of *Mansfield Park* I shall be drawing on this kind of pattern, rather than using the plot as a basis. As always, in the case of each extract I shall be asking questions about point of view, key words and oppositions and I shall be using as far as possible examples of different narrative methods, but my extracts will now be chosen solely because they illustrate particular issues I am interested in exploring, just as you will choose passages and incidents which illustrate your particular argument and subject when you write essays. The ability to see a novel as a whole, as a set of significant patterns rather than just as a sequence of events, is something you should aim for because it makes analysis and essay-writing so much easier (I shall be going into this again in the final chapter on essay-writing).

Mansfield Park is about Fanny Price, the poor niece of Sir Thomas and Lady Bertram of Mansfield Park, who is brought at the age of nine to live with her rich relations. At first she is very unhappy and the kindness of Edmund, the younger of the two Bertram sons, endears him to her and she eventually falls in love with him. When Fanny is sixteen Sir Thomas has to leave Mansfield for a long visit to his plantations in Antigua. While he is away Maria, his elder daughter, becomes engaged to the rather stupid Mr Rushworth through the machinations of her aunt, Mrs Norris; and Mary and Henry Crawford, brother and sister of the local rector's wife and rich members of London society, arrive in the neighbourhood. Henry trifles with the affections of both Maria and Julia Bertram, and, much to Fanny's distress and concern, Edmund becomes infatuated with Mary, who is totally unable to sympathise with his vocation as a clergyman.

When Sir Thomas returns he finds Mansfield disrupted by preparations for a play under the direction of Mr Yates, a friend of his dissolute elder son, Tom. Maria marries Mr Rushworth, in spite of her attraction to Henry Crawford, and goes to London. Henry turns his attentions, with some seriousness, to Fanny, who refuses his offer of marriage. While Fanny is on a visit to her parents in Portsmouth, Tom Bertram is brought home dangerously ill as a result of his profligate life-style, Maria elopes with Henry Crawford and Julia with Mr Yates. Edmund's shock at Mary Crawford's superficial attitude to these dreadful events cures him of his infatuation, Fanny returns to Mansfield as the much-needed comfort of Sir Thomas and his wife, and 'exactly at the time when it was quite natural that it should be so, and not a week earlier, Edmund . . . became as anxious to marry Fanny, as Fanny herself could desire' (ch. 48).

What then are the features of *Mansfield Park* which make it more complex and less immediately approachable than something like *Pride and Prejudice*? I think we can identify at least two problems. The first is the nature of the main characters – and particularly Fanny herself. Like many readers, you might have found it difficult to sympathise with Fanny, who is quiet and unassertive, physically weak, and apparently always in the right so that she can seem to be a rather unappealing prig. She couldn't be more different from the lively Elizabeth Bennet in *Pride and Prejudice* or the assertive Emma. Edmund Bertram can similarly seem a rather feeble hero compared with someone like Darcy. The problem is compounded by the fact that Fanny and Edmund are contrasted throughout the novel with the Crawfords, whose principles might be suspect but who are far more immediately attractive than the hero and heroine.

A second kind of difficulty you might have experienced with the novel is in some ways similar to the problem of Fanny. The novel contains several important events – the visit to Mr Rushworth's house, Sotherton; the theatricals; and Fanny's visit to her home in Portsmouth towards the end – where the judgements which seem to be demanded of us, often because they are Fanny's, are difficult either to agree with or to see the point of. And throughout the novel the characters discuss issues, such as the role of a good clergyman, which are evidently of thematic importance but which modern readers can find it difficult to relate to. In other words, that sense of remoteness which many readers feel from Jane Austen's concerns and values can be particularly acute in the case of *Mansfield Park*.

What I want to do in this chapter is to start with the problem of Fanny and see whether Jane Austen's presentation of her heroine throws any light on other elements in the book which can present difficulties. My aim is to raise various questions which you can then take further in your own work on the novel. I shall also be following the direction of the title and concentrating particularly on the importance of *place* in the novel. This is something I discussed briefly when I looked at Elizabeth's visit to Pemberley in *Pride and Prejudice* and in looking at *Persuasion* I suggested that different groups of characters, sometimes associated with particular places, can have particular thematic significance. All Jane Austen's novels at least refer to places other than the neighbourhood of the main characters and in most of them the main characters move away from home and back again in the course of the novel, so the significance of different locations is something you should always consider. This movement often involves going from country to town, usually London or Bath; from a small, close-knit community to the wider and less predictable society of a city. In the case of *Mansfield Park* two of the main characters, the heroine and her rival for Edmund's affections, come to Mansfield from other places: Fanny from Portsmouth and Mary Crawford from London.

So as I look at the presentation of Fanny, and especially at the contrast between Fanny and Mary, I shall in many cases be using passages which concern their relationships with place. I am going to start with a group of extracts which illustrate the attitudes of these two outsiders to Mansfield and its surroundings, beginning with their first impressions.

In the second chapter Fanny, aged nine, arrives at Mansfield from Portsmouth and we are shown her initial misery at having to leave home:

> Mrs Norris had been talking to her the whole way from Northampton of her wonderful good fortune, and the extraordinary degree of gratitude and good behaviour which it ought to produce, and her consciousness of misery was therefore increased by the idea of its being a wicked thing for her not to be happy.

Maria and Julia Bertram do nothing to ease her unhappiness:

> The holiday allowed to the Miss Bertrams the next day on purpose to afford leisure for getting acquainted with, and entertaining their young cousin, produced little union. They could not but hold her cheap on find-

ing that she had but two sashes, and had never learnt French; and when they perceived her to be little struck with the duet they were so good as to play, they could do no more than make her a generous present of some of their least valued toys, and leave her to herself, while they adjourned to whatever might be the favourite holiday sport of the moment, making artificial flowers or wasting gold paper.

Fanny, whether near or from her cousins, whether in the school-room, the drawing-room, or in the shrubbery, was equally forlorn, finding something to fear in every person and place. . . . and when to these sorrows was added the idea of the brothers and sisters among whom she had always been important as play-fellow, instructress, and nurse, the despondence that sunk her little heart was severe.

The grandeur of the house astonished, but could not console her. The rooms were too large for her to move in with ease; whatever she touched she expected to injure, and she crept about in constant terror of something or other; often retreating towards her own chamber to cry; and the little girl who was spoken of in the drawing-room when she left it at night, as seeming so desirably sensible of her peculiar good fortune, ended every day's sorrows by sobbing herself to sleep. A week had passed in this way, and no suspicion of it conveyed by her quiet passive manner, when she was found one morning by her cousin Edmund, the youngest of the sons, sitting crying on the attic stairs.

'My dear little cousin,' said he with all the gentleness of an excellent nature, 'what can be the matter?'

(ch. 2)

Whatever we might think of her later, the heart-rending presentation of Fanny's isolation here makes it very easy for readers to sympathise with her, so I am going to begin by analysing the reasons for Fanny's misery and the techniques which secure our sympathy. The narrative voice moves between an objective position (telling us Fanny sobbed herself to sleep) and one which takes on the point of view of Fanny herself (describing her 'terror of something or other', for example) or of the Bertram sisters (who were 'so good as to play' to her – surely their own assessment of their generosity). We are thus able to share Fanny's experience and, by seeing things more clearly than she does, to understand more fully the causes of her isolation. That isolation is both emotional: she is desperately missing the family where she is valued and needed; and social: she feels displaced in this grand house and the self-centred Bertram girls judge her according to her possessions ('but two sashes') and a superficial assessment of her accomplishments (her lack of French). As a result, they hold her 'cheap', a word which draws attention to the mercenary nature of their judgements, while we are so painfully aware of the power of her feelings. To add to her unhappiness, Fanny's social inferiority becomes a source of added emotional pressure: as the poor relation she is expected to be grateful for the move which is making her so miserable, and her misery is compounded by guilt at not feeling the gratitude she should. What Fanny evidently learns to do very quickly, however, is to *appear* grateful, she *seems* 'so desirably sensible of her peculiar good fortune', while remaining emotionally isolated and misunderstood.

When we examine the basis of our sympathy for Fanny in this passage, it becomes clear that familiar oppositions are operating: between *feeling* and *material* values – Fanny's grief at leaving her family compared with the Bertrams' assumption that social improvement should be her only concern; and between *inner reality* and *surface appearance* – Fanny's actual suffering, which we are shown, compared with the Bertrams' complacent idea that her deferential attitude means contentment. This gap between Fanny's external manner and the depth of her inner feelings is something the novel makes clear again and again, and though it is of course possible to accuse Fanny of hypocrisy in thus disguising her real feelings, the passage makes it very clear *why* Fanny retreats into herself. There are powerful pressures on her to please, so that though we might not *like* her any better, we can perhaps begin to understand some of the reasons for those passive, 'priggish' aspects of the older Fanny which can seem so unattractive.

Our sympathy here for the little girl who is so thoroughly misunderstood invites us to judge in favour of feeling and against the Bertram girls' thoughtless cruelty, and the narrative voice encourages that judgement in describing their holiday pastimes: 'making *artificial* flowers and *wasting* gold paper'. In this passage, then, Fanny represents feeling and affectionate family ties compared with the Bertram sisters and Mrs Norris who stand for social and economic snobbery. If we put this in terms of *place*, Portsmouth values are so far much preferable to those of Mansfield, and the poor outsider, little Cinderella, seems to have more to offer than her rich relations. The exception, of course, is Edmund, whose 'excellent nature' makes him sensitive to Fanny's feelings and able to comfort her. Because its inhabitants are so diverse, we perhaps need to reserve judgement here on the significance of Mansfield itself.

I want next to put this introduction of Fanny beside a passage in which Mary Crawford is introduced to Mansfield. In complete contrast to Fanny, Mary comes from wealthy society to stay at the Mansfield parsonage and her sister's 'chief anxiety was lest Mansfield should not satisfy the habits of a young woman who had been mostly used to London' (ch. 4). To her own surprise, however, Mary is very pleased with the place and particularly at first with the eldest son, Tom Bertram:

> Miss Crawford soon felt, that he and his situation might do. She looked about her with due consideration, and found almost every thing in his favour, a park, a real park five miles round, a spacious modern-built house, so well placed and well screened as to deserve to be in any collection of engravings of gentlemen's seats in the kingdom, and wanting only to be completely new furnished – pleasant sisters, a quiet mother, and an agreeable man himself – with the advantage of being tied up from much gaming at present, by a promise to his father, and of being Sir Thomas hereafter. It might do very well. . . .
>
> (ch. 5)

What impression of Mary Crawford do we get from this account of her reactions to Mansfield? Quite unlike Fanny, she has a fortune of twenty thousand pounds and the self-confidence which results from a position of economic superiority. She judges Tom Bertram 'and his situation' according to whether he will 'do' in her own scheme of things, and she is clearly much more interested in social status than in individuals: she is impressed by the thought of Tom becoming 'Sir Thomas hereafter' and by the fact that he and his family look as if they will be easy to manage. Compared with Fanny, then, she has a will and energy which have a certain attraction, though her interests are in public appearance rather than personal feeling. Her view of Mansfield itself confirms this impression. She sees it neither as a home nor as the awe-inspiring place which so frightened the young Fanny. Instead, she coolly judges its social position and its appearance, seeing the outside as a fit image of social authority in a 'collection of engravings of gentlemen's seats', and the inside as in need of total change, 'wanting only to be completely new furnished'. Fanny, even the older Fanny, would never dare suggest that anything at Mansfield might be changed; Mary's readiness to do so is a reminder of her wealth and of the familiarity with new fashions which life in London has given her. So, again putting our impressions in terms of place, we can say that Mansfield's *social status* is contrasted with the *money* and *modernity* of London.

Having established some interesting oppositions to do with place by comparing Fanny's and Mary's first impressions of Mansfield, I am going to choose two more passages which are similarly concerned with their reactions to Mansfield and the surrounding area, so that I can explore the comparison further. The first is from a conversation between Mary and Edmund about Mary's harp. She has had difficulty finding someone to transport it from Northampton and Edmund has to explain to her that all the local farmers need their horses and carts for haymaking.

> 'You could not be expected to have thought on the subject before, but when you *do* think of it, you must see the importance of getting in the grass. The hire of a cart at any time, might not be so easy as you suppose; our farmers are not in the habit of letting them out; but in harvest, it must be quite out of their power to spare a horse.'
>
> 'I shall understand all your ways in time; but coming down with the true London maxim, that every thing is to be got with money, I was a little embarrassed at first by the sturdy independence of your country customs.'

(Ch. 6)

What does this short conversation add to our impressions of Mary and, through her, of London values? In referring to the hay harvest as if it is a mere quaint 'custom', Mary shows a complete mis-understanding of the economic importance of such activities and her tone is patronising, suggesting that she has still failed to grasp Edmund's point. An opposition is set up between her London idea of money – that 'every thing is to be got' with it – and the rural aware-ness that money depends on hard work on the land. This is rein-forced by the fact that it is a *harp* that she wants to transport and which she sees as having a rival claim to the grass for which the farmers need their carts. If we generalise these contrasts, we can oppose country to city, Mansfield to London in terms of *work* and *leisure, use* and *decoration* and as representing two very different attitudes to money, as something that has to be *earned* and as something to be *spent.* Can we as yet choose between these alternatives? Edmund cer-tainly makes Mary's expectations seem rather selfishly unreasonable and her patronising tone is irritating, but on the other hand her skill on the harp is an attractive quality and both Edmund and Fanny look forward to hearing her play. Again at this stage we might reserve judgement.

But in a slightly later passage the narrative voice encourages us to judge by making an explicit comparison between Mary's and Fanny's responses to the countryside. They are on the way to visit Sotherton,

Mr Rushworth's house, and travel through areas which are new to Fanny:

> . . . in observing the appearance of the country, the bearings of the roads, the difference of soil, the stage of the harvest, the cottages, the cattle, the children, she found entertainment that could only have been heightened by having Edmund to speak to of what she felt. That was the only point of resemblance between her and the lady who sat by her; in every thing but a value for Edmund, Miss Crawford was very unlike her. She had none of Fanny's delicacy of taste, of mind, of feeling; she saw nature, inanimate nature, with little observation; her attention was all for men and women, her talents for the light and lively.
>
> (ch. 8)

The narrator is very obviously on Fanny's side here. Her response to her surroundings is described as evidence of her *delicacy* of taste, mind and, again, *feeling*. This is contrasted with Mary Crawford's lack of interest in 'nature, inanimate nature' and her 'talents for the *light* and *lively*'. What is Fanny's view of 'inanimate nature'? She is not looking at the view simply for its beauty. She is interested in the roads, the soil, the harvest, the cottages, cattle and children: in other words in the evidence of human *use* of nature (very similar to Elizabeth's appreciation of Pemberley in *Pride and Prejudice*), thus suggesting that, unlike Mary Crawford, she responds to both nature *and* 'men and women' and, furthermore, to nature as inseparable from people. She seems therefore to have the right appreciation of the countryside lacking in Mary's indifference to haymaking and in her preference here for the 'light and lively'. Because it is associated with 'lightness', liveliness is here seen as suspect. On the other hand, Fanny's seriousness, her 'delicacy' of taste and mind, are seen as qualities which we are encouraged to approve. As readers, we might feel that Fanny could do with some of Mary Crawford's liveliness, however untrustworthy, but what is clear is that the argument of the novel tends to favour Fanny's seriousness, and that this is associated with a particular view of the country as a place where people work for a living.

We get another view of the country in contrast with London in a conversation between Edmund and Mary later in the trip to Sotherton. Mary has discovered that Edmund is to be a clergyman – much to her distress, since she disagrees with his view that the clergy have an important status and influence on society. How, she demands, can they:

'. . . govern the conduct and fashion the manners of a large congregation for the rest of the week? One scarcely sees a clergyman out of his pulpit.'

'*You* are speaking of London, *I* am speaking of the nation at large.'

'The metropolis, I imagine, is a pretty fair sample of the rest.'

'Not, I should hope, of the proportion of virtue to vice throughout the kingdom. We do not look in great cities for our best morality. It is not there that respectable people of any denomination can do most good; and it is certainly not there, that the influence of the clergy can be most felt. A fine preacher is followed and admired; but it is not in fine preaching only that a good clergyman will be useful in his parish and his neighbourhood, where the parish and neighbourhood are of a size capable of knowing his private character, and observing his general conduct, which in London can rarely be the case.'

(ch. 9)

The opposition between *country* and *city* is given here in explicitly *moral* terms: Edmund suggests that 'the proportion of virtue to vice' in London is worse than in the rest of the country, that London ways cannot be looked to as a model of conduct. The passage thus brings out clearly the moral element which was implicit in the oppositions set up in the other extracts I have examined so far. The association of London with a superficial attitude to money and with a desire to use that money to modernise and change things (Mary's view that Mansfield should be completely refurnished) is here identified as *morally* dangerous. In contrast, small country neighbourhoods are seen as ideal for encouraging right standards of behaviour. Because people in those kinds of communities know each other well, the good clergyman's influence can be most effective. This is an argument against the *size* of London, in which it is difficult to know anyone well, and against the rapid *changes* in city life which also make it impossible to get to know people properly. Country communities are seen as attractive because of their *stability*. So *stability* and *change* are established as elements in the moral opposition of country and city. This moral opposition is confirmed later in the novel: London is the scene of Maria's elopement with Henry Crawford. Again, Edmund's views on the good clergyman repeat the opposition between *inner* and *outer* selves in his stress on the clergyman's 'private character', the fact that his 'general conduct' should confirm what he preaches. Mary, on the other hand, focuses simply on preaching, on the external show.

Modern readers sometimes find it difficult to see the point of the various discussions about the role of the clergyman which occur in the course of the novel. I hope my analysis of this particular passage has shown how you can begin to make sense of scenes like this one. If you analyse the thematic oppositions which are present in the scene and look for versions of oppositions you have already begun to see as part of the novel's overall *thematic pattern*, you will usually find that incidents which at first seem remote or pointless can be fitted into your view of the novel as a whole.

The whole business of Sotherton – both discussion about it and the visit itself – can present difficulties of this kind. I am not going to look in detail at the rest of the visit to Sotherton, from which the last two extracts were taken, because I hope that my exploration so far of some of the thematic oppositions associated with place will have given you a basis for your own analysis, both of the conversation about 'improvements' at the beginning of Chapter 6 and the visit itself in Chapters 9 and 10. The word 'improvements', for example, can immediately be associated with Mary Crawford's (by now suspect) desire to change or 'improve' the inside of Mansfield Park, and it's interesting that in the conversation about improving Sotherton she is in favour of simply paying someone to ' "give me as much beauty as he could for my money; and I should never look at it, till it was complete" ' (ch. 6). Fanny, on the other hand, is worried by the whole idea of change and particularly by Mr Rushworth's threat to cut down an avenue of trees: ' "I should like to see Sotherton before it is cut down, to see the place as it is now, in its old state" ' (ch. 6). The differences which we have already observed between the two characters are here very clear: Mary shows the city person's indifference to nature and stands for spending money to bring about change; Fanny, having lived in the country for eight years, is sensitive to nature and to the need for using it responsibly, and she is in favour of the stability and security of leaving things as they are.

So far in my consideration of characters and place in *Mansfield Park* I have mainly concentrated on the differences between Mansfield and London, as represented by Fanny and Mary Crawford. But, as the first passage made clear, at the beginning of the novel Fanny is associated not with Mansfield but with Portsmouth, so to complete my examination of place, I need to look at passages which will help me to understand the significance of Portsmouth.

At the beginning of the novel, when Fanny comes to Mansfield as a lonely outsider, Portsmouth seems to stand for warmth of feeling and family affection and, much later, when Fanny is to return for the first time to her family, she sees it in these terms: 'to feel affection without fear or restraint, to feel herself the equal of those who surrounded her' (ch. 37). Her impressions of Portsmouth itself, however, are a great disappointment: 'It was the abode of noise, disorder, and impropriety. Nobody was in their right place, nothing was done as it ought to be' (ch. 39), and she realises that Mansfield has become 'home'. Fanny's visit to Portsmouth is one of the most difficult parts of *Mansfield Park* to come to terms with. Many readers feel that both Fanny and Jane Austen are guilty of a snobbery which amounts to rejecting people simply for being poor, and they find the whole novel distasteful as a result. As always, if this is your reaction, do not assume it is wrong, but ask how you arrived at it and whether it can be used to help your understanding (if not your enjoyment) of the novel. With this in mind, I am going to look at two passages from Fanny's visit to Portsmouth in which she compares Portsmouth with Mansfield. The first comes soon after her arrival:

> . . . she could think of nothing but Mansfield, its beloved inmates, its happy ways. Every thing where she now was was in full contrast to it. The elegance, propriety, regularity, harmony – and perhaps, above all, the peace and tranquillity of Mansfield, were brought to her remembrance every hour of the day, by the prevalence of every thing opposite to them *here*.
>
> The living in incessant noise was to a frame and temper, delicate and nervous like Fanny's, an evil which no super-added elegance or harmony could have entirely atoned for. It was the greatest misery of all. At Mansfield, no sounds of contention, no raised voice, no abrupt bursts, no tread of violence was ever heard; all proceeded in a regular course of cheerful orderliness; every body had their due importance; every body's feelings were consulted. If tenderness could be ever supposed wanting, good sense and good breeding supplied its place; . . .
>
> (ch. 39)

The second when she has been there several weeks and has just had news of Tom Bertram's illness:

> It was sad to Fanny to lose all the pleasures of spring. She had not known before what pleasures she *had* to lose in passing March and April in a town. She had not known before, how much the beginnings and progress of vegetation had delighted her. – What animation both of body and mind, she had derived from watching the advance of that season which cannot, in spite of its capriciousness, be unlovely, and seeing its increasing beauties, from the earliest flowers, in the warmest divisions of her aunt's garden, to the opening of leaves of her uncle's plantations, and

the glory of his woods. – To be losing such pleasures was no trifle; to be losing them, because she was in the midst of closeness and noise, to have confinement, bad air, bad smells, substituted for liberty, freshness, fragrance, and verdure, was infinitely worse; – but even these incitements to regret were feeble, compared with what arose from the conviction of being missed, by her best friends, and the longing to be useful to those who were wanting her!
(ch. 45)

The passages are presented primarily from Fanny's point of view, but her assessment of Portsmouth seems to have the author's approval so that the reader is invited to share her judgement. In the second paragraph of the first passage, for example, the narrative voice defends Fanny's reaction by referring to her *delicacy* of temper (compare the description of her 'delicacy of taste, of mind, of feeling' on the way to Sotherton) and describes life in Portsmouth as an *evil* to someone with Fanny's temperament: 'It was the greatest misery of all'. The tone is authoritative, suggesting that this is not just Fanny's view, but a description of things as they really are. 'Evil' is a strong word which is later used of Maria's elopement and of Mrs Norris, but it is used here to describe *noise*. This might seem a bit excessive, but further analysis shows that noise is opposed not only to the 'peace and tranquillity of Mansfield', but to its '*elegance, propriety, regularity, harmony*', and that it is associated at Portsmouth with the sounds of *contention* and *violence* never heard at Mansfield. The opposition of noise and peace thus again takes on a *moral* dimension. Through its association with violent disagreement, noise becomes indicative of the wrong treatment of other people, whereas at Mansfield 'every body had their due importance; every body's *feelings* were consulted'.

The image of Mansfield, then, is one of thoughtfulness towards others compared with the self-interested quarrels of Portsmouth, and the suggestion seems to be that Portsmouth's failings are due not to poverty but to a lack of moral discipline; they are due, in other words, to the Price family's *internal* weaknesses rather than to the pressure of their circumstances. Fanny's 'delicacy', on the other hand, represents those inborn moral qualities her parents lack. In the second passage this is expressed through her response to nature, in the by now familiar opposition of *country* to *city*. The fact that she misses the spring in the town shows that her rightful place is in the country, at Mansfield. When Fanny arrives at Mansfield at the beginning of the novel, she is the outsider. Now she is the outsider in Portsmouth, having responded positively to Mansfield's environment and values. And what is more, as the second passage makes clear, she is *needed* there, needed because, with the exception of Edmund, the legal inheritors of Mansfield have failed to live up to their moral responsibilities. In other words, they show moral failings rather like those of the family in Portsmouth, except that the Bertrams' responsibilities are all the greater given their social privilege. It is Fanny who brings to Mansfield the moral feeling which is capable of appreciating and therefore fulfilling Mansfield's 'propriety, regularity, harmony'. Like Elizabeth at Pemberley, she finds her true home away from her actual family, something recognised by Sir Thomas himself when, at the end of the novel, he acknowledges that 'Fanny was indeed the daughter that he wanted' (ch. 48).

So Fanny's growing importance at Mansfield seems to suggest that the old country values can only be refreshed and made effective by a poor outsider, that it is the individual who has the right moral feeling, regardless of their social background, who is the true heir to Mansfield's 'elegance'. And this argument bears out our sympathy for Fanny at the beginning of the novel, when she was identified with *feeling* as opposed to the Bertrams' *material* values. Perhaps, then, far from being a snob, Jane Austen is suggesting the need for social change and mobility, rather as she does through her approval of the naval characters in *Persuasion?*

But is the presentation of Fanny's relationship to Mansfield quite so straightforward? We might well feel that in demonstrating Fanny's *inborn* sensitivity to right values, the novel underestimates the effects of *circumstances* on the way individuals behave. Again like Elizabeth at Pemberley, Fanny's responses to Mansfield could be *moral* but they could also be to *material* comforts. To try to deal with this uncertainty, I am going to look more closely at the words used to express Fanny's very positive image of Mansfield.

In the second passage, for example, the country is seen as offering *liberty* compared with the *confinement* of Portsmouth. It's hardly surprising if the house full of children in Portsmouth fails to give Fanny the sense of freedom and beauty she gets from 'her aunt's garden' and 'her uncle's plantations' and woods. It is, after all, easier to feel free if you live in a house that has, as Mary Crawford noted, 'a real park five miles round'. Like the first passage, the second passage is mainly presented from Fanny's point of view, so this could just be her idea of the shortcomings of Portsmouth, but we have already seen that in the first passage, the association of *noise* (a word which recurs here) with some kind of moral weakness seems to have authorial approval. There, the noise and *disorder* are opposed to the thoughtfulness and *order* ('cheerful orderliness') of Mansfield. The 'order' at Mansfield might be moral, but it is also *social.* 'Every body had their *due* importance', suggests that it is based on people knowing their place; and 'good *breeding*' supplies the place of 'tenderness' when necessary. This order is also *aesthetic,* associated with a pleasant environment, with *elegance,* for example. When I looked at Elizabeth's responses to Pemberley in *Pride and Prejudice,* I suggested that words like 'elegance' often have a moral meaning in Jane Austen's fiction and here, as in the description of Pemberley, 'elegance' is associated with 'propriety, regularity, harmony', suggesting a balanced combination which importantly includes moral elements. The suggestion is that it is this kind of order that Fanny misses in Portsmouth. But, again as with Pemberley, this morally harmonious way of life is associated with wealth and the social authority which comes with that. Wealth alone is certainly inadequate, as the behaviour of Henry Crawford or even the Bertrams themselves demonstrates, but in Fanny's final preference for Mansfield, like Elizabeth's removal to Pemberley, the identification of moral order with social privilege is still a problem, particularly for modern readers. It is certainly open to very different interpretations: the 'harmony' at Mansfield could be seen as an image of ideal balance in which moral behaviour matches social status; but it could also be seen as a confusion of social privilege with moral superiority. It is certainly the case that, again as in her treatment of Pemberley, Jane Austen's *moral* argument about treating other people properly becomes part of her defence of the *social* order as it is, part of her *conservative* position – and modern readers' unease with her 'snobbish' treatment of Portsmouth in *Mansfield Park* is a way of responding to this.

The opposition between Fanny and Mansfield's *stability, stillness* and *quietness* and Mary Crawford's *liveliness* and love of *change* in these passages about place can be seen as part of this conservative argument. Mary's modern London ideas (or Mr Rushworth's desire to 'improve' Sotherton at all costs) threaten the way of life at Mansfield, a way of life based on traditional social relationships and values, and implicit in the countryside itself as Fanny sees it. We have detected these concerns through close attention to our responses to the text, but it's interesting to note that Jane Austen's defence of the country against city values in *Mansfield Park* is very much part of the political arguments of her day. Country landowners like Sir Thomas Bertram were frightened of having their political and social power taken over by people who had made their money quickly through trade and financial speculation, people who were in many cases much richer than themselves. The country gentry's inherited wealth was tied up in land and farming; the city merchants had ready cash. Mary Crawford's assumption that she ought to be able to transport her harp by buying the use of a cart which is needed for the hay harvest can thus be seen as a representative image of this contemporary political conflict.

As the rightful inheritor of Mansfield (though she doesn't actually live there after her marriage – she and Edmund eventually move into the parsonage, not into Mansfield itself), Fanny represents Jane Austen's conservative defence of constancy and stability, values which it is difficult to dramatise in an attractive way because they are by definition inactive. Mary Crawford's liveliness is, in contrast, immediately (though dangerously?) attractive. When I looked at Fanny's arrival at Mansfield, I suggested social and psychological reasons for her submissiveness and apparent passivity. This analysis of the relationship between character and place supplies a *thematic* explanation of her behaviour. Again, it might not mean that you learn to *like* Fanny any better – indeed, you might actively disagree with the values she represents – but it is always helpful to understand *why* a character behaves in a certain way.

Because Fanny presents such a problem for so many readers of *Mansfield Park* I want to spend what is left of this chapter looking in more detail at the way she is presented, asking in particular whether quietness and stability are quite the same as the passivity of which she is so often accused, and whether Fanny changes in the course of the novel, something again often denied. I am going to use extracts from scenes which deal with Fanny's refusal of Henry Crawford's offer of marriage, and, first, a passage which illustrates the difference between her *outer* appearance and her *inner* feelings, an opposition already present in the first passage I looked at, showing her as a child. This extract examines Fanny's response when Edmund decides to join in with the amateur theatricals:

> She could not feel that she had done wrong herself, but she was disquieted in every other way. Her heart and her judgment were equally against Edmund's decision; she could not acquit his unsteadiness; and his happiness under it made her wretched. She was full of jealousy and agita-

tion. Miss Crawford came with looks of gaiety which seemed an insult, with friendly expressions towards herself which she could hardly answer calmly. Every body around her was gay and busy, prosperous and important, each had their object of interest, their part, their dress, their favourite scene, their friends and confederates, all were finding employment in consultations and comparisons, or diversion in the playful conceits they suggested. She alone was sad and insignificant; she had no share in any thing; she might go or stay, she might be in the midst of their noise, or retreat from it to the solitude of the East room, without being seen or missed. She could almost think any thing would have been preferable to this.

(ch. 17)

It's difficult for modern readers to understand why Fanny objects so strongly to the plan to perform *Lovers' Vows*, so the whole episode of the theatricals is one in which, to many readers, she appears at her most priggish. But is priggishness the main impression of Fanny given in this passage? Because it is presented from her point of view, the reader has access to the turmoil in Fanny's mind, beneath her quiet surface which makes the others unaware of whether or not she is even present. So we are made very much aware of how painful she finds her decision not to join in: 'She alone was sad and insignificant'. This sense of being excluded amounts almost to a temptation to give in to something she is sure is wrong. Real passivity would have meant that she simply went along with what the others were doing; to refuse, even though it means making herself miserable, is an act of will. And, making things worse for Fanny (though it might help to evoke our sympathy for her), she is jealous of Mary Crawford's influence over Edmund. We are told that 'her *heart* and her *judgement* were equally against Edmund's decision'. The stress on her *feelings* as well as her *reason* is a reminder of Fanny's capacity for passion, which often complicates her motives – and any idea we might have of her simply as boring and self-righteous.

Fanny does not object to acting itself – later in the novel she grudgingly admires Henry Crawford's reading of Shakespeare (ch. 34). Her objection is to this particular play, which gives Henry Crawford and Maria the opportunity to indulge their infatuation in spite of Maria's engagement to Mr Rushworth. It also gives Edmund and Mary a similar opportunity. The preparations which so disrupt Mansfield therefore suggest a threat to its *moral* stability – Fanny is concerned that even Edmund is affected with '*unsteadiness*', recalling again the opposition of *constancy* to *change* which runs throughout the novel.

So Fanny's inner suffering in this passage can be seen as due to both powerful emotion and a kind of moral heroism, the 'heroism of principle' referred to by the narrator on a later occasion (ch. 27). Bearing that term 'heroism' in mind, I am going now to turn to the effects on Fanny of refusing Henry Crawford to explore further in what sense Jane Austen's quiet heroine could be said to earn that title.

Henry's offer of marriage is again something for which Fanny is supposed to feel *grateful*, even though she cannot love him since she already loves Edmund, and she is convinced of his moral weakness, having seen the way he has played with Maria and Julia's feelings. Because she is the poor relation, his proposal is seen as a compliment she cannot refuse and in doing so, she isolates herself completely, even from Edmund. My final two extracts from *Mansfield Park* are confrontations between Fanny and her uncle and Fanny and Edmund about the proposal. Her uncle makes clear that it is not just because of her *social* inferiority that he is astounded by her refusal:

> 'I had thought you peculiarly free from wilfulness of temper, self conceit, and every tendency to that independence of spirit, which prevails so much in modern days, even in young women, and which in young women is offensive and disgusting beyond all common offence.'

Fanny is deeply upset by his fierce criticism:

> Her heart was almost broke by such a picture of what she appeared to him; by such accusations, so heavy, so multiplied, so rising in dreadful gradation! Self-willed, obstinate, selfish, and ungrateful. He thought her all this. She had deceived his expectations; she had lost his good opinion. What was to become of her?

> (ch. 32)

Sir Thomas clearly expects Fanny to conform to expectations and to accept Henry simply because that is her duty as a woman. Because she is a woman, her rebellion, as he sees it, is a social evil taken 'beyond all common offence'. So yet another source of pressure to be submissive is added to the social and psychological pressures which we have already seen working on Fanny from her arrival at Mansfield: that of her *gender* position, the social role expected of her as a woman. Most modern readers will find Sir Thomas's views and his extreme language absurd. It is perhaps less easy for us, then, to see why Fanny should be so upset by his accusations, but important that we should try to explain her reaction.

Fanny is particularly upset by the idea that she has 'deceived' Sir Thomas's expectations, that she has proved herself selfish and ungrateful. Having seen Fanny from the inside throughout the novel, we know this is not the case so we can share her sense of righteous indignation: Fanny actually wants to be approved *in Sir Thomas's terms*. She wants to belong to Mansfield for psychological reasons (we have already seen how painful she finds exclusion at the theatricals and how important it is to her to feel herself needed at Mansfield when she is in Portsmouth); but also because, again as we have seen, she identifies with Mansfield values and thus, ironically, with her uncle's objections to the modern 'independence of spirit' exemplified by someone like Mary Crawford. In other words, the pressures upon her to conform have resulted in her genuinely *wanting* to do so. Again, it is thus all the more heroic, because all the more difficult, for her to stick to her decision.

And particularly when Edmund, though in a more reasonable manner, apparently agrees with his father. This rouses Fanny to defend her right as a woman to have some say about the man she marries:

> 'I *should* have thought,' said Fanny, after a pause of recollection and exertion, 'that every woman must have felt the possibility of a man's not being approved, not being loved by some one of her sex, at least, let him be ever so generally agreeable. Let him have all the perfections in the world, I think it ought not to be set down as certain, that a man must be acceptable to every woman he may happen to like himself.'
>
> (ch. 35)

By the end of their conversation, we are told, 'Her feelings were all in revolt'.

In spite of her belief in tradition and authority, Fanny 'revolts' here on behalf of her *feelings* and on behalf of her *sex*. Fanny's view that women have as much right to their individuality and feelings as men seems self-evident to a modern reader, but it's important, I think, that we remember the difference between the position of women in Jane Austen's time and in our own, that we make the imaginative effort necessary to recognise the bravery of Fanny's self-defence. It's also important, when we feel irritated by Fanny's longing to conform, to ask whether similar social pressures to conform to gender roles, to behave in a generally accepted 'masculine' or 'feminine' way, don't still operate.

My analysis of the role of place in *Mansfield Park* tended to see Jane Austen as offering a socially conservative argument in the novel.

My analysis of the way in which Fanny learns self-assertion suggests that a more radical argument is also present. At the end of the novel we are invited to see Fanny, the socially disadvantaged woman, as the real heir to Mansfield. At the same time, of course, both her feelings and her social conservatism are satisfied by marrying Edmund, the man who has been mainly responsible for her education at Mansfield and whom she looks up to as an authority figure, just as Emma looked up to Mr Knightley. So again, as at the end of so many of the novels, we can see an interesting tension in Jane Austen's fiction between different political positions, and between the questions raised in the novel and the implications of the happy ending.

This kind of problem or tension is not something you should feel you have to 'solve'. It arises out of the different contemporary social and political pressures affecting Jane Austen's fiction and cannot be susceptible to any easy solution. What I hope you do feel by now is that you have an approach to Jane Austen's novels which helps to open up some of these interesting issues; that simply by applying a systematic and fairly simple analytic method, and by having the confidence to use your own reactions as the basis for further questions, you are not only ready to deal confidently with essay and exam questions on these texts but also to enjoy reading them more.

I deal with the practical problem of writing essays in my final chapter, and you might want to go straight on to read that. You might, however, feel ready to move on to develop your approach to Austen by reading some criticism. So in my next chapter I offer some guidelines on Austen criticism, and how to read it.

6

Moving on: Jane Austen and critical debate

YOU should by now be feeling fairly confident about reading and analysing Jane Austen's novels on your own. You are no doubt developing a sense of which issues seem to you most important, either in the particular novel you are studying, or in Austen's work more generally, and you can demonstrate how her use of language and plot seems to you to set up and develop those issues. You are, in fact, ready to leave this book behind and move on to read more widely in Jane Austen criticism. The aim of this chapter is to give you some guidance, partly in what criticism to read (there are other suggestions in the 'Further reading' section as well), but primarily in how to go about reading it in ways which will help you develop your own critical approach.

How to use criticism can be a problem. Some students (and some teachers) feel that using criticism is somehow 'cheating', that they should rely entirely on their own ideas. Others read too much criticism, or read it too slavishly, and lose all confidence in their own ability to say anything worth while about a text. Don't be afraid of reading criticism: literary studies depend on a stimulating exchange of ideas. But always *test* any critical reading of your set text against your own impressions and against the text itself – and don't worry if you disagree with the critic's view. Remember: criticism is opinion, not truth; it offers an *interpretation*. So don't assume, as sometimes happens, that critics must be right – since they often disagree with each other, that can hardly be the case! It's important to recognise from the start that in looking at critical readings of your set texts you will encounter very different, sometimes contradictory, responses to them. In other words, you will enter into a critical *debate*.

It might be helpful to think of your critical reading as working in three interrelated ways. Obviously, its most immediate effect will be to help you clarify and extend your own ideas about your set text and to stimulate new lines of thought. But by thinking from the start in terms of a critical debate, you will begin to see those particular points of view in a wider context, as part of more general arguments about Austen, arguments in which you will feel you want to take sides. And in negotiating or choosing between different critical readings, in discovering which kinds of critical readings you find most helpful and interesting, you will also begin to develop and define your own critical approach.

Bearing these important points about debate and choice in mind I suggest that, rather than starting with a single-authored book on Austen's work, you begin by looking at collections of essays by different critics – either on your set text, or on Austen more generally. Beginning with a collection of essays helps avoid the danger of simply accepting one particular point of view. More importantly, it will make the critical debate which I have been stressing evident from the start. Most collections of essays have helpful introductions which describe the way the articles they include fit into the wider history of Austen criticism, the ways in which different approaches to Austen have developed over time and in relation to each other. Reading collections of essays will also help you see how different readings of Austen reflect changing critical methodologies and so relate in turn to much wider critical arguments – about the definition and role of literature itself and about the methods and function of criticism.

Much of the material I'm going to focus on in this chapter – particularly at the beginning – is easily available in essay collections, and I shall be using it to demonstrate in detail what I mean by different kinds of readings and their wider critical contexts. My method will be very similar to that used throughout the book. I shall be choosing representative passages from the critics and analysing them in some detail – just as I have been doing for Austen's novels. I shall be suggesting how, by paying close attention to the style and vocabulary of a piece of criticism and asking questions about what it doesn't say as well as what it does, you can begin to recognise the assumptions on which it is working and so understand how it fits into a wider critical picture. By approaching criticism in this way from the beginning, you will quickly gain the confidence to read and use it in an active and discriminating way, rather than passively accepting everything it says.

The aim of the chapter, then, is to give you a confident start in reading criticism, and to do so by combining close analysis with a selective (but I hope fairly representative) history of Austen criticism over the past forty years or so. The chapter is divided into three sections. Each section looks at extracts from three critics, and takes a central critical question as its main focus: the question of *value* in the first section; the question of *historical context* in the second; and the question of *gender* in the third. By now, I hope, these issues will not be entirely unfamiliar to you anyway. Looking comparatively at how various critics have dealt with them will help make you more self-conscious about their relevance and importance to your own thinking about Austen. How we assess the status and value of Austen's work; how it relates to its social and political context; and the significance of Austen's gender to her writing and our reading of it: these are questions which constantly recur, in one form or another, in recent Austen criticism. It is, of course, impossible (and undesirable) to keep these issues separate from each other, and I shall be dealing with all three to some degree in each section. But I have separated them out initially here – partly for the sake of clarity, and partly because it reflects the chronological development of Austen criticism. This is obviously not meant to be an exclusive list of topics. I have tried to be as representative as possible in my choice of both topics and examples, but it inevitably reflects my own critical interests and approach, and there are other important issues which you will discover for yourselves.

One last point before I move on to my examples: in selecting extracts, I have tried as far as possible to avoid readings of particular novels and to choose passages which deal with Austen in general terms. So you should find the chapter relevant whether you are reading one, several or all of Austen's novels.

'3 or 4 Families in a Country Village': Austen and questions of value

The quotation in my subtitle comes from that famous letter of advice which Austen wrote to her niece Anna: 'You are now collecting your People delightfully, getting them exactly into such a spot as is the delight of my life; – 3 or 4 Families in a Country Village is the very thing to work on'.[1] A recurrent question in Austen criticism has been whether, and how, Austen's apparently limited subject-matter, her 'narrow' focus on three or four rural families, affects our assessment of her novels; whether novels which seem to be so restricted in their range of reference must necessarily be 'minor' works, however incisive and well-written they might be. Lying behind such questions – and the answers to them – are all sorts of assumptions about what is and is not 'important', about what does and does not constitute 'significant' subject-matter. So it's important always to ask *whose* version of what might be considered 'important' and 'wide-ranging' we are being given. The three critics represented in this section are all defenders of Austen, and I shall be paying particular attention to the grounds on which they defend her.

The extracts are from the work of three important male critics, from the 1940s and 1950s, whose work has attained a classic status in the history of Austen criticism. As we shall see, more recent Austen criticism is still very much concerned with the question of how to evaluate Austen, though the terms in which it is discussed have altered. But in the immediate post-war period the question was addressed particularly explicitly. My chosen critics in this section are: D. W. Harding, whose essay 'Regulated Hatred: An Aspect of the Work of Jane Austen' was first published in the journal *Scrutiny* in 1940; Lionel Trilling, whose essay on *Mansfield Park* first appeared in 1954, and who also wrote, among other things on Austen, an introduction to *Emma*; and Arnold Kettle, whose influential book *An Introduction to the English Novel* (1951) included a chapter on *Emma*. These essays have been widely anthologised and are easily available in various critical collections – notably the 'Casebooks', published by Macmillan, and 'Twentieth-Century Views', published by Prentice-Hall. I shall be giving page references to both these collections, and suggest that you read this chapter if at all possible in conjunction with the essay collection you find most relevant to your set text(s), so that you can follow up ideas and read further for yourselves.

If you are using one of these essay collections, you will see from the brief history of Austen criticism in the editor's general introduction that Harding, particularly, was defending Austen not so much against critics who *explicitly* dismissed her as limited, but against those Austen fans, often referred to as the 'Janeites', who idealised but also patronised her as a delightful, genial and essentially undisturbing miniaturist. Harding's essay begins with an account of this attitude to Austen:

> A. The impression of Jane Austen which has filtered through to the reading public, down from the first-hand critics, through histories of literature, university courses, literary journalism and polite allusion, deters many who might be her best readers from bothering with her at all. How can this popular impression be described? In my experience the first idea to be absorbed from the atmosphere surrounding her work was that she

offered exceptionally favourable openings to the exponents of urban-
ity. . . .

I was given to understand that her scope was of course extremely
restricted, but that within her limits she succeeded admirably in expressing the virtues of a civilised social order. . . . Chiefly, so I gathered, she
was a delicate satirist, revealing with inimitable lightness of touch the
comic foibles and amiable weaknesses of the people whom she lived
amongst and liked. (Lodge, 1991, pp. 69–70; Southam, 1976b, pp. 69–
70; Watt, 1963, pp. 166–7)[2]

In reaction against this comfortable image of Austen, Harding develops
a rather different idea of her as a much more complicated and potentially disruptive figure:

B. . . . the wide currency of this false impression is an indication of Jane
Austen's success in an essential part of her complex intention as a writer:
her books are, as she meant them to be, read and enjoyed by precisely
the sort of people whom she disliked; she is a literary classic of the society
which attitudes like hers, held widely enough, would undermine. (Lodge,
1991, p. 70; Southam, 1976b, p. 70; Watt, 1963, p. 167)

In support of this view, Harding offers various examples from the novels
where he sees Austen as recording what he calls the 'eruption of fear
and hatred into the relationships of everyday social life'. He goes on:

C. To speak of this aspect of her work as 'satire' is perhaps misleading.
She has none of the underlying didactic intention ordinarily attributed to
the satirist. Her object is not missionary; it is the more desperate one of
merely finding some mode of existence for her critical attitudes. To her
the first necessity was to keep on reasonably good terms with the associates of her everyday life; she had a deep need of their affection and a
genuine respect for the ordered, decent civilisation that they upheld. And
yet she was sensitive to their crudenesses and complacencies and knew
that her real existence depended on resisting many of the values they
implied. The novels gave her a way out of this dilemma. This, rather
than the ambition of entertaining a posterity of urbane gentlemen, was
her motive force in writing.

As a novelist, therefore, part of her aim was to find the means of
unobtrusive spiritual survival, without open conflict with the friendly
people around her whose standards in simpler things she could accept
and whose affection she greatly needed. (Lodge, 1991, p. 72; Watt, 1963,
p. 170)[3]

Once you feel you have a reasonable grasp of the basic argument
in a piece of critical writing, a good way to start analysing it in more

detail is to *identify its positive and negative terms*. Here, for example, 'urban-ity' and 'urbane', 'civilised', 'delicate', 'lightness' and 'gentleman' carry negative connotations through their association with what Harding confidently dismisses as the 'false impression' of Austen. Instead, Hard-ing sees Austen as 'complex', 'sensitive' to 'crudenesses and complacen-cies' and engaged in 'resisting' many of the values of her society. His positive assessment of her as a properly serious rather than a merely 'delicate' writer seems to depend, then, on proving that she felt alie-nated and isolated within her society, that her complex spiritual nature meant that she was in rebellion against society's superficiality, simpli-city and complacency.

The existence of some kind of limitation is not denied altogether in Harding's view, but it is located in Austen's society (and, by exten-sion, some of her critics), rather than Austen herself. Austen is 'saved' as a serious writer by separating her from her social context and making her into an *oppositional* figure – albeit an 'unobtrusive' one. Her 'real existence' and 'spiritual survival' (C) happen somewhere beyond the 'civilised social order' (A). 'Real' and 'spiritual', then, seem to be closely linked here as positive terms. 'Real' is a slippery word, which needs careful attention whenever it occurs in a critical work – and par-ticularly so for our purposes, since it is a word often associated with Jane Austen. Austen is often described as a 'realist' because of her close attention to the material details of a particular society. Here, however, 'real' implies quite the opposite. Harding uses it to mean 'sig-nificant' or 'meaningful' and associates it, as we have seen, with Aus-ten's non-material, spiritual existence, with her *transcendence* of and her *moral superiority* to social detail rather than her attention to it. For Hard-ing, then, Austen's importance as a writer depends on her being funda-mentally at odds with the dominant social order of 'urbane gentlemen'.

You will already be testing this view of Austen against your own impressions. (And if you have the complete text of Harding's essay you should, of course, look carefully at his use of examples from the novels to support his argument: how far do you agree with his interpreta-tions?) You might feel quite happy to endorse many of Harding's values: his impatience with complacency; his plea for Austen as a com-plex writer who demands more complex levels of reading. I would cer-tainly want to accept his central argument that Austen's work has a complicated and by no means wholly positive relationship with its society, for example. In assessing a piece of criticism, however, it's important to think not just about the particular points that the critic makes, but also about the critical assumptions which lie behind them: we should be sceptical about accepting any critic's view as a complete package. Critics often write as if they are describing the truth about an author, whereas in fact they are *constructing* an image of that author, persuading you to accept a version of them which is produced by the critic's own interests and preconceptions working on the writer's text. All criticism is *political* in this sense: whether it acknowledges it or not, it speaks from and for a particular cultural position and set of values. This is an inevitable process, but you will find that more recent critics (writing, say, within the past twenty years) tend to be more aware of its inevitability and more open about their own position than those from an earlier period. So having established the positive and negative terms in a piece of criticism, the next important question to ask is about its *value and ideology*. You should try to establish, in other words, where it is 'coming from' and how it goes about persuading us to accept its readings and arguments. What, then, can we learn about Harding's critical position from his account of Austen?

Harding's positive evaluation of Austen depends, as we have seen, on making her into a rebellious figure who uses her novels to channel and express her frustrations with society and so defend her private, spiritual life. Harding thus challenges not just the 'Janeite' view of Austen, but a point of view which would see literature more generally as defending the 'civilised', 'urbane' values (decorum, order, manners) associated with the dominant social class. For Harding, Austen's importance depends on identifying her with an *alternative* set of values, more 'sensitive', more 'real', and more spiritual. Indeed, if we take the implications of Harding's evaluation of Austen a bit further, we might suggest that, for him, good literature must by definition be opposed to any form of social or moral complacency. Good writers, it would seem, constitute a rival order, a spiritual alternative to the social dominance of that 'posterity of urbane gentlemen'.

We are beginning to develop here a sense of the principles lying behind Harding's judgement of a literary text, of his general *aesthetic* criteria. For him, it would seem, literary value is closely tied up with questions of moral and spiritual value. He doesn't, for example, defend Jane Austen because she writes beautifully: his defence of her depends on the *moral* rather than the purely *formal* qualities of her texts. He seems also to expect good literature to be subversive, to offer a challenge to dominant assumptions, and a marked parallel emerges between his description of Jane Austen's relationship with the more complacent members of her society and Harding's own position in relation to the comfortable 'Janeite' critics. So criticism, too, is by implication closely involved in this struggle over values.

This stress on literature as a site of moral judgement is characteristic of the period at which Harding was writing, and within that period it is associated particularly with the journal *Scrutiny*, in which Harding's article first appeared. *Scrutiny* was edited by the controversial and prolific critic F. R. Leavis who, in his influential book on the English novel, *The Great Tradition* (1948), confidently identified Jane Austen as 'one of the truly great writers' (Leavis, 1972, p. 13). What that meant for Leavis can be illustrated by a comment on *Emma*:

> . . . when we examine the formal perfection of *Emma*, we find that it can be appreciated only in terms of the moral preoccupations that characterize the novelist's peculiar interest in life. (Leavis, 1972, pp. 17–18)

For Leavisite critics, then, judgements about form and method, about a writer's 'formal perfection', can be made only in terms of their moral seriousness, their 'intense moral preoccupation' (Leavis, 1972, p. 16). I have not got space here to look at Leavis's work in any detail. If you are interested in the development of criticism, he is a figure you might want to follow up for yourselves. But I hope that even this brief quotation gives some sense of a critical context for Harding.

The insistence in the work of these critics that moral questions are at the centre of literary judgement is important and powerful. But their absolute confidence in the correctness of their own judgements can be worrying. More recent critics are much less willing to pronounce in this way on who are and are not 'truly great writers', on what does and does not constitute 'moral seriousness' or, to take a phrase from Harding, 'real existence'. We are now much more alert to the ways in which different cultural groups – women, men, people from different class or ethnic backgrounds – will judge writing according to different criteria; ideas of 'greatness' or of 'realness' have come to seem much less stable than Leavis or Harding might imply. What I want to do now is to examine in a bit more detail some of the effects which follow from Harding's tone of confident judgement.

Throughout the extracts I have quoted, Harding persuades his readers to accept his argument by implicitly assuming that we already do so, by implying that any intelligent or sensitive person must necessarily already think like he does. His voice is quietly authoritative; his views are presented as knowledge rather than interpretation. He knows exactly how Austen's 'best readers' will think, and we of course feel that we want to belong to that group. And because he is one of Austen's 'best readers', Harding can also claim to know about Austen's state of mind, to understand her 'complex intention as a writer'. These 'best readers' are set up in opposition to both that 'posterity of urbane gentlemen' whom, Harding claims, Austen did not want to entertain, and to the 'popular impression' of her. So, if we go along with Harding's persuasive rhetoric, we have accepted two implicit assumptions. The first is that Austen's values were virtually indistinguishable from our own – hence our ability to understand her 'complex intention'. We might not come from Austen's particular social class, but she and we are identified as members of the same cultural or intellectual grouping, a group defined not in visible, material ways, but in terms of its greater sensitivity and its superior understanding of 'real existence'. We are at one in our rejection of the dominant, 'urbane' consensus. The second assumption follows from that: good literature – and by extension good criticism – must be a subversive, and also a select, activity. We are being invited to help rescue Jane Austen from her superficial admirers by joining the small, sophisticated group who can really understand her – and who, if there were enough of them, could 'undermine' received ideas.

Harding's rhetoric is, as I have suggested, very persuasive, but it's important to ask of any piece of criticism what it *excludes*, what issues it can't or won't address. Before moving on then, I want very briefly to point out what seem to me to be some of the gaps and slippages involved in Harding's evaluation of Austen. My sense of what these issues are necessarily comes from my own critical principles, which have themselves been produced by many different factors – including, simply, the fact that I was brought up in a later critical tradition than that represented by Harding. One of those principles is that the critical process should be as rigorous, self-conscious and responsible as possible: responsible particularly to important *differences*, which make meaning possible – differences of meaning within *language* itself, as well as the differences of *history, gender, class,* and so on which produce different meanings. At this stage, I want to raise these ideas without much explanation. They will recur throughout the chapter, so my hope is that they will become clearer as they become more familiar.

Let me demonstrate something of what I mean by looking briefly at examples from Harding's text. At various points, Harding seems to me to confuse or conflate categories which should be kept separate. The first, and most basic, slippage is between his own position as *critic*, the reading he makes of what the *text* is saying, and the views attributed to the *author* as an individual. Thus Harding's own irritation with a particular view of Austen produces a certain reading of the novels as expressing 'fear and hatred', and those feelings are in turn attributed to Austen herself. It is as if proving Austen's status as a serious writer involves making her into as close a version as possible of Harding's own position.

One clear example of the slippage from text to author can be found in the first paragraph of passage C, where 'Austen' or 'she' starts out as a way of referring to Austen's writing and slips imperceptibly into commentary on Austen's state of mind. (You can trace the details of that shift for yourselves.) Mightn't we want to make distinctions between an author's private feelings – which must, anyway, always remain unknowable – and the texts they write? Texts are produced by a multiplicity of determining factors – including, of course, private feelings and experiences. But texts make any private input public; it is mediated and made available for interpretation through language.

Behind Harding's critic–text–author conflation lies another slippage: from past to present, ignoring *historical context*. The 'posterity of urbane gentlemen', for example, conveniently spans the hundred and fifty years between the early nineteenth and the mid-twentieth centuries. The implication seems to be that there has been an unbroken tradition of complacent urbanity between the two. That is, of course, part of Harding's point, central to the sense we get from the extract that he feels as alienated as a critic as Austen did as a novelist, and central to his view of good literature and sensitive critics as inhabiting a moral and spiritual space which transcends social and historical conditions. But I, at least, have problems with a sweep across history which suggests that nothing has really altered (and therefore, logically, never can), that social and moral categories are interchangeable across nearly two centuries.

One thing that clearly has changed, for example, is our critical sense of the relevance of *gender* in reading a text. Harding depicts Austen's 'desperate' isolation within her society of 'urbane gentlemen', but he nowhere suggests that it might at least in part be to do with her position as a *woman* in that society. For Harding, writing in 1940, 'gentlemen' has significant class resonances but gender remains as yet an invisible issue.

I am going to leave Harding there. I have devoted quite a lot of space to this first extract, simply because certain general points have to be made at the beginning. From now on, we can move more quickly through my examples. As far as Harding goes, it is for you to decide how useful or valid you find his work – or that of any other critic. My concern is that any judgement you make should be based on analysing the critic's values and criteria as thoroughly – and as sceptically – as possible.

Lionel Trilling's essay on *Mansfield Park* is one of the most frequently reprinted pieces of criticism on Austen. My examples of Trilling's criticism are taken both from that essay and from his introduction to *Emma*, published in 1957 and reprinted in Lodge's Casebook. Trilling's readings of both novels are based on the same general arguments about Austen's cultural importance, so can be applied to whatever novel you are studying. At the beginning of his introduction to *Emma*, Trilling signals his own concern with evaluating Austen by using Harding as a reference point. We are made immediately aware of critics in dialogue with each other, so we are prepared to pay particular attention to the similarities and differences between their positions:

> The impatience with the common admiring view of Jane Austen is not hard to understand and sympathize with, the less so because (as Mr Harding and Professor Mudrick say) admiration seems to stimulate self-congratulation in those who give it, and to carry a reproof of the deficient sensitivity, reasonableness, and even courtesy, of those who withhold their praise. (Lodge, 1991, p. 120)

Trilling picks up on Harding's characterisation of the 'Janeite' critics as complacent. His other reference is to Marvin Mudrick's book *Jane Austen: Irony as Defense and Discovery*, first published in 1952, which, like Harding, reacted against 'nostalgic latter-day enshrinements of [Austen] as the gentle-hearted chronicler of Regency order' (Mudrick, 1974, p. vii). (Chapters from Mudrick's book are widely available in essay collections, should you want to compare his version of Austen with Harding's). Harding and Mudrick simply dismiss the Janeite tendency to make unqualified admiration for Austen a test of moral maturity and good manners; Trilling, by contrast, is concerned to understand *why* readers react to Austen in this way – beyond attributing it merely to their 'impulse to self-flattery': 'Perhaps a reason is also to be found in the work itself, in some unusual promise that it seems to make, in some hope that it holds out' (Lodge, 1991, pp. 120–1).

This more conciliatory and exploratory approach might in part be to do with *where* this essay first appeared: the introduction to an edition of a popular Austen novel has to address a much wider range of readers than does an article in a specialist journal like *Scrutiny* (and the implied audience of a piece of criticism is always something worth considering). But it is also, as we shall see, a significant characteristic of Trilling's critical approach more generally. Trilling identified himself as spokesperson for, as he called it in the title of one of his most famous books, *The Liberal Imagination*, for an attitude of intellectual tolerance and understanding, and one particularly concerned with issues of freedom and its limits. More specifically, Trilling's essay on *Mansfield Park* is taken from his book, *The Opposing Self* (1954), which was written in the early Cold War period. In America at that time, liberal and left-wing intellectuals, including Trilling, were engaged in a very urgent political struggle against the McCarthyite persecution of anyone in public life suspected of 'communist' sympathies. In that context, Trilling's liberalism represents a committed alternative to public censorship and intolerance.

In the following passages, Trilling develops a quite complicated answer to his questions about why Austen's novels invite such devotion in some readers. Like Harding, he sees Austen primarily as a *moralist*. So, as you read, think particularly about whether and how, within that shared approach, Trilling's version of Austen differs from Harding's. The first two passages are from the essay on *Mansfield Park*; the second two are from the introduction to *Emma*.

A. Jane Austen's irony is . . . primarily . . . a method of comprehension. It perceives the world through an awareness of its contradictions, paradoxes, and anomalies. It is by no means detached. It is partisan with generosity of spirit – it is on the side of 'life', of 'affirmation'. But it is preoccupied not only with the charm of the expansive virtues but also with the cost at which they are to be gained and exercised. This cost is regarded as being at once ridiculously high and perfectly fair. What we may call Jane Austen's first or basic irony is the recognition of the fact that spirit is not free, that it is conditioned, that it is limited by circumstances. This, as everyone knows from childhood on, is indeed an anomaly. Her next and consequent irony has reference to the fact that only by reason of this anomaly does spirit have virtue and meaning. (Southam, 1976a, pp. 216–17; Watt, 1963, p. 124)

B. It was Jane Austen who first represented the specifically modern personality and the culture in which it had its being. Never before had the moral life been shown as she shows it to be, never before had it been conceived to be so complex and difficult and exhausting. (Southam, 1976a, p. 233; Watt, 1963, p. 138)

C. Jane Austen, conservative and even conventional as she was, perceived the nature of the deep psychological change which accompanied the establishment of democratic society – she was aware of the increase of the psychological burden of the individual, she understood the new necessity of conscious self-definition and self-criticism, the need to make private judgments of reality. And there is no reality about which the modern person is more uncertain and more anxious than the reality of himself. (Lodge, 1991, p. 129)

D. The impulse to believe that the world of Jane Austen really did exist leads to notable error. 'Jane Austen's England' . . . is an idyll. The error of identifying it with the actual England ought always to be remarked. Yet the same sense of actuality that corrects the error should not fail to recognize the remarkable force of the ideal that leads many to make the error. To represent the possibility of controlling the personal life, of being acquainted with ourselves, of creating a community of 'intelligent love' – this is indeed to make an extraordinary promise and to hold out a rare hope. (Lodge, 1991, pp. 135–6)

I have quoted quite extensively here because, as I have already suggested, Trilling's argument about Jane Austen's value and her peculiar appeal is quite complicated and it is difficult to represent it in any smaller space. I also want you to feel able to test and supplement my general suggestions with your own more detailed analysis, and to have enough evidence on which to base your assessment.

Bearing in mind my earlier emphasis on the importance of making careful comparisons between critics' methods and views, I am going to focus my discussion of Trilling's evaluation of Austen by way of a comparison with Harding. Like Harding, Trilling sees Austen's appreciation of complication and difficulty as positive qualities, but there is a striking difference between Harding's view of Austen as beleaguered and alienated in her society, and Trilling's presentation of her as a confident and generous sage, characterised by 'awareness' and 'generosity of spirit', and 'on the side of "life"' (passage A). Clearly, like Harding, Trilling rejects absolutely the idea that Austen herself is limited by the comparative narrowness of the society she depicts. Indeed, he seems even more confident than Harding of the general relevance and importance of her moral vision. For Harding, Austen's value was based on her ability to see through the superficialities of her particular society. Trilling's focus is different: he refers to the object of Austen's attention not as a particular social order, but as 'the world', suggesting that her perception, her 'method of comprehension', is much more wide-ranging and all-inclusive. The spiritual constraint which Harding saw as Austen's (and the sensitive critic's) personal response to particular conditions, Trilling sees as everyone's situation ('as everyone knows from childhood on'). For Trilling, then, Austen's achievement lies in her particularly sensitive insight into our shared human condition and her ability to describe it particularly eloquently. Like Harding, he produces Austen in his own terms, as a moralist and *humanist* − as, indeed, the ideal liberal intellectual.

How, then, does Trilling persuade his readers of his version of Austen, and with effects? Though his tone is less authoritative than Harding's, Trilling too persuades us of his point of view by addressing us as if we already agree. But, not surprisingly perhaps, he projects a more generous and inclusive view of the readership able to understand Austen properly: there is no explicit equivalent, for example, to that 'posterity of urbane gentlemen' for whom, according to Harding, Austen was *not* writing. Trilling comes closest to condemnation in passage D, when he describes the nostalgic tendency of some readers to believe that Austen's world really did exist as a 'notable error'. But his rhetorical effort is to understand rather than dismiss that reaction; he presents it as a mistaken but very possible response to the ideal community of moral tolerance and self-control which, according to Trilling, Austen's novels represent. The difference between readers is presented more as one of degree than of kind: between those who want to believe that this community was achieved in some better past; and those whose 'sense of actuality' is sufficiently developed to recognise it as a kind of utopia, as an ideal projection rather than a description of actual social conditions. But all readers are assumed to respond to the 'remarkable force of the ideal'. If, as is quite likely, we had not thought of the novels in these terms at all, the effort to do so becomes, implicitly, part of that 'complex and difficult' moral life which Trilling's version of Austen invites us to engage in. The possibility of disagreeing (as Harding would, for example) with what is in fact a quite idiosyncratic reading of Austen's novels is not considered.

Trilling's texts are committed and challenging and offer a powerful version of Austen which demands our serious attention. But the rhetoric of tolerance and generosity should make us particularly alert to any exclusions, slippages and conflations operating in Trilling's text. Inclusiveness operates as consensus; its powerful strategy is to turn disagreement into a version of itself, rather than addressing a different point of view in its own terms. As in Harding, historical (and certainly gender) differences are minimised or ignored; and once again, the effort to validate Austen seems to involve making her into a contemporary figure. Trilling does, though, appear to be much more explicitly concerned than Harding with historical change: his view of Austen's significance and greatness is largely dependent on the suggestion that she was the first writer to respond to 'the establishment of democratic society' and to represent 'the specifically modern personality' (passages C and B). But, like Harding's 'posterity of urbane gentlemen', this phenomenon appears to have remained essentially unchanged since Austen's day. Trilling's concern is with the 'modern personality' which emerged from a period of change, rather than with the historical process of change itself.

In passage C, for example, Trilling suggests that Austen might have been 'conservative and even conventional', but the specific historical and social implications of this observation are left unexplored. Instead, he depicts Austen as the first analyst of the 'psychological burden' experienced by 'the modern personality', implying that the most significant struggles take place within the individual. Thus Trilling makes Austen into a novelist of the *private* rather than the *public* life and stresses the *continuity* rather than any significant differences between her immediate situation and that of himself and his readers. So, though he emphasises different qualities – the 'expansive' rather than the 'critical' virtues – Trilling, like Harding, bases his aesthetic criteria in a writer's ability to *transcend* his or her immediate context and speak to like-minded readers across history.

Trilling's analysis raises exciting and challenging issues. The question of 'modernity', of how it is defined and when it might be said to have begun, is still an important focus of critical debate. More recently, however, critics have been less willing than Trilling to assume that 'the modern condition' affects or affected all social and national groups equally, and have raised questions about the universal relevance of that liberal struggle with individual identity to which Trilling gives such primary significance.

With these questions in mind, I want now to turn to my third and final example in this section, Arnold Kettle's essay on *Emma*. Kettle confronts the question of limitation in Austen more explicitly and more openly than either Trilling or Harding. Like them, he is a defender of Austen and he shares many of their critical assumptions, but he is nevertheless prepared to contemplate the possibility that there could be some justification for accusations of narrowness. As you read the extracts, pay particular attention to the details of vocabulary and argument which differentiate Kettle's version of Austen from those you have encountered so far:

A. How does Jane Austen succeed in thus combining intensity with precision, emotional involvement with objective judgement? Part of the answer lies, I think, in her almost complete lack of idealism, the delicate and unpretentious materialism of her outlook. (Lodge, 1991, pp. 85–6; Watt, 1963, p. 114)

B. She examines with a scrupulous yet passionate and critical precision the actual problems of her world. That this world is narrow cannot be denied. How far its narrowness matters is an important question.

Its *smallness* does not matter at all. There is no means of measuring importance by size. What is valuable in a work of art is the depth and truth of the experience it communicates, and such qualities cannot be identified with the breadth of the panorama.

The limitation and the narrowness of the Highbury world [in *Emma*] is the limitation of class society. And the one important criticism of Jane Austen (we will suspend judgment for the moment on its truth) is that her vision is limited by her unquestioning acceptance of class society. That she did not write about the French Revolution or the Industrial Revolution is as irrelevant as that she did not write about the Holy Roman Empire; they were not her subjects. But Highbury is her subject and no sensitive contemporary reader can fail to sense here an inadequacy (again, we will suspend judgment on its validity). It is necessary to insist, at this point, that the question at issue is not Jane Austen's failure to suggest a *solution* to the problem of class divisions but her apparent failure to notice the *existence* of the problem. (Lodge, 1991, pp. 89–90; Watt, 1963, pp. 118–19)

C. The truth is that in so far as *Emma* does reveal her as a conventional member of her class, blindly accepting its position and ideology, the value of *Emma* is limited, not just relatively, but objectively and always. But the truth is also that this is not the principal or most important revelation of *Emma*. (Lodge, 1991, p. 93; Watt, 1963, p. 121)

D. So that when we think back on *Emma* we do not think principally of the narrow inadequacies of Highbury society but of the delight we have known in growing more intimately and wisely sensitive to the way men and women in a particular, given situation, work out their problems of living. (Lodge, 1991, p. 95; Watt, 1963, p. 123)

What, then, are the grounds on which Kettle defends Austen? Kettle's political allegiance is more immediately obvious than that of either Harding or Trilling. His assumption that class is a central issue identifies him as a socialist or Marxist critic, concerned with the ways in which *material* conditions affect and produce literary works, and with the ways in which literary works perpetuate or disrupt the dominant structures of power in society. This produces a rather different view of Austen from that offered by either Harding or Trilling. Harding saw Austen as fundamentally dissatisfied with her society, even though she had to be strategically complicit with it in order to survive; Kettle writes of her 'objective judgement' and her 'critical precision', but also of her 'unquestioning acceptance of class society'. Trilling suggested that Austen's novels project a social ideal which never existed; Kettle sees in her an 'almost complete lack of idealism' and praises her 'unpretentious materialism'. Both Trilling and Harding present Austen as primarily interested in the private life of the 'spirit'; Kettle stresses her concern with the 'actual problems of her world'. For Kettle, then, Austen is primarily a *social realist*: her value rests on the *precision* (a word which recurs in the extract) with which she depicts and judges her society.

To what extent do these differences of emphasis represent fundamentally opposed assessments – both of Austen, and of what constitutes 'great literature'? We can approach that question best by comparing the different ways in which these three critics deal with the question of 'narrowness' and value. As we have seen, both Harding and Trilling dismiss any suggestion that Austen herself might be narrow. Harding does imply that her society might be so, but for him Austen's greatness is assured precisely because she saw through and rejected society's 'crudeness and complacencies'. Trilling, too, registers a kind of narrowness but, in passage D, he argues that Austen's society is unreal rather than narrow, that it should be read as a moral symbol of the possibility of harmonious community, rather than taken as an accurate representation.

Because of his political concern with the social, material conditions which surround a work of literature, Kettle addresses the question in a much more direct and sustained way. He makes careful distinctions between categories which the other two critics tend to gloss over, and introduces different criteria by which to judge. The most obvious of these is the way in which he redefines Austen's 'narrowness' by making a distinction between 'narrowness' and what he calls 'smallness' of subject-matter. When other critics describe Austen as 'narrow' they are usually referring to her limited range of subject-matter: the '3 or 4 Families' with which her novels are concerned, as compared with 'important' contemporary events like the French or Industrial Revolutions. This is what Kettle means by 'smallness' and he dismisses the idea that a writer's importance has anything to do with the breadth of their subject-matter. I shall be coming back to the important issue of Austen and wider historical events at the beginning of my next section. For the moment, I want to look more closely at Kettle's definition of 'narrowness'. Kettle argues that writers must be judged on the *accuracy* with which they deal with their chosen subject-matter; that they should be evaluated not on *what* they deal with but on *how truthfully* they do so. And it is according to this criterion that Austen's depiction of her society is judged to be narrow. She is seen as failing to tell the truth about the injustices inherent in class society; she accepts 'the assumption that it is right and proper for a minority of the community to live at the expense of the majority', as Kettle puts it elsewhere in the essay (Lodge, 1991, pp. 90–1; Watt, 1963, p. 119).

It is interesting to compare Kettle's explicit stress on injustice with Harding's treatment of the limitations of Austen's 'civilised social order'. As we have seen, Harding's text does have a class dimension: his dislike of the 'posterity of urbane gentlemen' suggests opposition to the fact that forms of cultural power are often class-based. But the terms which Harding uses to express his critique locate the problem in *individual moral inadequacies* ('crudeness and complacencies'), rather than in *structural social inequality* as Kettle sees it. Their solutions to the problem and their views of what role literature might play in that process are therefore, by implication, very different. Harding would want to change individuals and raise moral awareness; Kettle would want to alter the structure of society itself. Harding presents literature as an *alternative* to society; Kettle wants works of literature to be more openly and directly *engaged* in the struggle for social change: he sees the value of *Emma* as limited 'objectively and always' because it fails to point out social inequalities.

And though Trilling writes very persuasively of Austen's acute awareness of the difficult shift to a more democratic social structure, the fact that he can read her depiction of Highbury society as an image of ideal community must mean that, from Kettle's point of view, he is accepting, *colluding with*, that society's inequalities. In Marxist terms, both Austen and Trilling suffer from *false consciousness*: that is, they are unaware of the true nature of class society, 'blindly accepting its position and ideology', as Kettle puts it.

Overtly political critics are often accused of being biased and dogmatic, of imposing their own particular ideas of truth and accuracy on literary texts. But we should beware of assuming that critics whose political positions are less immediately obvious or less openly acknowledged are any less coercive. As we have seen, Trilling and Harding are as confident about their moral judgements, about who are the 'best readers', about what 'everyone knows', as Kettle is about the injustices of class society and 'the one important criticism of Jane Austen'. But because their views are less disruptive it is easy to present them as common sense rather than opinion, as the way in which any sensible, sensitive reader will inevitably see things. If anything, Harding and Trilling are much more inclined than Kettle to turn Austen into a version of themselves. In the fourth paragraph of the extract, Kettle adopts the dominant critical terminology when he suggests that 'no sensitive contemporary reader' can fail to sense an inadequacy in Austen's Highbury. But the addition of 'contemporary' to 'sensitive' is significant. Unlike Harding and Trilling, whose critical discourse tends, as we have seen, to minimise historical differences between Austen and modern readers, Kettle implies that a modern perspective does make a difference: that it ought to make the 'sensitive reader' more alert to social limitations, and thus able to make distinctions between, for example, mere 'smallness' and more serious 'narrowness'.

What, then, are the criteria which underpin Kettle's ultimate evaluation of Austen, and how are they affected by this awareness of historical difference? To answer this question, we need to look closely at the two final paragraphs of the extract. By this stage, Kettle's confident assertion of what 'the truth is' comes supported by a process of careful distinctions and logical argument. The reader has been taken step by step through various critical possibilities (which are, of course, much more extensive and thoroughly argued than this extract can show). Unlike the other two critics we have looked at so far, Kettle reaches the conclusion that at one level – that of political awareness – Austen's value *is* limited. He also makes it clear that this is an 'objective' and permanent limitation, not a 'relative' judgement. In other words, though the historical and social context in which Austen wrote might *explain* her blindness to class injustice, it does not *excuse* it. Elsewhere in the essay, Kettle attacks critics who would want to 'make a certain allowance', given Austen's historical context:

This represents a view of literature which, behind an apparently historical approach, debases and nullifies the effects of art. It invites us to read *Emma* not as a living, vital novel, relevant to our own lives and problems, but as a dead historical 'document'. (Lodge, 1991, p. 92; Watt, 1963, pp. 120–1)

For Kettle, judging *Emma* as 'a living, vital novel' means being prepared to condemn its blind spots, to judge it by immediate, urgent standards of social and moral responsibility. But what he does not want is that *Emma* should therefore be condemned outright. *Emma* is a 'living, vital novel' precisely because, Kettle claims, its social narrowness is not 'its principal or most important revelation'. For Kettle, that 'most important revelation' is an interesting combination of the by now familiar criterion of moral sensitivity ('more intimately and wisely sensitive') with a concern for social specificity ('a particular, given situation').

On the one hand, then, Kettle wants to hold on to an idea of art as *transhistorical*, as rising above and able to communicate across history – and here his aesthetic criteria are very close to those of Harding and Trilling. On the other hand, he wants to stress *historical difference*, and draw attention to the ways in which 'a particular, given situation' will produce particular problems, a situation which it is the work of art's responsibility to depict with as much critical 'depth and truth' as possible. Elsewhere in the essay, for example, Kettle lists some of the 'positive forces' at work in Austen, including 'her highly critical concern over the fate of women in her society, a concern which involves a reconsideration of its basic values' (Lodge, 1991, pp. 94–5; Watt, 1963, p. 122). So Kettle's essay negotiates between rather different – some might even say incompatible – aesthetic criteria. It combines a *liberal humanist* vocabulary, which works on the premise that human nature and moral issues are universal, that they remain constant for all times and places, with a *socialist materialist* position, which would argue that 'human nature' is historically constructed, that it is different for different groups and at different historical moments. This mixture of critical criteria is itself typical of the historical moment at which the essay was written: in his attempt to work out a socialist aesthetic position Kettle draws heavily on, but also of course modifies, the more dominant vocabulary of humanist criticism.

Central to Kettle's position is the belief that the value of a work of literature cannot be judged without addressing the question of how the work relates to its social context. His essay thus provides a useful point of transition into the next section of this chapter, where I shall be taking that issue as my main focus for discussion.

Kettle's book on the novel, from which his essay on *Emma* is taken, was published in 1951. His concern with literature in its social context pointed forward to the important developments, certainly in Austen criticism, which were to take place during the next twenty or so years. In 1957, Ian Watt published his book on eighteenth-century fiction, *The Rise of the Novel*. Though it has now been superseded in many ways, this remains one of the most important books to be written on the fiction of the period. It argues that the rise of the novel, as a literary form, is directly related to the rise to social prominence of the individualist, capitalist middle class during the eighteenth century. In other words, it insists that there is a direct relation between *genre*, the kind and form of a work of literature, and *social formations*. And it ends with some brief remarks on Jane Austen. Watt suggests, for example, that Austen's novels face 'the social and moral problems raised by economic individualisms and the middle-class quest for improved status'; he also describes them as representative of 'the process whereby . . . women were playing an increasingly important part in the literary scene' (Watt, 1972, p. 339).

The most important and interesting criticism on Jane Austen since Watt's book was written has taken up, developed and/or challenged one, or both, of these ideas. I shall be focusing on the question of gender in my third section. But I want to look first at the work of three critics whose concern is to explore ways in which Austen's novels engage with the social and political issues of her time.

'A neighbourhood of voluntary spies': Austen and questions of historical context

For this section, I have taken the quotation in my subtitle from Austen's earliest completed novel, *Northanger Abbey*. As those of you who have read the novel will know, the heroine Catherine Morland, under the influence of novel-reading, becomes convinced that her host, General Tilney, has murdered his wife. She is put right by the hero, Henry, who is the General's son:

'Could [such atrocities] be perpetrated without being known in a country like this, where social and literary intercourse is on such a footing; where every man is surrounded by a neighbourhood of voluntary spies; and where roads and newspapers lay everything open? Dearest Miss Morland, what ideas have you been admitting?' (*Northanger Abbey*, ch. 24)

In his article 'Regulated Hatred', D. W. Harding describes this reference to 'voluntary spies' as a 'touch of paranoia' which is 'badly out of tune with 'Henry's astonishing generosity and nobleness of conduct' (Southam, 1976b, p. 71; Watt, 1963, p. 167). Harding uses this as one of his examples of 'the eruption of fear and hatred' into Austen's novels, as evidence of Austen's own bitter, even paranoid, reaction to a claustrophobic society.

Harding's response to a phrase he can't understand, a phrase apparently so out of keeping with his idea of Henry's character, is to explain it as a symptom of Jane Austen's *psychology*. The mind of the author is, for him, the source – consciously or unconsciously – for everything in the novel. For a later generation of critics, however, the main strategy on finding anything that is difficult to explain or understand has been to look for an answer in Austen's *historical context*, to assume that the reason a reference might be obscure to a modern reader is that we are no longer in direct touch with Austen's social and political world. So after research into the historical background, more recent critics have read the 'neighbourhood of voluntary spies' as an all-too-accurate description of the political atmosphere which characterised the 1790s, the decade when *Northanger Abbey* was largely written. This was the decade following the French Revolution of 1789, when the British government, anxious about the possibility of a similar event in Britain and actually at war with France by the end of the decade, passed fierce censorship laws and set up a kind of secret service whose task was to detect and report revolutionary sympathisers.

One thing which the case of the 'voluntary spies' makes immediately apparent is that, though contemporary events might not appear in Austen's novels in a direct way, they are certainly not irrelevant to her fiction. At the end of the previous section, we saw that even a critic like Arnold Kettle, who is very much aware of the relevance of contemporary issues of social class in Austen's novels, can confidently assert that Austen 'did not write about the French Revolution or the Industrial Revolution'. As far as most of the critics I shall be discussing in this and the following section are concerned, that is a nonsense. They are working with a different model of how social 'context' manifests itself in literary texts – a model which assumes that the fact that these events *appear* to be absent from a novel does not mean that they are really so: significant contemporary events and debates are inevitably present, either through shorthand references like the 'voluntary spies', which a contemporary audience would immediately recognise, or – more indirectly – through details of language, literary form, or characterisation, all of which, historicist critics argue, are inevitably moulded by their immediate cultural and political context. These critics also tend to assume, therefore, that literary texts cannot be neutral or impartial on political and social issues. They are much less likely to argue, as even Kettle does, that Austen's focus on 'problems of living' allows her texts to transcend their 'narrowness' on questions of social inequality.

The particular example of the 'voluntary spies' has, I hope, provided a useful illustration of the way in which attention to historical context can alter our sense of what a text is about. It's important, however, not to allow a critic's historical expertise to intimidate you. We might feel that Harding's indifference to, or perhaps even ignorance of, the revolutionary context impoverishes his interpretation of the way the phrase 'voluntary spies' works in the novel – but it does not wholly invalidate that interpretation. Simply to 'spot' and point out contextual references is not in itself sufficient: historical awareness can – even should – be a major factor in interpreting texts, but it is not a substitute for the process of interpretation. So that basic habit of *testing* a critic's view of a text against your own remains just as important when you read historically-based criticism.

What's more, contextual material is used very differently within different critical approaches, as we shall see. Again, then, it's important to be aware of this, and to make your own mind up about what *version* of history – and therefore of Jane Austen – you find most interesting. In this section, in order to explore some of those differences, I shall be looking at the work of three critics from the 1970s whose main concern is to *contextualise* Austen's novels. My chosen passages are from: Alistair M. Duckworth's *The Improvement of the Estate: A Study of Jane Austen's Novels* (1971); Raymond Williams's *The Country and the City* (1973); and Marilyn Butler's *Jane Austen and the War of Ideas* (1975).[4] In looking at each, I shall have three broad questions in mind: about just what is meant in each case by 'history' or 'context'; about how the relationship between text and context is assumed to work; and about what this suggests about the critic's own political stance. And these are questions which can be applied, of course, to any criticism you read.

As its title suggests, Duckworth's study, *The Improvement of the Estate*, has a very specific historical focus. It reads Austen's fiction in terms of the contemporary practice of property 'improvement', of the development, design and creation of the country estates which are the main settings of many of Austen's novels. Those of you who know *Mansfield Park* will already be familiar with landscape design as an important focus of moral and political debate, and Duckworth uses that novel extensively in his first chapter. But the argument which Duckworth develops out of this quite specific focus is relevant to Austen as a whole, and the book discusses all the major novels. Duckworth uses the actuality of estate improvement, as well as its possible metaphorical and ideological meanings, to establish his central point: that Austen was 'an author whose deepest impulse was not to *subvert* but to maintain and properly *improve* a social heritage' (p. 80; my emphasis). Thus the 'estate' becomes a metaphor for tradition, for inherited values.

My chosen extracts are from Duckworth's 'Introduction':

A. The extreme opinion of the 'subversive' critics – that Jane Austen undermines the social values she seems to affirm, that she can discover personal equilibrium in a society she detests only through the secret ironies of her art – are implicitly opposed throughout this study. Here the emphasis which this criticism places on Jane Austen's moral individualism, on 'the detachment and autonomy of the individual as a centre of self-responsible moral judgment', in D. W. Harding's words, may be briefly questioned. There are occasions, indubitably, where such individualism is admirable . . . and a recurring requirement of Jane Austen's moral vision is that the formal and static façade of authority be enlivened and regenerated by individual energy. But this is a long way from saying that individual action of a subversive or anti-social nature is sanctioned, even unconsciously, in Jane Austen's novels. . . . Given the irresponsibility of others, we might say, it is the more incumbent upon the Austen heroine to support and maintain an inherited structure of values and behaviour.
. . . Against the regulated hatred, the detached irony, and the subversive morality that much recent criticism has stressed, it is necessary to take more seriously a Jane Austen 'thoroughly religious and devout', who has the additional 'merit . . . of being evidently a Christian writer'.[5] (Duckworth, 1971, pp. 7–8)

B. Nor, in asking that Jane Austen be read as an author who affirms society, do I wish to ignore her keen awareness of the dangers of automatic formality and a complacent pride in status. Conscious of the possible weakening of external structures and of the possibility of an economic transvaluation of morality, however, she insists on individual commitment to, rather than mere acceptance of society. Her novels may be seen as the continuing record of a responsible woman concerned with right conduct in 'such days as these'.[6] (Duckworth, 1971, p. 32)

C. The ungrounded imagination is as dangerous for an author as it is for a character within the novel, and imaginative limitation is welcome, for it is proof that there is a centre to reality other than the individual mind. In her close attention to physical fact Jane Austen declares her belief, not in man as the creator of order but in man's freedom to create within a prior order. Thus her individualism as author, like the individualism of her heroines, respects finally the given structure of her world. Her careful attention to topographical details . . . takes on in this regard something of an ontological significance. (Duckworth, 1971, p. 34)

Like Harding attacking the 'Janeites', Duckworth immediately locates himself within a critical debate. But this time it is Harding's 'subversive' approach which is seen as in need of correction. Harding's approach is dismissed as 'extreme', in the first sentence of passage A; and we are told that it is 'necessary' that we should take a rather different view of Austen, 'more seriously'. Like the other critics we have seen so far, then, Duckworth writes in an authoritative idiom, as if he has privileged access to the 'right' Austen, to her 'deepest impulse', as he puts it in the comment I quoted just before the extracts themselves. So what version of Austen is Duckworth offering as a corrective to the 'subversive' view, and what is the implicit basis of his confident authority?

Unlike Harding, Duckworth presents Austen as essentially conservative – a view which recalls Trilling's sense of her as 'conservative and even conventional' (see above, p. 118). Working within the familiar individual/society opposition, he defines Austen as 'an author who affirms society': he stresses her commitment to 'an *inherited* structure of values and behaviour'; and reads her novels as expressions of a belief in 'man's freedom to create *within a prior order*' (my emphasis). For Duckworth, then, Austen can be described as an individualist only in so far as that 'individual energy' is committed to the 'regeneration' of the existing social structure: she wants reform from within, rather than any radical change to things as they are. And this commitment to 'enliven and regenerate' traditional structures is presented very much as a *moral* obligation. Duckworth refers explicitly to Austen's 'moral vision' (A); he describes her novels as the record of 'a responsible woman' (B); and it is 'incumbent' on her heroines to support inherited values (A).

In this sense, in spite of his vehement opposition to Harding's view of Austen as 'subversive', Duckworth's approach still has much in common with Harding's (and Trilling's) treatment of the novels as essentially moral debates. What distinguishes Duckworth from these two earlier critics – and brings him closer to Kettle's concern with material conditions – is his insistence that Austen's moral position must be understood in terms of the preoccupations and practices of her time. For example, in passage A Duckworth supports his argument by quoting contemporary opinions about Austen's religious commitment, as if the views of people at the time necessarily carry more authority than those of modern commentators; in B, he alludes confidently to her immediate content, ' "such days as these" ', characterising it as a period of social change in which 'external structures', social hierarchies, codes of behaviour, are under threat. And elsewhere in the book, as I have suggested, he draws on specialised knowledge of an actual social practice, 'the improvement of the estate', and connects that metaphorically with those threatened structures: 'the "estate" . . . is symbolic of a whole social and moral inheritance' (p. 31).

Duckworth bases his authority as a critic, then, on historical knowledge. As we saw in the previous section, Harding and Trilling persuaded us to accept their interpretation by implicitly including us in an imagined, but often not very clearly defined, community of morally sensitive readers. In contrast, Duckworth's claim that he can offer a 'better', more accurate, understanding of Austen is based on demonstrating knowledge of her contemporary context. He suggests, in other words, that right reading depends on historical awareness and accuracy – indeed, that such awareness is itself a moral issue, a kind of critical duty. In passage C, Duckworth insists on Austen's realism, her 'close attention to physical fact', as an expression of her belief in a 'prior order'. Ostensibly, Duckworth is describing Austen's 'belief', but – again as we saw in Harding and Trilling – there seems to be a slippage between Duckworth's version of Austen and his own views. The first sentence has the ring of generalisation. It expresses a deep scepticism of what Duckworth calls the 'ungrounded imagination': of characters or authors (or critics?) who try to escape the constraints of the immediate context. It's difficult to avoid the sense that, at this point, the description of Austen's 'belief' slips also into a manifesto for Duckworth's own critical position. Harding's reading of Austen's subversive individualism would thus be 'dangerous' and 'ungrounded', compared with Duckworth's responsible historical, 'respect' for 'the given structure of her world'.

But what exactly does that 'world' consist of for Duckworth? And how does that differ from the 'world' evoked by other historical critics?

In order to examine that question more closely, I want at this point to bring in my second 'contextual' critic, Raymond Williams, as a point of comparison. Williams's book *The Country and the City* (1973), from which the extracts are taken, is an exciting and wide-ranging study of cultural change. It examines literary representations of rural and metropolitan communities from the sixteenth right through to the twentieth century. Necessarily, then, Williams deals only briefly with Jane Austen, but – like so much of Williams's work – his reading of Austen is powerfully suggestive, and has significantly influenced subsequent criticism. It's particularly useful to compare his account of the major preoccupations in Austen's fiction with Duckworth's, since Williams, too, is concerned with 'improvement':

> A. It is not personal relationships, in the abstracted sense of observed psychological process, that preoccupy Jane Austen. It is, rather, personal *conduct*: a testing and discovery of the standards which govern human behaviour in certain real situations. To the social considerations already implicit in the examination of conduct, with its strong sense and exploration of the adequacy of social norms, we must add, from the evidence of the novels, a direct preoccupation with estates, incomes and social position, which are seen as indispensable elements of all the relationships that are projected and formed. Nor is this a preoccupation within a settled 'traditional' world; indeed much of the interest, and many of the sources of the action, in Jane Austen's novels, lie in the changes of fortune – the facts of general change and of a certain mobility – which were affecting the landed families at this time. (Williams, 1973, p. 113)

> B. . . . it must be clear that it is no single, settled society, it is an active, complicated, sharply speculative process. It is indeed that most difficult world to describe, in English social history: an acquisitive, high bourgeois society at the point of its most evident interlocking with an agrarian capitalism that is itself mediated by inherited titles and by the making of family names. . . . The social confusions and contradictions of this complicated process are then the true source of many of the problems of human conduct and valuation, which the personal actions dramatise. An openly acquisitive society, which is concerned with the transmission of wealth, is trying to judge itself at once by an inherited code and by the morality of improvement.
> . . . Jane Austen reminds us, yet again, of the two meanings of improvement, which were historically linked but in practice so often contradictory. There is the improvement of soil, stock, yields, in a working agriculture. And there is the improvement of houses, parks, artificial landscapes, which absorbed so much of the actually increasing wealth.
> . . . The working improvement, which is not seen at all, is the means to social improvement, which is seen very clearly indeed.

It is not seen flatteringly. The conversion of good income to good conduct was no automatic process. Some of the conscious improvers are seen as they were: greedy and calculating materialists. But what is crucial is that the moral pretension is taken so seriously that it becomes a critique: never of the basis of the formula, but coolly and determinedly of its results, its character and action. (Williams, 1973, pp. 115–16)

Duckworth and Williams share the assumption that Austen's novels can only be understood as the products of her specific time and place: the rural upper-middle class or lower gentry in the early nineteenth century, at a moment of instability and change – perhaps of 'improvement'. And they agree that Jane Austen's subject is 'conduct': that, in this period of social crisis, her fiction sees standards of behaviour as centrally important for the survival of her class group. But for Williams, conduct is not the whole story. 'We must add', he insists, Austen's equal preoccupation with economic questions. 'estates, incomes and social position' (A). He uses a quite specialised socioeconomic vocabulary to define the complex social negotiations taking place within Austen's world: 'an acquisitive, high bourgeois society at the point of its most evident interlocking with an agrarian capitalism', and so on (B). This is very different from Duckworth's critical vocabulary which, as we have seen, is dominantly moral, evoking a 'world' where these changes are experienced and understood primarily through ethical, even religious, categories: 'the irresponsibility of others'; the 'transvaluation of morality'.

Like Kettle's concern with class, Williams's emphasis on precise social definition identifies him as a Marxist critic, for whom, as he says, economic conditions are the '*true* source' of problems of human conduct (my emphasis). For Duckworth, history is a story about abstract categories: 'individual', 'society', 'authority', 'order', 'freedom'. His critical commitment to historical context is evident in his scrupulous concern to 'ground' those categories in the practices and debates of a specific moment, but this material evidence is ultimately given significance within the *history of ideas*. We can see this very clearly at the end of passage C (which concludes Duckworth's introductory argument), in his rather grandiose assertion that Austen's 'careful attention to *topographical* details' takes on '*ontological* significance' (my emphasis). Critical interpretation here involves a move from the concrete to the abstract: 'topographical' refers to landscape; 'ontological' is a specialist term from philosophy meaning 'a concern with being, with the essence of things'.

For Williams, those abstract categories are certainly important, but they are a function of other forces. Williams is writing a *material history*, an account of history as a process of economic change and class struggle, in which abstract categories are firmly identified as an effect of economic and social conditions. To use Marxist terms, they are part of the cultural and ideological *superstructure* produced by the economic *base*. According to this approach, ideas, ideology, will primarily serve the interests of the dominant class, and so will tend to obscure the 'real' power relations governing the historical process. Broadly speaking, it is this assumption which underpins Williams's quite complicated assessment of Austen as a social critic in these passages, and I want now to look at his argument, as it develops in passage B, in more detail.

Williams's account of Austen's critical relationship with her social group is complex and subtle. He is not interested simply in dismissing her as the representative of ruling-class values. Rather, he uses her fiction as a means to *understand* the terms through which that class justified its position to itself; he wants to understand, in other words, the ideological process through which social power relations were maintained. He sees the 'morality of improvement' as central to this self-justification. By the 'morality of improvement', Williams means what Duckworth calls Austen's 'moral vision': the novels' suggestion that 'personal conduct' can regenerate 'an inherited code' of traditional values and so can reform ('improve') her 'openly acquisitive society'. Duckworth is content to describe, and even, implicitly, to approve this project of reform. Williams, however, is also interested in its limitations, its blind spots; he is concerned not simply to explicate, but to *critique* Austen's position as he sees it. In the final paragraph of the extract Williams carefully defines the objects and nature of Austen's own critique. He approves her clear-sighted attack on the 'greedy and calculating materialists', who represent a blatantly self-interested version of 'social improvement'. But in focusing simply on 'results', on how people behave, Williams suggests, Austen doesn't go far enough. She fails to question what he calls 'the formula': she accepts the 'moral pretension' that conduct can be judged *independently* of economic forces. What she doesn't judge, doesn't even see or show, is the dependency of both social and moral 'improvement' on another form of 'improvement': the developments in agricultural practice, involving working-class labour, which are the real source of the wealth which makes 'social improvement' possible. In other words, to use the terms I introduced earlier, Austen's critique remains at the *superstructural* level; it does not move outside its class ideology to address the 'reality' of the economic *base*.

Williams's approach represents, then, a theoretically more sophisticated and a more consistently materialist analysis of what Kettle described, twenty years earlier, as Austen's 'unquestioning acceptance of class society' (see above, p. 121). Williams shares Kettle's overtly political approach to Austen, but, paradoxically perhaps, he seems much less anxious, much less judgemental, than Kettle about Austen's conservatism. As I suggested earlier, he is more interested in tracing broad historical and political processes than in evaluating individual authors. Though he talks constantly about 'Jane Austen', we sense that he uses the term to refer not to Austen as an individual, but to her work as a whole, using the author's name as a convenient label. Her novels are read as *symptoms* of her social context; they are complex documents, giving us access to history, not to individual psychology. And what the novels don't say is thus potentially as interesting as what they do address.

So it's not contradictory for Williams to claim on the one hand that in Austen 'working improvement' is 'not seen at all', and on the other that she actually 'reminds us' of the two meanings of improvement. Her novels 'remind us' of the two types precisely *because* they ignore one of them. Knowledge of what Austen ignores must, of course, be supplied from outside her texts. Because Williams is a Marxist, he is committed to uncovering working-class histories, so that outside knowledge comes partly from his prior sense of what is significant in the rural community which Austen describes; because he is a literary critic, he is committed to using literary texts as sources of evidence, so in *The Country and the City* – as you will see if you go on to read more – he looks at Austen alongside other writers (notably, in this case, the political journalist and activist William Cobbett who spoke for the rural labouring class), whose work offers a very different perspective on the same agricultural landscape at the same historical moment. Rather than treating Austen in isolation as a 'great author' who is assumed to have privileged access to 'truth', Williams – like a good historian – gathers evidence from as many sources as possible.

In Williams's criticism, the historicist approach is very obviously a function of his own political commitment. For Williams, writers illuminate the historical process to which they are subject; Duckworth's contextualisation of Austen, on the other hand, uses history to illuminate the literary text. Duckworth's apparently neutral account of Austen and 'improvement' is no less political, of course: in Williams's terms it endorses that ideological 'moral pretension' which minimises 'real' historical process. But whatever their evaluation of her position, both critics take it for granted that Austen's concern with 'the social history of the landed families' (Williams, p. 113) means that her novels are very directly involved with significant current issues – even if they don't refer directly to the Napoleonic Wars.

Marilyn Butler, my third example of contextual criticism, shares that view, but she presents Austen's involvement with current issues as more *self-conscious* than either Duckworth or Williams suggests. Like Duckworth and Williams, Butler characterises Austen as conservative, but in *Jane Austen and the War of Ideas* (1975), she defines that conservatism in more specific terms than we have so far seen. Butler uses her contextual knowledge to argue that there is a very direct relationship between fictional *form* and contemporary political debates: in choosing to write a particular kind of novel, Butler suggests, Austen very clearly takes sides politically. The title of Butler's book gives a useful indication of her critical approach: it connects Duckworth-type *history of ideas* criticism with the more overtly *political* resonances of 'war', thus drawing our attention to the inescapable political identity of 'ideas'. At the same time, in suggesting that 'ideas', rather than just economics and class, are an area where significant debate and change take place, Butler distinguishes her historical and political approach to literary texts from that of traditional Marxist criticism.

I have chosen extracts from Butler's original 'Introduction',[7] and from her 'Conclusion', in an attempt to represent her book's main argument:

> A. The novel of Jane Austen's day was not just didactic. It was also seen as relevant to contemporary issues, and, since these issues were unusually deep and clearcut, inevitably partisan. Indeed, at the period when Jane Austen began to write, literature as a whole was partisan, in England as well as on the Continent. . . . There may well have been artists who thought relatively little about politics. But some artistic forms implicitly seemed to convey certain general principles or prepossessions about man, and if, in this sensitive period, an artist did not care much for what they were, his critics and readers were liable to care for him. As it happens, Jane Austen's novels belong decisively to one class of partisan novels, the conservative. Intellectually she is orthodox . . . Her important innovations are technical and stylistic modifications within a clearly defined and accepted genre. (Butler, 1975, p. 3)

B. If Jane Austen's historical context is correctly defined in these terms, some of the commonest critical assumptions about her need re-examination. The first, obviously, is that she does not involve herself in the events and issues of her time. The crucial action of her novels is in itself expressive of the conservative side in an active war of ideas. So, too, is the stylized opposition in her fictional world between certain kinds of virtuous characters, and certain kinds of villains. The heroine who is fallible and learns, and the heroine who is Christian and exemplary, are the standard heroine-types of the reactionary novels of the 1790s. In Jane Austen's novels they confront, equally typically, the villains of the anti-jacobin period – plausible, attractive strangers, penetrating a community from abroad, or from dangerously up-to-date London, like wolves entering a sheepfold; and bent, especially, on winning the affections of the heroine. . . . Technically the striking thing about her novels is indeed that they do not mention the French Revolution and barely allude to the Napoleonic Wars. (Butler, 1975, p. 294)

C. At some point it is necessary to come to terms with what cannot be explained away. Jane Austen is conservative in a sense no longer current. Her morality is preconceived and inflexible. She is firm in identifying error, and less interested than other great novelists in that type of perception for which the novel is so peculiarly well adapted – the perception that thoroughly to understand a character is to forgive him. But if this is true, are we right to call her a great novelist at all?

Of greater imaginative importance to us than Jane Austen's answer should be her question. In her day the very form of the novel prompted an inquiry of central importance and urgency: what was the moral nature of the individual, and what his true role in society? The novelist who evaded, or simply did not notice that he was called upon to put the question, was the true artistic cripple. The willingness of Jane Austen's admirers to concede that she escaped the ferment of ideas in the revolutionary period damages her more than the attempt to show that she was, in fact, a partisan. (Butler, 1975, p. 298)

If we look for the positive terms in these passages, one of the most obvious is 'partisan'. This is unexpected: we tend to assume that to be partisan is a bad thing, because it suggests bias, an inability to judge things fairly. But in the final sentence of passage C, Butler begins to reassess the usual view with her suggestion that it's far less damaging to describe Austen as 'partisan' than to suggest that she is uninvolved in 'the ferment of ideas'. This is typical of Butler's method throughout. She is very much aware of contradicting received opinion on Austen, of reversing the usual criteria of judgement. She sticks her neck out and risks what look at first like negative opinions: that Jane Austen is 'partisan'; that she is 'orthodox'; that her morality is 'preconceived and inflexible'; that we might even be wrong to call her a 'great novelist'. In other words, she rejects the traditional critical view that 'great' literature must be impartial, original, and morally generous. This polemical, confrontational voice is different from either Duckworth or Williams, both of whom maintain a more decorous tone of authority, confident of their historical material. Like them, Butler relies on historical knowledge to justify her claims, but her critical style mirrors the energy and urgency which she attributes to Austen, and in doing so enacts her own critical commitment. She is even prepared, at one point, to risk her whole project, in an effective polemical move which dares us to disagree: '*If* Jane Austen's historical context is correctly defined in these terms . . .' (B; my emphasis).

So in what terms does Butler define that historical context, and how are they distinguished from the other two examples of historical criticism we have looked at? It's helpful here to follow up Butler's judgement of Austen as 'partisan'. In passage A, we are told that it is not just Austen, but the novel of her day, that is 'inevitably partisan'. It is 'inevitably' so for two reasons: because contemporary issues were 'unusually deep and clearcut'; and because the novel was more likely than other genres to be read politically in terms of those issues. Butler refers here to the French Revolution of 1789, and to the fierce pro- and anti-revolutionary debates which it triggered in Britain, both during the 1790s when Austen was first writing, and into the period of the Napoleonic Wars. The term 'anti-jacobin' in passage B, for example, means anti-revolutionary, since the French revolutionaries were often referred to as the 'jacobins'. Butler's book is based on a categorisation of novels as either jacobin or anti-jacobin – judged according to how they 'convey certain general principles and prepossessions about man', as she puts it in passage A. Because novels deal with individuals in a social setting, Butler argues, they raise in a very direct way issues of social responsibility. In a revolutionary context, such issues become particularly charged: novels seen to favour individual freedom are identified as supporting revolutionary principles; novels which emphasise tradition and social responsibility are read as anti-revolutionary.

Butler makes particular claims, then, both for the historical moment ('*unusually* deep and clearcut'), and for Austen's chosen form. At certain times, she suggests, certain literary forms will become inescapably politicised, and the novel in Austen's day was just such a form. In Butler's account, Austen's familiar concern with individual social conduct is inextricable from the very specific context of 'the

Revolution controversy'. The class anxieties and changes which were seen by Duckworth and Williams as part of gradual historical processes are here firmly located in an immediate political debate. Passage B provides more detailed examples of how this politicisation of fictional forms might work. Certain plot-lines or character-types – notably the heroine who learns to recognise her shortcomings and control her will – conveyed, Butler argues, an unambiguous political message. Because she chose those plots and those characters, Austen's novels can be confidently categorised as 'conservative'.

Butler's evidence for her reading of Austen comes mainly from contemporary fiction. The first half of *Jane Austen and the War of Ideas* is devoted to analysing novels from the period, and to demonstrating those features which identify them as jacobin or anti-jacobin. Among the jacobin writers are William Godwin, Mary Wollstonecraft, Mary Hays and Elizabeth Inchbald; the anti-jacobins include Jane West and Elizabeth Hamilton. Several of these names will very probably be unfamiliar to you. Though well-known at the time, much of their work was for a long time forgotten or ignored. Over the past few years, however, because of critics like Butler, some of their novels have become available again in modern editions and a few are being taught at university level, though they remain very much a specialist interest. Butler's point is that we can have only a very imperfect sense of any writer if we are largely ignorant of their immediate literary context, of the writing which was popular at the time. For her, one of the primary meanings of 'history' for literary studies is the recovery of texts which allow us to understand precisely how a writer's work was read and understood by a contemporary audience.

This clearly raises a very important wider question about what and why we read. Do we read and study texts for their aesthetic qualities, or for historical reasons? And are those two things necessarily separable? Butler would argue that they cannot and should not be entirely separated; in her view, the common assumption that aesthetic judgements transcend history results in misjudgements – of both texts and contexts. To illustrate the point, we can usefully return to Butler's controversial judgements of Austen as 'partisan', 'orthodox', and 'inflexible', and to the question of whether Austen can still be described as a 'great' novelist. From a contemporary perspective, Butler suggests, Austen would be valued for qualities very different from those praised by modern critics. In the context of a war of ideas, the best, or the most significant, novels, would be self-consciously partisan, so a rather 'inflexible' and judgemental morality becomes under-standable. Similarly, to be strikingly original in such a context would be an irrelevance: innovation within 'a clearly defined and accepted genre' is thus a more impressive achievement. And, at the end of pas-sage B, Butler gives a different twist to the by now familiar issue of Austen's 'narrowness', turning what some critics had seen as a failure into one of Austen's 'striking' achievements. A properly historicised appreciation, she argues, will recognise that Austen's 'technical' skill lies *precisely* in addressing the politics of the French Revolution or the Napoleonic Wars without actually mentioning them.

In passage C, Butler pursues this question of literary value – a question which was largely avoided by Duckworth and Williams. Typi-cally, historical critics (and more recent critics generally) are less con-cerned with issues of explicit evaluation: in focusing on how literary texts fit into their cultural context, they are much more likely to find writers 'interesting' than 'great'. But Butler manifests, perhaps, a more traditional side to her critical approach in still wanting to pose the question of value. Her answer, as we might expect, is rather less tradi-tional. She uses Austen's 'partisan' quality to test our definition of the novel form itself. *If* we follow the dominantly nineteenth-century view that fiction is about moral sympathy, then Austen – according to Butler – falls short. But again, the novel 'in her day' is taken to be the relevant criterion, and Butler neatly concludes by *both* saving Austen for 'great literature', and refuting those critics who want to tie the novel down to a single definition and so separate Austen, and ques-tions of literary value, from questions of history and context.

Butler's judgement of Austen assumes that, though Austen could not avoid her novels being read politically, she was free to *choose* whether or not to engage consciously with the 'urgent and important' contemporary questions. Butler's judgement also relies heavily on her contention that those questions were 'deep and clearcut'. This stress on the writer's choice differentiates Butler from a critic like Williams, for whom writers do not necessarily have such freedom. For the Marxist critic, writers and their texts are products of a historical process, and questions of will and responsibility become much more problematic.

Many Marxist and non-Marxist critics (including, perhaps, both Williams and Duckworth) would want to question Butler's simple binary account of political debate, her division of writers and texts into just two camps; they would want to suggest a much more com-plex model of how culture and politics actually work. But *Jane Austen and the War of Ideas* remains an important and, as intended, a controversial book, stimulating subsequent critics to develop, qualify, or refute Butler's challenging claim that Austen is an unavoidably political writer.

Though they focus on different aspects, all three critics in this section agree that Austen's novels must be read in terms of her social, economic, and political context. They agree, too, in characterising Austen as an essentially conservative representative of the landed or leisured classes – though, again, they choose different ways of 'proving' their case. This insistence on history as the proper context in which to read literary texts is representative of that important critical reaction which took place in the early 1970s, against the 'liberal humanist' critics of my previous section. Criticism of Austen since the 1970s has remained dominantly historicist, with critics building on this earlier work in an attempt to define ever more precisely Austen's position within her class, in relation to contemporary politics and with other writers – and as a woman. What each of the critics in this section most startlingly lacks is any sense that Austen's gender might have affected her moral, social, or political landscape. For the feminist critics in my third and final section, gender is a necessary starting-point for any understanding of Austen's novels.

'An accomplished woman': Austen and questions of gender

In *Pride and Prejudice*, there is a scene in which various characters discuss what it might mean to be 'an accomplished woman'. Mr Bingley, pleasant but unexacting, is impressed by decorative 'feminine' skills like painting tables or making net purses; his worldly sisters expect a fashionable education – singing, drawing, dancing – and elegant manners. Darcy, the hero, demands 'something yet more substantial, in the improvement of her mind by extensive reading' (*Pride and Prejudice*, ch. 8). The discussion provides an appropriate subtitle for my third section. It reminds us that the status and education of women is one of Austen's main subjects, in a world where the definition of 'proper' womanhood was much discussed. As Austen's novels so clearly show, middle- and upper-class women particularly were dependent on their fathers or on marriage for their livelihood; as far as some commentators were concerned, it was not proper for women to write or for their work to appear in print; and though radical women of the period, like Mary Wollstonecraft, defended women as 'rational creatures' with a right to self-expression, it was generally agreed that the private, domestic sphere was the only appropriate place for even the most 'accomplished' women.

For feminist critics, a proper approach to Austen's novels must recognise the effect of these circumstances and the importance of this subject-matter; how the novels define and represent femininity must be a primary focus of any critical interpretation. As we shall see, feminist critics have approached these questions in a variety of ways, and the critical debates which by now are familiar to you – about Austen's attitude to her social group; about the place of history; about Austen's political identity – recur in this new critical context. 'Feminist criticism' includes a great variety of critical approaches. Indeed, perhaps the only thing feminist critics have in common is the basic assumption that sexual difference, and the inequalities that have resulted from it, inevitably affect the way texts are both written and read. In that sense, they all see criticism – as Marxist critics do – as an inherently political activity, concerned to explore, expose and thereby, perhaps, to help change, sexual inequality. Feminist critics draw widely on other critical approaches, and they argue with each other, in a continuing effort to understand how sexual difference affects social structures, how it constructs *subjectivity*, our sense of individual identity, and what role literary texts play in these processes.

For this section, I have chosen passages from books that have become feminist classics, and which – apart from a focus on issues of gender – are clearly distinct in critical method. The first extracts are from Sandra Gilbert and Susan Gubar's famous study *The Madwoman in the Attic* (1979), which explores how nineteenth-century women writers negotiate the male-defined literary imagination. My second example is Mary Poovey's *The Proper Lady and the Woman Writer* (1984), a Marxist–feminist analysis of the way the middle-class ideology of female 'propriety' affects the work of three women writers – Mary Wollstonecraft, Mary Shelley, and Jane Austen. And finally, I shall look at passages from Nancy Armstrong's *Desire and Domestic Fiction* (1987), which argues that the 'feminine' domestic novel of the eighteenth and early nineteenth centuries was a major force in shaping the dominant cultural identity of that period.[8]

The aim of this section is to help you identify some of the significant differences between these examples of feminist criticism, and to suggest connections and comparisons between them and some of the critics we have looked at already.

The full title of Gilbert and Gubar's study is *The Madwoman in the Attic: The Woman Writer and the Nineteenth-Century Literary Imagination*. In the opening chapters of their book, Gilbert and Gubar argue that during the period in which Austen wrote, the 'fundamental definitions of literary authority are . . . both overtly and covertly patriarchal' (Gilbert and Gubar, 1979, pp. 45–6). Literary creation is represented, they suggest, as a God-like fathering of texts, a process which effectively denies any female involvement: women are its objects rather than active creative subjects. If, then, *author*ship suggests masculine *authori*ty and ownership of a text, women find it difficult to think of themselves as authors in a world which denies them those forms of power. They also find it difficult to express themselves openly and directly within existing literary forms which must also, by definition, be 'patriarchal'. As a result women's writing is characterised, Gilbert and Gubar argue, by strategies of indirection and subversion – irony, symbolism, a fraught fascination with monstrosity – through which they find a way of expressing female identity, frustration, and anger. This general argument lies behind their account of Jane Austen:

> A. Austen's propriety is most apparent in the overt lesson she sets out to teach in all of her mature novels. Aware that male superiority is far more than a fiction, she always defers to the economic, social, and political power of men as she dramatizes how and why female survival depends on gaining male approval and protection. . . . Whereas becoming a man means proving or testing oneself or earning a vocation, becoming a woman means relinquishing achievement and accommodating oneself to men and the spaces they provide.
>
> Dramatizing the necessity of female submission for female survival, Austen's story is especially flattering to male readers because it describes the taming not just of any woman but specifically of a rebellious, imaginative girl who is amorously mastered by a sensible man. No less than the blotter held over the manuscript on her writing desk, Austen's cover story of the necessity for silence and submission reinforces women's subordinate position in patriarchal culture. . . .
>
> At the same time, however, we shall see that Austen 'performs everything' under this cover story. . . . Undoubtedly a useful acknowledgement of her own ladylike submission and her acquiescence to masculine values, this plot also allows Austen to consider her own anxiety about female assertion and expression, to dramatise her doubts about the possibility of being both a woman and a writer. She describes both her own dilemma and, by extension, that of all women who experience themselves as divided, caught in the contradiction between their status as human beings

and their vocation as females. (Gilbert and Gubar, 1979, pp. 154–5; Lodge, 1991, pp. 203–4)

B. In all six of Austen's novels women who are refused the means of self-definition are shown to be fatally drawn to the dangerous delights of impersonation and pretence. But Austen's profession depends on just these disguises. What else, if not impersonation, is characterisation? What is plot, if not pretence? In all the novels, the narrator's voice is witty, assertive, spirited, independent, even (as D. W. Harding has shown) arrogant and nasty. . . .

Using her characters to castigate the imaginative invention that informs her own novels, Austen is involved in a contradiction that, as we have seen, she approves as the only solution available to her heroines. Just as they manage to survive only by seeming to submit, she succeeds in maintaining the double consciousness in fiction that proclaims its docility and restraint even as it uncovers the delights of assertion and rebellion. Indeed the comedy of Austen's novels explores the tensions between the freedom of her art and the dependency of her characters: while they stutter and sputter and lapse into silence and even hasten to perfect felicity, she attains a woman's language that is magnificently duplicitous. (Gilbert and Gubar, 1979, pp. 168–9)

In order to explore the assumptions underlying Gilbert and Gubar's argument in more detail, it might be helpful to look first for similarities and differences between their account and some of the versions of Austen we have already seen. Essentially, there seem to be two Jane Austens here: the one who in the first paragraph of passage A 'defers to the economic, social, and political power of men'; and the one who, in the final paragraph of B, 'uncovers the delights of assertion and rebellion'. The first bears some resemblance to Marilyn Butler's description of Austen as an anti-revolutionary novelist. Gilbert and Gubar's stress on Austen's 'deference' reworks Butler's identification of Austen's plots as anti-revolutionary; her characterisation of the ideal anti-jacobin heroine, 'who is fallible and learns' (see above, p. 137), reappears here as 'the taming . . . of a rebellious, imaginative girl'. But, unlike Butler, Gilbert and Gubar are not prepared to accept that Austen wholly approves of this story – and they are certainly not interested in the contemporary political debates which Butler cites to support her reading. As far as they are concerned, the relevant 'war' is not about French Revolutionary ideas, but between women and men.

They describe a guerilla war rather than open battle. For Gilbert and Gubar, Austen conforms to male power – but on the surface only. She teaches an 'overt' lesson of 'propriety', of 'submission' and 'acquiescence to masculine values', which is 'flattering to male readers'. But in fact, as we learn in the third paragraph of A, her novels dramatise 'anxiety' and 'doubts'; she maintains a 'double consciousness', as Gilbert and Gubar put it in passage B. This is much closer to D. W. Harding's 'subversive' Austen, the Austen whose object was the 'desperate one of merely finding some mode of existence for her critical attitudes' (see above, p. 110). It's no coincidence, I think, that Harding is the only other critic named in these passages. For Harding, Austen was working out 'unobtrusive spiritual survival' in a society whose goodwill she needed; she spoke for an elite, sensitive group alienated from 'a posterity of urbane gentlemen'. But in Harding gender remained insignificant: 'gentlemen' was a description of class only. Gilbert and Gubar translate this characterisation of a divided Austen into the language of sexual politics: for them, Austen describes the situation of 'all women' who experience 'the contradiction' of being human, but also fe male

So in Gilbert and Gubar's reading, attention to the problem of gender brings together two versions of Austen which we identified earlier as being on opposite sides of the critical debate. The critics in the previous section who used historical evidence to stress Austen's conformism (in their cases, conformism within her class position) were explicitly rejecting Harding's 'subversive' Austen. But a focus on Austen as a woman writer disturbs and complicates existing critical categories and judgements because it introduces a different, and previously invisible, point of view. (The same would be true of a similar focus on any other position – ethnic identity or sexual orientation, for example – which is outside the social norm.) Feminist critics have argued that to be a woman, particularly in the past when opportunities for women were much more limited, is to live a contradiction; that women occupy a *liminal* position on the boundaries of cultural categories, a position which escapes definition. As Gilbert and Gubar put it here, women are struck between their 'status as human beings and their vocation as females'. In other words, they both are and are not 'human' in a culture which implicitly defines the 'human' in masculine terms. Instead, as the word 'vocation' suggests, they are called to the more restricted role of being a woman. Gilbert and Gubar take the view that when a woman writes, this split, liminal, identity will necessarily make itself felt in her writing. They use ideas from *psychoanalysis* to argue that her repressed energies will find a way of returning into her text. So, even though Austen's plots are very conventional, with her heroines 'amorously mastered by a sensible man' (A), this is just a 'cover story'. The real drama is located in the 'witty, assertive, spirited, independent' voice of the narrator (B).

For Gilbert and Gubar, then, women are always already repressed – being a woman means 'relinquishing achievement' (A) – and women's writing is always already potentially subversive. The feminist critic's job is to discover how that subversion manifests itself. Even a writer like Austen, who has been read by so many critics as supporting things as they are and speaking the language of the dominant class, can be redefined as actually speaking a deceptive 'woman's language'. Rather like Harding wanting to get Austen back from the 'Janeites', Gilbert and Gubar want to get her back from masculinist critics who don't appreciate that she is, above all, a woman. And they want to celebrate women's survival strategies: they describe Austen at the end of passage B as 'magnificently duplicitous'.

Gilbert and Gubar's insistence on reading Austen as a woman writer represents a vital corrective to the gender-blindness in many earlier studies. It makes them much more open than Butler, for example, to the possibility that Austen's fiction might involve significant tensions, contradictions, and inconsistencies. But, as with all critical readings, we again need to ask about the limits of this approach. Where Butler ignored gender, Gilbert and Gubar privilege it over any other category. Their method tends to assume the existence of subversion and then set out to prove it. Gilbert and Gubar's readings of Austen's novels are original and challenging but I for one feel anxious about their comparative indifference to any question of historical specificity – particularly in the light of the convincingly detailed contextual studies of Austen, including Butler's, which we have already looked at. Are all women, at all times, really the same? Are they always equally disadvantaged – as individuals or as writers? Other feminist critics have certainly questioned the transhistorical tendency of Gilbert and Gubar's criticism, and I want now to turn to Mary Poovey, whose work combines sexual difference with differences of history and class.

Mary Poovey's *The Proper Lady and the Woman Writer: Ideology as Style in the Works of Mary Wollstonecraft, Mary Shelley, and Jane Austen* comes from a different critical tradition from that which informs Gilbert and Gubar's study – though Poovey is at times influenced by some of Gilbert and Gubar's ideas. As the word 'ideology' in the subtitle of her book suggests, Poovey is a Marxist–feminist critic. So she is committed to working out the complex, and sometimes contradictory, relationships between ideologies of class and of gender, and to exploring the ways in which they manifest themselves in literary texts. In her first chapter, Poovey analyses the middle-class ideology of feminine *propriety* or *decorum*: she describes how the figure of 'the Proper Lady' emerged, during the eighteenth century, as the ideal form of middle-class femininity – chaste, modest, domestic, and self-effacing. (A version, in fact, of the 'Christian and exemplary' anti-revolutionary heroine whom Butler describes above (p. 137). This ideal is most clearly evident in the popular advice books, or 'conduct books', of the time, but its repressive *effects* can be traced, Poovey argues, in women's writing. To write for the public was to refuse to behave like a Proper Lady, so women's texts tend to bear the scars of their author's defiance of convention. It is here that Poovey draws most obviously on Gilbert and Gubar's characterisations of women's texts as 'double': as expressions of both repression and resistance. She argues, for example, that Jane Austen, 'gradually perfected a form of irony that enabled her to present her personal values in such a way as to make them seem natural correctives to the restrictions of decorum' (Poovey, 1984, p. 47). In other words, she offers a gender-based twist to the view (as argued by Duckworth and Williams, for example) that Austen was committed to a reformed version of traditional values.

But, as I have suggested, Poovey is much more concerned than Gilbert and Gubar with the way ideologies work at specific historical moments. Like Butler, Poovey reads Austen's novels in the context of French Revolutionary debates; like Duckworth and Williams, she focuses particularly on the challenge to traditional social structures which came from an increasingly commercial society. But unlike Butler, Duckworth or Williams, Poovey also explores the effect of these crises on ideas about the social roles of men and women. Like many recent Marxist critics, Poovey is interested in defining why it is that people believe in ideologies which perpetuate their inequality, why they *internalise*, identify with, ideas which contribute to their own repression. As a Marxist–feminist, she is particularly concerned with how women are persuaded to accept ideologies of gender which perpetuate inequalities between the sexes. Why was it, for example, that at this period women believed in the Proper Lady, and were so profoundly affected by such a restrictive ideal? Poovey's answer is that it offered the illusion of power within a new family structure, and that it was sold to women through the ideology of romantic love. My chosen passages are from Poovey's discussion of that ideology:

A. In retaining the premises and promises of romantic love . . . Jane Austen perpetuates one of the fundamental myths of bourgeois society. . . . in the absence of institutions that actually link the private and the public spheres, romantic relationships, by their very nature, cannot materially affect society. . . . by focusing on courtship, the myth of romantic love tends to freeze the relationship between a man and a woman at its moment of greatest intensity, when both partners are seen (and see themselves) in the most flattering light, and – what is perhaps most important – when women seem to exercise their greatest power. Romantic love, in other words, seems to promise to women in particular an emotional intensity that ideally compensates for all the practical opportunities they are denied. All that it can actually yield, however, is the immediate gratification of believing that this single moment of apparent autonomy will endure, that the fact that a woman seems most desirable when she is most powerful will continue on in marriage and in society. In Jane Austen's society, of course, romantic love did not alter the institutions of marriage or property or female dependence. Even the private gratification available in the domestic sphere could not live up to the intensity and power promised by romantic love; for as a wife and mother, a woman could at best act indirectly: through her children, through sacrifice, through duty. Romantic love, finally, had its most vital, most satisfying existence, not in society, but in art. (Poovey, 1984, p. 237)

B. Because bourgeois society defined women in terms of their relationships (specifically, their conjugal or familial relationships), because they were granted power within the 'proper sphere' of the home, and because the theory of 'influence' postulated a model for the dissemination of domestic virtues throughout society, women had a particular investment in conceptualizing their space as special and as containing special moral authority. More generally, however, we should remember that the cultural ideology that encompassed both propriety and romantic love had at its heart the same separation of spheres that we see in women's novels. For bourgeois ideology held out the promise that every individual would have an equal opportunity to work for equal material rewards – a promise that the limitations of natural resources and the inherent inequalities of class society rendered particularly false. The existence of a private sphere, replete with the resources of boundless love and uncritical sympathy, promised a compensatory substitute for other kinds of unavailable gratification – for men as well as women. (Poovey, 1984, p. 240)

One of the most important features of Austen's novels – and one of the major reasons for their continuing success with modern readers – is that they are romantic love stories. For many feminist critics, however, this has been one of their more worrying aspects, since they therefore seem to perpetuate a very conventional view of sexual relationships. For Gilbert and Gubar, for example, as we have seen, Austen's official plot is a story about 'female submission': about 'a rebellious, imaginative girl who is amorously mastered by a sensible man' (see above, p. 143). Poovey would broadly agree with that description, but she is also concerned to locate romantic love more firmly in terms of history and class. As she suggests in the opening of passage A, for example, Austen's use of the romance plot perpetuates not simply a conventional view of sexual relationships, but 'bourgeois society' itself, since for the Marxist–feminist the two are inseparable. What Poovey rejects, is any idea that women and men are *naturally* suited for the roles society allots to them; she believes that gender is a *constructed*, and therefore a changing and changeable, category. There is nothing inevitable about romantic love, therefore. It's just a social *myth*, an ideology which supports a particular form of social organisation: in this case, the new bourgeois consumer society, and the nuclear family which is its ideal unit. The basis of that society is an absolute separation of the public and private worlds, work and home, production and consumption; within that division, women are restricted to 'power' over the private, domestic sphere only, and romantic love persuades them to accept that role as 'natural'. The fact that many people *experience* romantic love as a very powerful emotional event does not make it 'true'. Ideology is at its most effective when it operates through what we like to think of as our most private, most spontaneous, feelings.

In passage A, we see Poovey trying to answer the question as to why this particular ideological myth is so persuasive, particularly for women. Her answer is that it uses pleasure to give an illusion of power. The kind of love story that Austen writes, 'tends to freeze the relationship between a man and a woman at its moment of greatest intensity'; and this is also the moment when 'women seem to exercise their greatest power'. So romantic love persuades women to settle for a conventional, domestic existence, by holding out a false promise that marriage will involve both the 'emotional intensity' of romance and more extensive social 'influence' (passage B). The promise of female 'influence' brings us back to the Proper Lady: women are told that they are responsible for 'the dissemination of domestic virtue throughout society', and that this moral task can be fulfilled only by a properly decorous and domesticated wife. As far as Poovey is concerned, this kind of power and influence is dangerously illusory. Romantic love, like Austen's acceptance of class society in Kettle's analysis, or like her belief in the 'moral pretension' of the ruling class in Williams (see above, pp. 121, 133), is a form of *false consciousness*, blinding its subjects to the realities of social power – and powerlessness.

According to Poovey's analysis, then, romance and the Proper Lady were devices which kept women safely away from any real power, because they directed their energies and desires towards the private world of the emotions and the family (the world of the novel), and away from the public sphere of economic production. The private sphere, she argues, was actually powerless to exert any kind of influence for change. Like Williams, Poovey still implies that the 'real' world, the world where significant things happen, is the world of the economic base, a world which, in Austen's time, excluded middle-class women. According to this model, novels are influential vehicles of ideology, so Austen's novels have a lot to tell us about the mechanisms of social change. But they remain *symptoms* of those processes; they do not participate actively in them. In Poovey's reading, both Austen and her writing are ultimately subject to the ideology of orthodox femininity.

Poovey's work illustrates the crucial Marxist–feminist recognition that analysis of capitalist society cannot ignore the gendered relationship between the public world of economic production and the private world of domestic affections; that it must take account of gender as well as class oppression. Poovey exposes the public/private division as the production of bourgeois ideology, but, like Williams, she nevertheless continues to imply that the economic is more 'real', that it is of greater historical significance, than the domestic. Many feminists would want to question that gendered hierarchy, and to disagree with Poovey's view that, for example, romantic relationships 'cannot materially affect society'. Nancy Armstrong, my final critical example, is one of these, and I want now to compare her view of women's 'influence' with Poovey's rather negative conclusion that it can only ever be illusory.

In *Desire and Domestic Fiction: A Political History of the Novel* (1987), Armstrong introduces a more dynamic and flexible model of historical and cultural change. She agrees that the separation of the public and private spheres was an important ideological feature of Austen's period, but she does not accept that the division between the two was therefore absolute, in the way Poovey suggests. Armstrong's challenging argument is that the new bourgeois culture was produced, that it identified itself in the first place, through the figure of the domestic woman and in the private sphere. And novels like Austen's, she argues, were absolutely central in that process. My extracts are taken from Armstrong's conclusion to her discussion of Austen.

> A. I mean to refute the idea that Austen was an ardent little Tory who sought to make fiction justify a traditional notion of rank and status. But in opposing this position, I do not subscribe to the view of Austen as a proto-feminist rebel who thrashed against the constraints that bound an author of her sex unwillingly to convention. (Armstrong, 1987, p. 156; Monaghan, 1992, p. 160)

> B. Austen proposes a form of authority – a form of political authority – that works through literacy rather than through means to maintain social relations. If, by Austen's time, sexual relations are assumed to be the specialized knowledge of the female, and if it is in female writing that the terms of such relationships are figured out, then fiction fulfils its discursive function by exemplifying the conduct of relationships between men and women. Novels do not have to launch elaborate self-defences any more, for they have appropriated the strategies of conduct books to such a degree that fiction – instead of conduct books – can claim the authority to regulate reading. . . . I am suggesting that with Austen . . . the novel supplants the conduct book as that writing which declares an alternative, female standard of polite writing. (Armstrong, 1987, pp. 157–8; Monaghan, 1992, pp. 160–1)

> C. I am quite certain that Austen understood as well as anyone could the power of fiction to constitute things, truth, and reality. It was not the country gentry and their specific interests that she promoted as the best life for everyone to live. The ways of the town and the city and their connection with commerce abroad always hover at the borders of the elite community to remind and assure us of its limitations. It was not this particular segment of society that she idealized, then, but rather the language that constituted the nuances of emotion and the ethical refinements that seemed to arise from within to modify the political meaning of signs, a new language of kinship relations capable of reproducing this privileged community on a personal scale within society at large. It is in this respect that Austen's writing implies the presence of a new linguistic community, a class that was neither gentry nor nobility as the eighteenth century knew them, yet one that was clearly a leisure class and thus a paradoxical configuration that can only be called a middle-class aristocracy. (Armstrong, 1987, pp. 159–60; Monaghan, 1992, pp. 162–3)

In passage A, Armstrong locates herself in relation to by now familiar critical positions. She rejects first the view of Austen as 'an ardent little Tory' who defends traditional values: the view, broadly speaking, of historical critics like Butler or Duckworth, who interpret Austen in relation to contemporary political controversies, or in terms of her class position. As we see at the beginning of passage B, Armstrong suggests that such critics understand Austen's 'political' identity in much narrower terms than Armstrong herself wants to establish. She then goes on, in passage A, to dissociate herself at the same time from the kind of feminism represented by Gilbert and Gubar – a feminism which, as we have seen, is ahistorical in its desire to see all women writers as 'proto-feminist rebels'. Armstrong thus implicitly locates herself – and Austen – somewhere between these two approaches.

Like Poovey, then, Armstrong's critical method is both historicist and feminist, but it combines gender with history in a very different way. I want to explore that critical difference, and define Armstrong's method more closely, by comparing a key statement from each. The first is Poovey's assertion that romantic relationships (and by extension, of course, romantic fiction) 'cannot *materially* affect society' (Poovey, passage A; my emphasis). The second is Armstrong's view, from the beginning of passage C, that Austen understood 'the power of fiction to *constitute* things, truth, and reality' (my emphasis). Clearly, Poovey and Armstrong are working with two very different models of the relationship between literary texts and society, between language and experience. For Poovey, as we have seen, literary texts, and ideas like romantic love, cannot 'materially' affect society because they are *effects* of social and economic conditions; they are outside the (masculine) world of economics and political institutions. Armstrong, on the other hand, draws on the *poststructuralist* idea that language 'constitutes' experience; that events, experiences, personal identity, can only be understood – and in that sense, only exist – when they are given meaning in language.[9] For Armstrong, then, texts can actually *produce* social 'reality'; they are one of the mechanisms through which a culture imagines, and thus defines, itself. So for Armstrong ideas and language, as well as economics and class, are part of 'material' history.

How does all this affect the way we might think about Jane Austen? In immediate contrast to Poovey, Armstrong claims that Austen's novels exert 'a form of political authority', which works not through the usual political and social institutions, but through 'literacy' (B). Like Poovey, Armstrong is interested both in Austen as a writer of love stories and in her relationship with the Proper Lady, the ideal domestic woman, of the conduct books. And she argues with Poovey that, 'by Austen's time, sexual relations are assumed to be the specialized knowledge of the female' (B). But Armstrong goes on to suggest that novels have therefore come to 'exemplif[y] the conduct of relationships between men and women'; that fiction – 'female writing' – has become the place where the social codes which govern sexual relationships are *made*. Novels, which deal with this area of 'feminine' expertise, have a profound effect on how society conducts itself: they teach men what kind of woman to desire, and they teach women what to desire to be. They teach, in other words, how to become a member of the newly emerging respectable bourgeois class, by showing you how to organise your private life in a particular way. For Poovey, romance and domesticity were merely false forms of compensation for women – and for men – when the material promises of success in the public world failed them. But Armstrong argues that it was not in the public sphere of commerce, but in the sphere of private relationships and behaviour, learned from conduct books and then novels, that a new class identity was produced. Within this model, the desirable, domestic woman becomes a central rather than a marginal figure, and women's writing, with its expertise in sexual relationships and in domestic decorum, takes on great cultural authority.

In the passages I have quoted for you, Armstrong concentrates her argument on questions of language. Like Duckworth and Williams, she sees Austen's novels as centrally concerned with conduct, with 'the best life for everyone to live' (C). But conduct has now become a gendered issue, and a matter of language. Austen's 'ideal community' (to go back to a phrase from Trilling) is located not in a particular social group, but in a way of speaking and thinking. It is located, as she puts it, in the (feminine) language of 'emotion and ethical refinements', in a language which gives the personal, moral life power over the external social world. Though these ideas – and some of Armstrong's own language – might seem difficult, we are actually on quite familiar ground here. We are used to thinking about Austen as a writer who makes careful, nuanced moral judgements. For Armstrong, however, Austen's language of careful judgement and discrimination is not simply a *critique* of her social group, as Duckworth and Williams would argue; it *is* that social group: it 'implies the presence of a new linguistic community', to which readers aspire to belong and through which they identify themselves.

Armstrong's suggestion, then, is that Austen is one of the writers responsible for producing a new social grouping at the beginning of the nineteenth century. This group transcended external social signs of status by identifying itself, precisely, in terms of the personal life, in terms of the emotions and 'ethical refinements', areas of experience often identified as 'feminine'. She describes, in other words, a 'feminisation' of culture. This doesn't mean that Armstrong sees Austen as politically radical, or that she approves of this identification of women and femininity with the emotional life: quite the reverse. Like Williams, for example, Armstrong offers a descriptive critique of historical processes, which is a very different thing from approving of them. What Armstrong does, however, is to put gender issues at the centre of historical processes in a way which daringly reverses Poovey's masculinist account, in which women tend to be victims of ideology rather than creators of cultural meaning.

In many senses, we have come a long way from the work of Harding and Trilling where we began. In spite of differences of vocabulary and approach, however, it is possible to trace connections through the criticism of the past forty years or so, and I hope that by focusing on particular critical *debates*, this chapter has helped you get a useful sense of where some of those connections might lie. In broad terms, for example, Armstrong would endorse Trilling's view that, 'It was Jane Austen who first represented the specifically modern personality . . . Never before had the moral life been shown as she shows it to be' (see above, p. 118) – though she might strongly disagree with him on just how the 'modern personality' or 'the moral life' should be defined or evaluated.

Over recent years, literary criticism has certainly become more self-conscious about its theoretical assumptions and about its political position – and rightly so. This self-consciousness has also meant that critical vocabulary has tended to become increasingly specialised (Armstrong would be an obvious example here), and this can make reading recent criticism seem quite daunting. But as I pointed out at the beginning of this chapter, all criticism works within some kind of theoretical position, even if it is not always overtly acknowledged. This is why I have encouraged you throughout to think about the assumptions underlying the readings of Austen we have looked at, and I hope that, as a result, the more specialised recent criticism begins to look more approachable.

You will inevitably find some critics more sympathetic than others, and some readings of Austen more convincing than others. I hope that this chapter has helped you feel more confident about the reasons for those responses, and those choices. Above all, I hope that it has encouraged you to take part in the exciting critical discussions which Austen's novels continue to inspire. That's what you're doing, after all, when you sit down to write an essay, and my final chapter offers some help with the practical problem of essay-writing.

Notes

1. *Jane Austen's Letters*, collected and edited by Deirdre Le Faye, 3rd edn (Oxford University Press, 1995) p. 275.
2. Full details of the books referred to are given in the 'References' below. This method of quick referencing which identifies a book by the author or editor's name and the date of publication is commonly used in modern criticism.
3. Lodge does not include the second paragraph of quotation C.
4. Extracts from Duckworth and Butler on *Sense and Sensibility*, and from Duckworth on *Emma* are included in the New Casebooks on those novels: see Clark, 1994, pp. 26–37, 38–52; Monaghan, 1992, pp. 35–51.
5. Duckworth quotes from contemporary responses to Austen's novels. 'Contemporary' can be an ambiguous term. I shall use it throughout to refer exclusively to the period contemporary with Jane Austen.
6. The quotation is from *Pride and Prejudice*, ch. 8.
7. *Jane Austen and the War of Ideas* was reissued in 1987 with an additional new Introduction, in which Butler gives a very useful overview of Austen criticism in the intervening period.
8. There is an extract from Gilbert and Gubar, which includes one of the passages I have used, in the Casebook on *Emma*. Extracts from Poovey on *Sense and Sensibility* and *Pride and Prejudice*, and from Armstrong on *Emma*, including those I have used, are reprinted in the New Casebooks on those novels. See Lodge, 1991, pp. 203–12; Clark, 1994, pp. 83–118; Monaghan, 1992, pp. 148–64.
9. More specifically, she is using the work of the influential French historian, Michel Foucault, who argues that political power doesn't work by *repressing* and controlling people's real, pe-existent identities and desires; rather, through 'discourse' and through various disciplinary mechanisms – prisons, asylums, the discourse of sexuality – it *produces* identities and desires as either 'normal' or 'deviant'.

References

Armstrong, Nancy (1987) *Desire and Domestic Fiction: A Political History of the Novel* (New York and Oxford: Oxford University Press).

Butler, Marilyn (1975) *Jane Austen and the War of Ideas* (reissued with a new introduction, 1987) (Oxford: Clarendon Press).

Clark, Robert (ed.) (1994) *New Casebooks: Sense and Sensibility and Pride and Prejudice* (London: Macmillan).

Duckworth, Alistair M. (1971) *The Improvement of the Estate: A Study of Jane Austen's Novels* (Baltimore, Md., and London: Johns Hopkins Press).

Gilbert, Sandra and Susan Gubar (1979) *The Madwoman in the Attic: The Woman Writer and the Nineteenth-Century Literary Imagination* (New Haven, Conn., and London: Yale University Press).

Leavis, F. R. (1972) *The Great Tradition* (first published 1948) (Harmondsworth: Penguin).

Lodge, David (ed.) (1991) *Jane Austen: Emma*, Casebook Series, revised edn (London: Macmillan).

Monaghan, David (ed.) (1992) *New Casebooks: Emma* (London: Macmillan).

Mudrick, Marvin (1974) *Jane Austen: Irony as Defense and Discovery* (first published 1952) (Berkeley, Los Angeles, London: University of California Press).

Poovey, Mary (1984) *The Proper Lady and the Woman Writer: Ideology as Style in the Works of Mary Wollstonecraft, Mary Shelley, and Jane Austen* (Chicago, Ill., and London: University of Chicago Press).

Southam, B. C. (ed.) (1976a) *Jane Austen: Sense and Sensibility, Pride and Prejudice and Mansfield Park*, Casebook Series (London: Macmillan).

Southam, B. C. (ed.) (1976b) *Jane Austen: Northanger Abbey and Persuasion*, Casebook Series (London: Macmillan).

Watt, Ian (ed.) (1963) *Jane Austen: A Collection of Critical Essays*, Twentieth Century Views Series (Englewood Cliffs, NJ: Prentice-Hall).

Watt, Ian (1972) *The Rise of the Novel: Studies in Defoe, Richardson and Fielding* (first published 1957) (Harmondsworth: Penguin).

Williams, Raymond (1973) *The Country and the City* (Oxford: Oxford University Press).

7

Writing an essay

SOONER or later your reading and ideas about your set novel have to be put into the form of an essay – something many students dread or find difficult. The aim of this final chapter is to help you to feel more confident about essay-writing. I am going to suggest some guidelines which I hope you will find helpful both when you are writing essays as part of your course work, and when you are answering exam questions, since the same basic methods of planning and organisation apply to both. In the first part of this chapter I shall be dealing with essay-writing in general, and though my examples are drawn from questions on Jane Austen, I hope you will find my suggestions useful whatever your essay topic. In the second part of the chapter I shall be looking more specifically at the kinds of questions commonly set on Jane Austen's novels. As I have stressed throughout the book, my aim is not to supply 'answers' to questions, to tell you what to think or write, but to offer a method which will help you to organise your own ideas into an effective essay.

But before going on to the practicalities of essay-writing, it's worth considering briefly the reasoning behind essay questions from the point of view of someone setting them. Some students feel that essay questions are unnecessarily restrictive, that they should be left to put forward their own ideas more freely, and that the aim of questions is to get them to make mistakes or reveal their ignorance. Questions are not, or certainly shouldn't be, out to 'trick' you in any way. They should give you the opportunity to explore a significant aspect of a particular text or topic and to express your views about it. If you are writing a course-work essay, this might be the first time you have considered this particular aspect and the essay title stimulates you into doing so; if you are answering an exam question and have prepared your material well, it will probably be something you have already considered. The particular phrasing of individual questions is intended to help stimulate your ideas and to help you organise your material. A question which simply asked you to 'Write all you know about . . . could be extremely daunting, not least because in offering no framework for your ideas, it could result in a very disorganised essay. So a good essay question should strike a balance between giving you the freedom to discuss an interesting topic in a way which interests you and providing a framework which helps you to discipline your discussion. It tests both your knowledge of the text and your ability to adapt that knowledge, to use it relevantly to respond to the slightly different perspective of a particular question.

Writing is rarely a totally painless process, but the challenge of working out the implications of an essay question and how best to tackle it so that you can still say what *you* want to say can make essay work enjoyable, even exciting. I hope the practical guidelines offered here will help you not only to write better essays, but to enjoy writing them.

General guidelines

Two particular complaints appear again and again in the reports of English literature examiners. The first is that many candidates ignore the question: instead of answering in the terms set, they regurgitate a learned answer or, particularly in the case of novels, simply retell the story. The second is that many answers are just lists of examples from the text – they might be relevant to the question, but they are not organised into a clear argument. So I'm going to begin with three rules which you should bear in mind constantly when you are writing essays. You have no doubt heard them many times already but they are important enough to bear a lot of repetition:

1. **Answer the question.**
2. **Organise your answer into a clear argument.**
3. **Illustrate your argument with relevant examples from the text and, if appropriate, from your critical reading.**

In other words, relevance and clarity are two of the most important qualities in a good literary essay. In this first section, I am going to divide the process of writing essays into three main stages and to suggest ways of approaching each stage which should help you to produce essays which have both those qualities. The three stages are: analysis of the title; thinking and rereading; and planning what to write.

1. *Analysis of the title.* When you start work on an essay, the first thing to do is to make sure you have a clear idea of exactly what you are being asked. Read the title carefully – and that means thinking about every bit of the title and resisting the temptation to focus on just one element which looks familiar. Ask yourself the following questions: 'Which main aspect of the text does this question want me to focus on?' and 'What particular approach to that does this question invite me to take?'

In answering the first of these questions, it's worth bearing in mind that certain aspects of texts reliably recur as the subjects of essay titles. Questions on novels, for example, fall broadly into five categories: questions on what happens and how those events are organised, on *plot*; questions on who it happens to, on *character*; questions on where it happens, on *place* or on the *society* of the novel; questions on what the novel seems to be saying and the issues it raises, on its argument or *values*; questions on how the novel is written, on *style* and *method*. To some extent, these are false distinctions. An essay on character or on the society of the novel, for example, will almost inevitably want to deal with the values the novel seems to be expressing through its treatment of those things; and without exception, essays should take some account of how the novel is written, how it organises its material. But these categories are useful in helping you to decide which aspect is the main focus of any particular title, and therefore which aspect should be central to the argument of your essay.

Having decided on the main focus of the title, you can move on to the second question about how you are being invited to approach it. Your answer to this will probably have two elements: first, identification of the title's particular perspective on character or place or method; and then identification of what the title is asking you to do. To help you to decide, it's a good idea to underline the words in the title which seem to you particularly important and of which your essay must take account. The majority of questions, particularly at A-level, ask you to agree or disagree with a statement about the novel, or to decide 'how far' something is true. (The common formula for this kind of question is a statement followed by the word 'Discuss'.) So you must be sure that your essay is organised in response to this: an essay which dealt with the subject of the statement, but failed to make clear whether or not you agreed with it would not be answering this kind of question adequately. Another very common formula is 'Show how', inviting you to pay attention to the *method* by which a particular aspect of the text is communicated. Again, answers which discuss subject-matter but not method are not answering the question.

How does this work in practice? This question on *Emma* was recently set in an exam:

> 'We end by liking Emma.' How far do you agree with this statement and what relevance do you think it has to Jane Austen's purpose?

This is a pretty straightforward question, and its main focus is easily identified as character, the character of the heroine. But someone who was not in the habit of fully analysing the question's demands might well plunge into an essay which simply described Emma's personality, or into one which did answer the bit about liking her, but ignored the second half of the question. By asking our second question, about how we are invited to approach the subject of character, we can avoid making those mistakes. Which words ought we to underline as indicative of the question's main concerns? My suggestion would be:

> 'We *end* by *liking* Emma.' *How far do you agree* with this statement and what *relevance* do you think it has to Jane Austen's *purpose*?

This tells us at a glance that a full answer should deal not simply with how likeable Emma is, but with the statement's assumption that though we like her at the end of the book, we hadn't done so at the beginning. Our answer must make clear *how* far we agree with this, then go on to discuss the part this plays in Jane Austen's *purpose*. At this point, a question on character becomes also a question on the novel's argument, on Jane Austen's didactic message. We are asked to decide on *how* Jane Austen's presentation of her heroine as increasingly likeable contributes to getting her message across. To do that of course, we must first decide what we think her message is, and make that clear in our essay.

Though this analysis makes it look a bit more complicated, this is still a pretty straightforward question. It deals with aspects of the novel – what the heroine is like and what the novel seems to be saying – which any careful reading will have considered already. The important point to recognise is that the question asks us to bring these two aspects together in a meaningful way.

Here's a slightly less straightforward example, again set recently on *Emma*:

Emma has been likened to a detective story because of its complicated plot and the importance of suspense. How far do you see the comparison to be true and how much do these qualities contribute to the novel?

Essentially, this is a question about plot and method, about the novel's organisation of events, a topic which should by now be fairly familiar since it has been central to our approach to the novels throughout this book. To clarify this title's particular perspective and demands, I would underline as follows:

> *Emma* has been likened to a detective story because of its *complicated plot* and the *importance of suspense*. *How far* do you see the comparison to be *true* and *how much* do these qualities *contribute to the novel?*

I have chosen this title as an example because it seems to me to illustrate two areas of possible confusion which thought and careful analysis will help you to avoid. The first arises from the title's main point, its comparison of *Emma* to a detective story. You might be worried that you are expected to write about detective stories as well as about *Emma*, something you might feel unable to do. This is a danger with any question which makes this kind of specific comparison, or which says something like 'Jane Austen tells us more about upper-middle-class society than any other novelist of her generation'. The point to remember is that you are writing an essay or sitting an exam on Jane Austen, and not on detective fiction or on all the other novelists of Jane Austen's generation, so you can't reasonably be expected to deal with those things. Concentrate on the point that's being made by the comparison. You can safely assume that's what you are being asked to discuss. You will notice that here, for example, I haven't underlined 'detective story', but the features which characterise detective stories, complicated plots and suspense, and it's *how far* these are also features of *Emma* which your essay should consider.

The second difficulty with this question is to decide exactly what is meant by 'contribute to the novel'. This could be interpreted in various ways. It could be taken to refer to the quality of the novel, or possibly to our enjoyment of it, or, like the previous question, to what the novel seems to be saying, to the values it is advocating. The last of these would probably produce the most interesting essay, but the point to remember is that if a question is phrased as vaguely as this it is up to you to interpret it in the way you find most appropriate or useful, as long as you make it clear in your essay exactly *how* you have interpreted it. The important thing is that you don't just avoid that part of the question altogether.

2. *Thinking and rereading.* This stage can be dealt with quite quickly here, since it's really what this whole book has been about. If you have read the novel carefully, constantly asking yourself *why* you are reacting in particular ways as I have suggested, then going back to the novel and to your notes with particular essay questions in mind should present little difficulty. Essentially you are engaged in the same process of response and explanation of that response, but this time to the essay question as well as to the novel itself. This is what I mean by calling this stage '*thinking* and rereading'. Once you have analysed the essay question so that you are clear about exactly what you think it is asking, analyse your response to the question equally carefully.

You will have thought about the novel's major aspects already, during your initial reading and analysis, and will have some sense of what you feel is important about each of them, what you would like to say about them in an essay. So, faced with an essay title, ask 'What is my immediate reaction to this?' 'Do I agree or disagree?' 'How far does this coincide with the conclusions I had already reached about plot/character/place/values/style?'. Rely on your immediate response to these questions to get you started. Just as when you were reading the novel itself, it's *your* ideas you should start from, and explore further. Don't assume that the person who set the question is looking for a 'right' answer – or that the statement in the title will inevitably be true, or even that its terms are necessarily useful. In most cases, you will probably find that the terms are fairly familiar, and coincide to a greater or lesser extent with your own ideas. But if your immediate reaction is strong disagreement with the title's assumptions, or with its terms, this is an equally valid basis for an essay, as long as you justify your own position by clear argument and illustrations from the text. Be careful though! Disagreement with the terms of the question is not an excuse for ignoring them. Your essay must still be recognisably working within the framework of the question.

Here's a question on *Pride and Prejudice*, for example:

'In *Pride and Prejudice* the plot is secondary, both in importance and interest, to character and dialogue.' Discuss this view.

This is a statement with which you might very well want to disagree, or which you might at least want to qualify. You might feel that plot –

particularly, for example, Lydia's eloping with Wickham and Darcy's involvement with that − is very important to the novel's purpose. Or that it's really very difficult to separate 'plot', in the way I have been using the term, from 'character and dialogue' since the relationship between Elizabeth and Darcy which depends on their respective characters and is conducted largely through their conversations *is* the novel's main plot. The invitation to 'discuss this view' allows you to develop these points, and though the title separates plot, character and dialogue whereas you might want to see them as less easily separable, the fact that the title uses those terms makes it easy to keep your discussion well within the terms of the question.

Here's another question, this time on *Emma*:

> 'One of the kindest, most gentle men in English fiction, yet he always gets his own way.' Discuss this view of Mr Knightley. Do you find him 'too good to be true'?

This seems to me a very limiting question. An answer of the kind it seems to demand would simply be an illustrated character sketch based on your opinion of Mr Knightley. But as we have seen throughout, Jane Austen's characters are part of the pattern of values in her novels so that the most interesting character-based questions will allow you the scope to extend your discussion to consider this function in the novel as a whole. The danger here could be that in doing that you might easily stray too far from the terms of the question. What you should try to do in a case like this, is to *use* those terms imaginatively in order to strike a balance between acknowledging the question and developing your essay in what you feel to be the most interesting way. Here, for example, you could use the description of Mr Knightley in the quotation to discuss his moral role in the novel, the fact that he is, literally, a 'gentleman', and the significance of that term for Jane Austen, and to consider the effects of allowing him to 'get his own way' on the novel's moral purpose. And the question about him being too good to be true could be answered not just by offering your opinion on his character, but by opening out your discussion to consider the wider problems of the relationship between Mr Knightley and Emma and whether Jane Austen's happy ending is wholly satisfactory.

Whether your answer to the set question is basically 'yes' or 'no' or, as will very often be the case, 'to some extent', the important thing is to justify your view by close reference to the text. If you are writing an essay as part of your course-work, your next step should be rereading. You might already have a clear idea of what your basic argument is going to be. If so, your rereading will simply be a matter of choosing passages which seem best to illustrate that argument. If you are still uncertain how to answer, your rereading will be more detailed, a further exploration of the text in the light of the question in order to clarify your ideas. In either case, you will be *selecting material for its relevance to the question* in the way that I chose passages from *Pride and Prejudice*, *Persuasion* and *Mansfield Park* to illustrate themes I was interested in. If you have already analysed the novel in the way I have suggested, so that you have a full and clear sense of its overall patterns of plot and argument, you should find it fairly easy to adapt your material to the particular question and the selection of relevant passages should present little problem. If you have read some criticism on Austen to help further in clarifying your ideas, you might occasionally want to quote from that in support of your argument: 'As so-and-so says', etc. But quotations from critics are like quotations from the text: they should *support*, not substitute for, your own argument. And as a rule of thumb, you should quote from critics far less than from the text itself.

If you are sitting an exam without your text the rereading stage isn't left out – it's just a matter of memory rather than actuality. This doesn't of course mean that you must memorise the whole novel! When you are preparing for an exam you should aim for a thorough knowledge of the novel but try to remember it in terms of the patterns of plot and argument I have been exploring throughout this book, and, within that broad outline, to focus on those five major aspects of a novel which tend to underlie most essay questions. To help you do this, concentrate on scenes and passages which you find particularly important and which illustrate for you various aspects of the novel. This way, you will be prepared for most questions and you will have examples ready to illustrate your argument. Obviously, in an exam – or even in a course-work essay – there isn't time to repeat the kind of detailed analysis of these passages which you will have given them when you were reading and preparing the novel. You can only refer to a few selected aspects in order to make your points, but having your full analysis to draw on will make that selection much easier and give your essay confidence and conviction.

3. *Planning what to write.* The only thing left to do now is to write your essay plan, to decide exactly how you are going to organise your argument and in what order you should use your examples. *Don't* be

tempted to skip this stage and go straight into your essay, however sure you are of what you are going to say. Different people write different kinds of essay plans, some much fuller than others. You will probably know from experience whether you need a detailed plan to help you keep your essay clear and well-organised, or whether you can manage with a few jotted ideas. But whichever is the case, the time spent planning is important – don't be unnerved if in an exam the person next to you has written two sides before you have started your essay. Length is not a guarantee of quality, and essays gain enormously from having been properly planned.

Think of your essay in terms of several paragraphs, each paragraph covering one main point which develops your argument by discussing another aspect of the topic, or offers a new example which extends or qualifies what you have already said. You should aim for a pattern of: introductory paragraph; the main core of the essay (say five or six paragraphs) which develop and illustrate the argument; concluding paragraph.

In the introductory paragraph you should aim to offer a broad outline of your answer to the question, of what line your argument is going to take. Or, if you are challenging the terms of the question, an indication of the basis of that challenge. Don't bring particular examples in at this point. Keep the paragraph general and fairly short. The aim is to give your reader a sense of what to expect from the rest of the essay – and to make them interested enough to read on, so try to present your argument in a forceful and interesting way. For example, you might want to begin with a generalisation, or a quotation – about Jane Austen, or this particular novel, or novels in general – which is relevant to the topic but approaches it from a slightly unexpected angle. If you were answering the question above on plot, character and dialogue in *Pride and Prejudice*, for example, you could begin with Henry James's famous question, 'What is character but the determination of incident? What is incident but the illustration of character?'

The main part of the essay is where you develop your argument in detail, moving from a clear presentation of your main points in the first two or three paragraphs to a discussion of qualifications, complications or even contradictions in later paragraphs. You should aim to illustrate each stage in your argument with an example from the text, but don't just repeat a pattern of point-illustration in each paragraph. This makes for a very jerky essay style. Each paragraph should be a bit like a mini-essay, containing an introduction of the main point, an illustrative example, and analytic commentary on the example to prove and extend the main point. One of the most important rules for writing literary essays is that *each quotation or example should be followed by analysis* to show *how* you have reached your conclusions. Which brings us to the question of quotations. Students often ask how much they ought to be able to quote accurately from the text in exams. There is no definite answer to this. Different topics will require different amounts of quotation. Essays on some aspects of style will obviously need more detailed quotation to illustrate their arguments than essays on a text's implicit values. But generally speaking, when you are writing about novels the important thing to aim for is the ability to refer confidently to particular incidents in a way which makes it clear that you know the passage in detail but without quoting huge chunks of the text word for word. If you do quote, try to do it as accurately as possible, so be realistic about how much you can learn. (Again this will vary from person to person.) Aim to be able to back up your detailed knowledge of the text with a few key phrases which you have learned because they sum up particular points you want to make.

Like the introductory paragraph, your concluding paragraph should be general rather than specific, offering a brief summary of your argument. Again, interesting and forceful expression will make more impression on the reader than a bland repetition of the question. If you didn't start with a quotation, for example, you might consider finishing with one. In some circumstances you might even want to conclude with a question. If you are writing on a particularly difficult or problematic text which seems to contain unresolved contradictions (I suggested that *Mansfield Park* or Jane Austen's happy endings, have something of this quality) don't be afraid to leave questions unanswered – as long as the argument of your essay has prepared for this kind of conclusion.

Essay-writing is a bit like swimming or riding a bike – once you can do it you never forget how and the essential method remains the same however good at it you go on to become. So if you find essay-writing difficult, I hope these guidelines will help you make that breakthrough in confidence. Remember: the basic method applies whatever the subject of your essay, and however simple or complex your argument. It remains for me now to apply some of these points to essays on Jane Austen.

Essays on Jane Austen

I have already suggested that questions on novels can be broadly divided into five types according to which aspect of the novel they focus on. This is certainly true of questions on Jane Austen, so I have organised the rest of the chapter according to those five categories and under each heading I have suggested common types of question and comments which mainly take the form of warnings about what mistakes to avoid in answering this kind of question. But I want to begin with a warning against categories altogether. They are of course schematic and artificial, an aid to clarity in essay-writing rather than an accurate reflection of the way the novels work. Plot, character, setting, and the values the novels discuss and promote are inextricably inter-related; and *what* the novels have to say cannot be separated from *how* they say it. In other words, questions on content cannot be properly answered without some consideration of method, and vice versa. So my major warning when you are writing on Jane Austen is: *Don't be restricted by the terms of the question.* Though the focus of your argument should reflect the focus of the question, aim to extend your discussion to as much of the novel as possible.

1. *Plot.* Questions focusing mainly on plot in Jane Austen's novels, with the possible exception of *Emma*, are not particularly frequent, but a typical formula would be:

> How do Catherine's experiences in Bath and at Northanger Abbey contribute to Jane Austen's purpose in this novel?

Other examples are the questions on plot, character and dialogue in *Pride and Prejudice* and that comparing *Emma* with a detective story which I quoted in the first part of the chapter. When you are answering questions focusing on plot, remember the distinction between 'plot' and 'story' which I have used throughout this book. If you bear that in mind, it will help to prevent you from simply retelling the story, one of the main dangers in answering this kind of question. As the question above on *Northanger Abbey* reminds us by asking *how* Catherine's experiences *contribute* to the novel's *purpose*, Jane Austen's plots, the way events are organised, are a major source of meaning in her novels and you should aim to *show the relationship* between plot and meaning in your essay. Also worth bearing in mind when you're answering on plot is the difference between a first reading and subsequent readings when we know what happens in the end.

2. *Character.* Questions focusing on character are extremely common. Here is a very straightforward example:

> Consider the way in which Jane Austen presents the Crawfords in *Mansfield Park* and their importance to the novel as a whole.

As in the question on plot in *Northanger Abbey,* the phrasing of the question is a reminder of the way in which character in Jane Austen's novels is *part of the overall pattern of values,* something I have stressed throughout this book. So in answering this kind of question don't just offer a straightforward character sketch. Always ask yourself what *function* the character(s) under discussion have in the novel. Here's another character question, more complicated but illustrating the same point:

> 'She prized the frank, the open-hearted, the eager character beyond all others. Warmth and enthusiasm did captivate her still.' To what extent do you think the characters in *Persuasion* are to be judged by these standards?

Here the question actually draws our attention to some of the values discussed in *Persuasion,* terms which are familiar from our analysis in Chapter 4 of the oppositions in the novel. The question is asking about the way in which the novel invites us to *judge* its characters (not just, note, about how Anne judges them). Remember, in answering a question like this, Jane Austen's technique of comparing and contrasting individuals and groups of characters in order to judge both them and the values they represent.

3. *Place.* As I suggested when I looked at *Mansfield Park* and at Pemberley in *Pride and Prejudice,* the same is true of Jane Austen's treatment of place, and the same kinds of warnings apply when you are answering questions with place as their focus: you should aim to consider its function in the novel. Here's an example of a question on *Mansfield Park* which should look pretty straightforward in the light of the analysis in Chapter 5:

> 'The stable and conservative values of Mansfield Park itself are those against which all other values in the novel are tested.' Discuss.

Here is a slightly different kind of question on place or society in Jane Austen's novels which appears fairly frequently:

> Discuss the view that Jane Austen's achievement as a novelist is inevitably limited because of the restricted world she presents.

This is something which, directly or indirectly, I have been encouraging you to consider throughout this book. The danger, if you are answering the question in defence of Jane Austen, is that your essay might become disorganised because you have too much material – in some ways it's a vague question, rather similar to something like 'Say why you think Jane Austen's novels are worth reading'. Beware of this danger if you have to answer a question like this. You might want to consider the possibility of answering it in very specific terms – by concentrating on the restrictions imposed by being a *woman* novelist, for example.

4. *Values.* Questions on the values discussed and advocated in Jane Austen's fiction are a favourite with examiners. Sometimes the focus is on specific values, as in this question on *Persuasion*:

> Jane Austen tells us that Anne was 'on the side of honesty against importance'. How are these values contrasted in the unfolding of the novel?

More often, questions are a version of the following in which you are expected to make clear which values you consider important:

> Discuss the values that Jane Austen seems to prize and consider the ways in which these are given expression in *Mansfield Park*.

This question on *Pride and Prejudice* offers a slightly different formula:

> Jane Austen is often described as a moralist. Does your reading of *Pride and Prejudice* lead you to support such a view?

The important thing to note about all three examples is that they do *not* expect you simply to describe Jane Austen's moral values, but to say *how* they are communicated: to consider, in other words, the roles of plot, character and dialogue, place and vocabulary in getting her message across. The constant analysis of oppositions and key words which I have suggested as the basis of your study of Jane Austen should give you ample material to answer this kind of question. And when you are answering a value question, don't necessarily expect Jane Austen's values to be wholly straightforward and consistent. As we have seen, one of the most interesting things about her novels is the way in which her conservatism can sometimes be at odds with other elements in the novels.

5. *Style and method.* All questions, as I have already said, are to some extent questions on method since a full answer to any question must consider *how* the material of a novel is presented. Questions which focus specifically on Jane Austen's method commonly ask you to discuss her irony, or the humour in her novels, or her comic vision (remember that those are not quite the same thing), or, more vaguely, her 'narrative skills'. Again, the habit of close analysis which I have been encouraging you to adopt should prepare you to answer this kind of question. Here, to end with, is a 'method question' on *Pride and Prejudice,* though it could have been set on any of the novels:

> 'Jane Austen's art is a highly serious criticism of life expressed in terms of comedy.' Discuss this view with reference to *Pride and Prejudice.*

The formula 'Jane Austen's art' should alert you to the fact that this is probably going to be a question focusing on method. The rest of the question narrows this down to the relationship between ('expressed in terms of') her 'serious criticism of life' and her 'comedy'. In other words, it illustrates a feature common to almost all method questions: their tendency to invite you to focus on aspect(s) of Jane Austen's technique, but as they contribute to the meaning of her novels. Meaning and method are here expressed in terms of an opposition: a '*serious* criticism of life' and '*comedy*'. You are invited to consider in your essay how, or whether, the novel you are discussing brings the two together. An essay which catalogued the terms of Jane Austen's 'criticism of life' and then gave examples of her comic method would not be answering the question properly. As always, the aim should be to show the *relationship* between the two, to consider the ways in which Jane Austen's comedy (meaning both her humour and her reconciliatory form) is used to express strong criticism of her society and to promote alternative values.

I'm not going to tell you how to answer that question. As I said at the beginning, my aim in this chapter – and throughout the book –

has been to give you not answers but the confidence to find and express your own answers. As with so many things, proper preparation is half the battle and this is certainly the case with essay and exam questions. If you think in advance about the kinds of question which are often set, the kinds of question I have illustrated here, then you will find it easier to recognise just what you are being asked when you face versions of those questions in an exam. One of my main aims in this book has been to help you not just to study Jane Austen's novels more efficiently, but also to enjoy them more. Perhaps with the help of this chapter you might even be able to enjoy essay-writing.

Further reading

As I suggested at the beginning of Chapter 6, a good way to start your critical reading is by looking at a collection of essays – either on your set text, or on Austen in general – which will give you a sense of different interpretations and critical approaches. Two of the most widely available and most useful series of essays are the Casebooks and the New Casebooks, published by Macmillan. There are Casebooks on *Emma*, edited by David Lodge (and now available in a revised edition); on *Sense and Sensibility, Pride and Prejudice* and *Mansfield Park*, edited by B. C. Southam; and on *Northanger Abbey* and *Persuasion*, also edited by Southam. There are New Casebooks available on *Emma*, edited by David Monaghan, and on *Sense and Sensibility* and *Pride and Prejudice*, edited by Robert Clark (see References, pp. 155–6), and a volume on *Mansfield Park* is planned. In spite of the fact that a couple of them might look rather out of date (the volumes edited by Southam were published in 1976), the original Casebooks are still a very good starting-point for your exploration of Austen criticism. They organise their material on a historical basis, giving you a clear sense of the development of critical comment; they are also, as the series title suggests, very much concerned with argument and debate in the way that I emphasise in Chapter 6. The New Casebooks concentrate on more recent critical approaches, so they very usefully complement the old series.

Other useful collections of essays include: *Jane Austen: Bicentenary Essays*, edited by John Halperin (Cambridge: Cambridge University Press, 1975); and *Jane Austen in a Social Context*, edited by David Monaghan (London: Macmillan, 1981). There is also a collection of interesting new essays on *Mansfield Park*, edited by Nigel Wood for the Theory in Practice series (Buckingham: Open University Press, 1993), and those of you with access to a good library might be able to get hold of *Jane Austen: New Perspectives*, edited by Janet Todd (New York and London: Holmes & Meier, 1983). *The Jane Austen Handbook*, edited by

David Grey (London: Athlone Press, 1986), includes some very good essays on all sorts of aspects of her work and its background.

Moving on to full-length studies of Austen, one of the best is Tony Tanner's *Jane Austen* (London: Macmillan, 1986). Tanner's book is based on his excellent introductions to several of Austen's novels in the old Penguin edition, and usefully contextualises her fiction, drawing on a wide range of material in a very available way. More specialised historical studies include of course, Butler's *Jane Austen and the War of Ideas* and Duckworth's *The Improvement of the Estate* (see Chapter 6), as well as David Monaghan's *Jane Austen: Structure and Social Vision* (London: Macmillan, 1980). Two particularly interesting feminist studies which extend and challenge the work of Gilbert and Gubar, Poovey, and Armstrong (see Chapter 6) are Claudia Johnson's *Jane Austen: Women, Politics, and the Novel* (Chicago, Ill., and London: University of Chicago Press, 1988) and Deborah Kaplan's *Jane Austen Among Women* (Baltimore, Md.: Johns Hopkins University Press, 1992).

One of the most interesting ways of approaching a particular novelist through criticism is to read general books on the novel as a form, such as David Lodge's *Language of Fiction* (1966; new edition, London: Routledge, 1984). Historical studies of the novel which you might find interesting include Gary Kelly's *English Fiction of the Romantic Period 1789–1830* (London and New York: Longman, 1989), a stimulating study of the novel in Austen's period which includes some very interesting comments on Austen; and Jane Spencer's *The Rise of the Woman Novelist* (Oxford: Blackwell, 1986) which, as the title suggests, examines women's role in the rise of the novel during the eighteenth century, and deals with Austen in that context. Ellen Moers's *Literary Women* (London: Women's Press, 1978) is a very readable account of women's writing across history, and again includes some very interesting comments on Austen.